Deception!

Happy reading!

Elizabeth Ducie

Elizabeth.

A Chudleigh Phoenix Publications Book

Cover design: Berni Stevens

ISBN: 978-0-9569508-7-1

Printed by Hedgerow Print, Crediton, Devon, EX17 1ES

Chudleigh Phoenix Publications

For the Sao Paulo team;
you made me feel at home.

ACKNOWLEDGMENTS

I am once again very grateful for all the support provided by my friends in the thriving community of writers and readers, both in Devon and beyond. In particular, my thanks go to Margaret Barnes for being my writing partner during the editing of our books; to my friends in Chudleigh Writers' Circle and Exeter Writers; to Sue, Clare and Helen, my MA buddies; and to Jenny Benjamin, Jo Cole, Mary Anne McFarlane, Heather Morgan and Richard Morgan, my beta readers.

I have fond memories of business trips to Brazil in the 1990s and 2000s; they were always great fun as well as hard work. *The Rough Guide to Brazil; Brazil (Footprint Handbook);* and *DK EYEWITNESS Top 10 Rio De Janeiro* helped supplement my notes on Sao Paulo and Rio. And the Berlitz *Cape Town Pocket Guide* was invaluable for travelling back to 1960s South Africa. I am grateful to Graham Walker who shared with me his encyclopaedic knowledge of steam railways.

Berni Stevens (@circleoflebanon) is responsible for the beautiful cover; Julia Gibbs (@ProofreadJulia) made sure the final text is as error-free as possible. My thanks go to both of them. I also owe a huge debt of gratitude to my sisters, Margaret Andow and Sheila Pearson, for their analytical reading skills and ongoing cheerleading.

Finally, my thanks go, as always, to my husband Michael McCormick, my fiercest critic and strongest supporter, who read the manuscript 'a million times' before we were both happy with it.

PROLOGUE

São Paulo, October 2005

It was a little after ten in the morning when he reached the square. The locals had all passed through on their way to work, while the tourists had yet to start arriving. For the moment he shared this central point in the old city with a handful of pigeons flying among the branches of the plane trees, and the old beggar from the *favela* who spent each day crouched in the shade of the monumental cathedral, preying on the guilt of the well-heeled visitors.

He threw his customary coin into the tin cup but didn't smile or return the man's greeting. He never smiled at him. He always made a gesture to help those less fortunate than himself, and the larger the audience, the bigger the gesture, but he believed there must be a reason why the old man was in such dire straits—and that somehow, he only had himself to blame.

He paused at a small doorway to the right of the cathedral steps and turned slowly, casually, in a full circle. His glance, hidden behind gold-framed sunglasses, took in every corner of the square, every place where an adversary or a spy might be hiding. He didn't expect to see anyone—and he wasn't disappointed—but it was a habit born of being on the run; a habit he was never likely to break.

He had to stoop slightly to enter the doorway. The interior was dim after the bright sunshine and he pulled off his sunglasses, blinking rapidly until gradually, the interior of the small café bar became clear. He snaked his way around the small round tables, pushing stools out of the way, to reach the counter at the back of the room.

In the evenings, this place was heaving with locals and tourists taking an aperitif before heading out to the restaurants for dinner. Then, the smells were of beer, wine and cigarettes. But this early in the day, he was alone. And there was a smell of coffee, good, fresh coffee, coming from the jug on the bar; and something else, warm, baked: croissants or maybe doughnuts. He felt his mouth water, as he knocked on the empty bar.

'Good morning, Alvar.'

'Good morning, Michael,' came a voice from the back room. 'Help yourself to coffee and I'll have one too.'

He was well known in this bar; he took breakfast there most mornings and often returned in the evening too. Now he poured two tiny cups of the strong black coffee and carried one over to a table in the corner. Usually he would sit at the bar and chat with Alvar, turning over the latest news stories, putting the world to rights. But not today. Today he was expecting company. And this was one conversation he didn't necessarily want to share.

He didn't have long to wait. A shadow blocked out the square of sunshine showing through the doorway. The resemblance to his old friend and ally was striking. There was the same stooping gait, the same cautious look; and, when he spoke, the same Ukrainian accent.

'Mr Hawkins?' It was not really a question; Hawkins knew Stefano Mladov kept a picture of the pair of them on his dresser and all the family had heard the stories of the 'good old days' in Africa many times. Now he just inclined his head and pointed to the chair opposite him. At a twitch of his finger, Alvar brought across the coffee jug, another cup and a plate of warm doughnuts, then retired to his back room again.

'Well?' Just one word, but it held so many questions for him. The young man nodded.

'I found her.' Hawkins let out a long breath he'd not realised he was holding. It was not the end of the story; it was only the beginning, but at least it had begun.

'She continued to live in Maputo, or Lourenço Marques as it was then, once you left. It seems life was hard and she had to make some difficult choices.' Hawkins thought he detected just a hint of condemnation in the young man's voice, but decided to ignore it. How could he hope to make him understand what it was like in Mozambique back in those days? 'She became a waitress and then a prostitute. My father tried to help her, but she was very independent. He thinks she blamed him for your disappearance.' The young man shrugged. 'But then she managed to find herself a benefactor who set her up in an apartment. No more working on the streets and in doorways for her.'

'But she can't still be doing that; she must be in her sixties by now,' Hawkins said.

The young man shook his head.

'I'm sorry, Mr Hawkins, but Grace Gove passed away twenty years ago.'

Hawkins said nothing but felt his shoulders slump. He was surprised at how the news affected him. It had been such a long time since he'd seen his first wife. As he left home that final morning, his lies tasted sour on his tongue and the hope in her face, tempered with just a touch of doubt, screamed out to him to turn back. To expect to be able to find her after all this time had been a long shot; to expect her to be happy to hear from him, an even longer one. He wasn't even sure why he'd commissioned this search in the first place. Guilt? Hardly. Regret? Maybe. Loneliness? Not likely. He could get all the companionship he wanted from the women of São Paulo. So, no, he didn't know why this had been so important to him; he just knew it was. But now it was over. He stood and held out his hand.

'Thank you for everything you've done, Mikhail. Your father must be very proud of you. Give him my best wishes.' He gestured towards the back room. 'Ask him for anything else you want. And have a good journey home.'

But the young man put his hand on Hawkins' arm to stop him walking away.

'Mr Hawkins, wait, there's something more I must tell you.' He reached into his jacket pocket and retrieved a photograph which he held out. It was a landscape picture taken with a telephoto lens from a long way away. The sea was rolling in and the sun was starting to sink below the horizon. There was a single person on the beach, staring out to sea. Her face was turned away from the camera, but she appeared to be quite young. There was a hauteur about her and a real sense of being alone. He looked enquiringly at the young Ukrainian.

'Her name is Mercy, Mr Hawkins, Mercy Gove. She's thirty-five years old.' He felt the breath catch in his throat and stared at the youth, saying nothing. 'Grace had a child a few months after you left Mozambique. She's your daughter, Mr Hawkins. And I know where she is, if you want to meet her.'

PART I

CHAPTER 1

São Paulo, January 2007

Suzanne Jones felt her stomach lurch as she watched the elderly white man walk across the grass and greet the young mixed race woman with a kiss on the cheek. It wasn't a lover's greeting; it was more familial: the greeting of an uncle to his niece or a father to his daughter. Charlie's fingers were digging into her arm and Suzanne realised both of them were holding their breath.

'I was right,' hissed Charlie. 'It's Hawkins, isn't it?'

'Hush, Charlie, he'll hear you; and if he looks this way, he'll spot us.'

'Relax, sis. In this get-up, even our own mother wouldn't recognise us!'

In large floppy hats and sunglasses they'd been watching for more than an hour, hoping—maybe not even daring to hope—that Charlie's hunch was right, and it looked like it was.

It was the Saturday of Marathon Weekend and although the main event wasn't until the next day, there was a carnival atmosphere at the sports ground and quite a crowd had gathered to take part in the fun run and children's races. In the mid-morning sunshine around twenty young people, mainly students by their clothing, were relaxing on the grass. One strummed a guitar and they hummed along to the tune. The woman had been sitting near the edge of the group, part of the crowd and yet seeming completely alone. They recognised Mercy Gove Hawkins from the picture Charlie had found in the race brochure. Suzanne had been sure the name was just a coincidence; wish fulfilment in fact. But as Charlie had pointed out, Hawkins might be a fairly common name back home, but here in Brazil it was rare.

Then, Mercy had uncoiled herself, stood and waved, a cool smile flitting across her face. The man walking towards her was clean-shaven, he wasn't wearing glasses and his hair was a close-clipped sandy blond rather than his trademark grey mane, but Suzanne was sure she was looking at her former boss, Sir Fredrick Michaels, now living as Michael Hawkins. The official reports were wrong and Charlie was right. He had fled to Brazil and he was standing just a few metres away from them at this very moment.

Suzanne kept absolutely still as they watched the couple chatting, not wanting any sudden movements to give them away. As Charlie would have put it, they'd found their prey. And with Mercy being one of the local entrants in tomorrow's marathon, they were fairly certain where he was going to be. For today, that was enough.

Hawkins looked at his watch and said something to Mercy. She nodded and the pair started walking towards the car park. Then Hawkins stopped and turned in a full circle, slowly scanning the crowd as though looking for someone. The Jones sisters froze. But his gaze slipped past them without pausing and when he'd completed his survey, he shrugged and continued on his way.

'Okay, what now?' asked Charlie. 'Stay here or go back to the hotel? We've got some planning to do.'

'Stay here for a bit, I think,' said Suzanne. 'I want to take a look around the sponsors' marquee; see if I can pick up anything on Sunshine Supplements. After all, that's why we're supposed to be here, remember?'

'Okay, I'm going to watch some of the children's races. I'll meet you outside the marquee in around an hour.' Charlie gave a wave and wandered off in the direction of the main arena.

As Suzanne strolled across the grass towards the large yellow tent festooned with advertisements and logos, there was a shout followed by a roar of anger. Turning, she was in time to see two young men in running kit grappling with each other, tearing at hair, clothes, anything to get a hold, before they fell to the ground and disappeared from sight behind the rapidly growing crowd of spectators.

Suzanne pushed her way through the crush until she was able to get a clear view of the two young men rolling around on the grass, clutching at each other, pulling hair and trying to throw punches. One had blood pouring down his face from a gash on his scalp, while the other seemed to have taken a punch in the eye and was squinting through puffed up lids. Both men were wearing the colours of the Indian team. From all sides, people came running, attracted by the shouting. Charlie arrived at full pelt, followed moments later by Damien Bradley Smithson, their client, the man who had brought them to Brazil in the first place.

'Suzanne, what's going on?' panted Charlie, 'are you alright?'

'Sure, I'm fine.'

'What happened?' asked Damien.

Suzanne shrugged.

'I really have no idea. I was just walking past and heard the shouting. I don't know what started it; when I looked, they were already going at it hammer and tongs.'

There was a bellow from behind them and a slim, neat little man forced his way through the crowd.

'That's Ravi, he's a sort of unofficial coach for all the Indian runners,' said Damien. 'He'll soon sort them out.'

The coach stood over the two men and shouted at

them to stop. But they ignored him and carried on brawling. Ravi strode over to a nearby drinks table. Ignoring the young waitress, he grabbed a large pitcher of water. With a flick of his hand, he deposited the contents of the jug over the two athletes.

They both yelled in shock and stopped fighting, looking around them and blinking as though just waking up. Then they rolled apart and scrambled to their feet.

'What happened?' screamed Ravi, 'What are you doing?' But the two men just stood there panting and hanging their heads. Ravi pointed at the taller of the pair. 'You, explain!'

'I can't, boss,' came back the reply, so quietly it was almost a whisper. Suzanne moved closer to catch the rest of his words. 'I don't remember anything after bumping into Manfred here and shaking his hand to wish him luck.'

The other man nodded his head.

'That's the truth, Ravi. I don't remember anything either.'

The two looked down at their feet like naughty schoolboys, seemingly oblivious to the sweat and blood trickling down their cheeks.

'Well, you'll need to come up with a better explanation than that,' said Ravi. He grabbed each one by an arm and started to march them away. 'You've let yourselves down and disgraced the entire Indian team. We'll talk about this when you've got yourselves cleaned up.'

With the excitement dying down, the crowd gradually drifted away, back to the races or their drinks, leaving Suzanne, Charlie and Damien staring after the departing Indians. Damien turned to Suzanne.

'Well, now you've seen it for yourself. This is what I've been observing for months, the reason I approached you in the first place: sudden unexplained violence, over as quickly as it starts and leaving everyone, including the main protagonists, confused as to the cause. Any thoughts?'

CHAPTER 2

Two weeks earlier
The call came in to the office, just off Vauxhall Bridge in London, as Charlie was briefing Suzanne on the parlous state of their finances.

'It's no good, Suzanne,' she said, 'either we get some more work soon, or we're going to have to change our office arrangements.' Her sister had her head buried in the latest issue of *GMP Review* and didn't move until Charlie rapped sharply on the desk. 'Earth to Suzanne Jones!'

'Sorry, Charlie, did you say something?'

'I was bemoaning the state of our finances. We've not earned anything for a couple of months now.'

'But we got all those fees from the project in Rome...'

'Just about gone, I'm afraid.'

'And the job in Russia?'

'What, all three days of it? Sorry, that's all gone too.'

'Well, we've got those three proposals in for the European Union projects. We've a good chance of getting at least one of those—and they're all due to kick off in the next couple of weeks.'

'Yeah, right,' Charlie said with an unladylike snort. 'When do you ever remember one of those starting on time?' She grabbed a pencil and a scrap of paper, made yet another list of figures, then looked around the room, regretting what she was about to say, even before the words left her mouth.

'I think we're going to have to get rid of this office.'

As she expected, that got her sister's attention. The tall blonde woman turned rapidly in her seat and held her hands up.

'No, Charlie, we are NOT moving all this stuff back into my flat. You know what it was like when we first started the business; it took over everything. That's why we rented this extra space in the first place.'

Charlie held her hands up in submission.

'No, I'm not suggesting we do without an office altogether. But there are other buildings, other options, rather than an expensive space in one of the up and coming areas of the capital.' She got up and went to stand at her sister's side. 'Look, sis, I know you love it here, but you'd still have your flat. It just means you'd have a slightly longer commute to work—and maybe,' she went on with a laugh, 'I could end up with a shorter one. There are loads of office buildings offering good deals over by Elephant and Castle.'

The telephone rang, shattering the sombre atmosphere in the office. Charlie picked up the receiver, automatically switching from sister to efficient personal assistant in the blink of an eye.

'Jones Technical Partnership; good afternoon. Charlie Jones speaking, how can I help you?'

She pulled the diary across to her as she listened to the voice on the other end. Then she held the receiver close to the pages as she riffled through them, pretending to look for a free space.

'Well, let me see, Mr Smithson; our diary is usually booked well in advance, but it so happens we've had a cancellation tomorrow morning. Shall we say ten-thirty? You know how to find us? Great. See you then.' Dropping the phone back onto the cradle, Charlie let out a whoop and grabbing her sister's hand, pulled her to her feet.

'Charlie, what is it? Who was that?'

'That, my dear sister, might just be the answer to our problems.' She let go of Suzanne's hand and picked up the diary, clearing her throat. 'Tomorrow morning, at ten-thirty precisely, you have a meeting with Mr Damien Bradley Smithson the Second from New York, New York (so good they named it twice) in the good ole U S of A. He wants to talk to you about a commission he has for us!'

'Damien Bradley Smithson..?'

'The Second; don't forget the Second! And he has some work he wants to put our way. Maybe we won't have to move after all. The one thing we know about American clients is they have money and they're not afraid to spend it!'

Damien Bradley Smithson II sounded quite mature on the phone and Charlie had visualised someone in their forties. So the man who strolled into the office the following morning was a complete surprise to her. For a start, he looked young, very young; almost too young to be wandering around London on his own, in fact. But his air of confidence far outshone his years. Charlie realised this was a man who was used to having his own way. But not, she suspected, in a bad way. His smile was easy, self-assured and reached the very depths of his dark blue eyes which shone through tortoiseshell-framed glasses. She was no real judge of fashion, but guessed his dark blue jacket and tailored slacks were made to measure, rather than off the peg. *And you won't get a pair of shoes like that in Marks and Sparks*, she thought.

While Suzanne settled their visitor in a chair, Charlie made them all a drink: fresh coffee, black, no sugar for Smithson; the same, but with a dash of skimmed milk for Suzanne; and a mug of instant with three sugars for herself. She decided the possibility of a new client and some paid work justified pushing the boat out, so she opened their last packet of chocolate biscuits and piled some on a plate. Smithson was telling Suzanne he was a student at Duke University in North Carolina and Charlie wondered what he was doing in that case visiting a technical consultancy in London.

'I'm a keen runner—have been all my life—and since I've been at Duke, I've had some success with the athletics team, particularly in long distance.' As he went on to talk about the medals he'd won representing the university and the state in national and international competitions, Charlie realised the phrase 'some success' was quite an understatement. This was a young man who loved his sport and seemed to be a bit of a rising star on the American horizon. She took her mug of coffee over to the window seat, sipped the drink and studied him as he continued speaking.

'Three months ago, a new runner joined Duke University Athletics Club. Her name was Lulana and she was Brazilian, on an exchange visit from University of São Paulo. She was supposed to be there for a year.'

'Supposed to be?' murmured Suzanne.

But Smithson held up his hand and carried on.

'We hit it off, right from the start and I asked her out the second time I met her. She agreed and we were having a great time—until we got close to the next important tournament, which was the National Varsity Meeting. She turned moody, started picking fights at everything I said then throwing herself at me afterwards until we made up. I put it down to a combination of nerves and her Latin temperament, but I have to admit it was starting to get difficult to spend time with her; not to mention the effect it was having on my own training regime. In the end, my coach put his foot down and told me I was to stop seeing her—at least until after the National Varsity Meeting.'

He bit his lip and stared down at his coffee in silence. Then he looked up and smiled at both of them—but to

Charlie, there was a wry tinge to the smile that hadn't been there before.

'I wonder whether I was to blame,' he said. 'If I'd been there, maybe I could have helped.' Suzanne leaned forward and put her hand on the young man's arm.

'What happened?' she said quietly.

'She got thrown out,' he said, 'sent back home in disgrace for fighting with another athlete.'

'And why do you think you could have changed things?'

'Well, I heard afterwards she'd been going right over the top with her training, pushing herself ever harder, ever faster. Friends said they tried to reason with her, but she wouldn't rest; it was as though she was addicted to the exercise. And on the day, the training seemed to have paid off. Not only did she win her race, she did so in the fastest time ever for a university event. Her time was international level. Then afterwards she was moody again, wouldn't talk to anyone, didn't seem to realise she'd won, and attacked someone who tried to congratulate her.'

'How strange,' said Suzanne. Damien nodded.

'Yes, and she's not the first to behave like this. I'd heard rumours in the past couple of years. Nothing concrete; friends of friends knew someone who had a friend; that sort of thing. So after Lulana got thrown out, I did some digging around. I've come up with at least half a dozen other runners who've behaved the same way.

'Sounds like some sort of epidemic,' said Charlie.

'And there was one odd thing,' he went on. 'All of them had been in Brazil at some point in the past two years.'

'All of them?' said Charlie. 'That sounds a bit too much of a coincidence.'

'It does, doesn't it?' agreed Suzanne.

'Lulana used to talk about a company back home, Sunshine Supplements. They've developed a sort of health drink, based on *yerba maté*, the South American herbal tea.

It's supposed to enhance performance in a legal way. She swore by it and always had a flask of the stuff with her. I think there may be a connection. She left some in my bathroom cabinet when we split up—and I've given it to a friend to get it analysed.'

'And how is Lulana these days?' asked Charlie. 'Are you in touch with her?'

'I've tried to contact her several times. But she seems to have dropped right off the radar. She didn't return to USP when she went home and none of the friends she made at Duke have heard from her either.'

'This is all very interesting,' said Suzanne, 'but why have you come to see us?'

'I'm over here visiting my aunt,' he explained. 'My father's quite a bit older than her. We've always been close; she's more like a big sister to me than an aunt. Well, I was telling her all about Lulana and my concerns over the health drink—and she suggested I come and talk to you guys.'

'Us? But we don't know your aunt, as far as I'm aware; why would she have heard of us?'

'Aunt Jo-Jo works at the Victoria and Albert Museum; she's a textile expert. And in the evenings, she helps run craft workshops, and what I believe are called 'stitch and bitch sessions'. She runs one in Dolphin Square.'

Charlie and Suzanne looked at each other and said in unison: 'Francine Matheson!'

Their visitor nodded.

'That's right. Jo-Jo and Francine have become quite friendly and we were all having supper together the other evening, when we were talking about Lulana. Francine mentioned the great things you guys did in Africa a couple of years back and that you've since set up on your own. Then Jo-Jo suggested I come and talk to you.'

'That's very kind of her,' said Suzanne, 'but I still don't see what we can do to help you.' Charlie hoped her more cautious younger sister wasn't going to scare this potential client away with her reluctance; after all, they really did need the money.

'I want someone to take a look at the company in Brazil; see if there's anything dodgy going on. I only have a suspicion at the moment and no-one is going to listen to me on the basis of that.'

'But exactly what do you want us to do?' Suzanne asked again.

'I'm going to São Paulo later this month to compete in the marathon. I'd like you, Suzanne, to come with me and find some way of getting into the company, have a look around, see what you can find out. You understand the pharmaceutical industry; you'll have more chance of spotting if something's not right.'

But Suzanne was shaking her head even before he'd finished speaking.

'I really don't think—'

'Now, don't let's be too hasty, Suzanne,' broke in Charlie. 'Let's ask Mr Smithson why he thinks you can help.' She nodded encouragingly at the young man, ignoring the frown she could feel coming across the room from her sister.

'Damien, please call me Damien,' he said. 'I'm afraid I've made a bit of a nuisance for myself, contacting the company, and asking questions. I've rather put them on their guard. I figured a British woman, with no connection to me, to athletics at all, would have more of a chance of getting in there.'

'But how?'

'Well, it might sound a little 'cloak and dagger' but I thought you might pose as a reporter and try to make contact with the guy who runs the company. He's an American, called Nigel Atkinson. He fancies himself as another Donald Trump from what I can find out. I reckon he would jump at the chance of being interviewed by, say, a freelance reporter.'

He stopped and looked at Suzanne, who was still

looking unconvinced. 'Look, I know it's a long shot—and I may well be making something out of nothing here—but I feel I owe it to Lulana to look at the company. If you can't find anything, I'll let it drop.' He looked across at Charlie. 'And I wouldn't ask you to come out on your own, Suzanne. Charlie could come with you—unless you're too busy running the office to leave it for a couple of weeks,' he said with just a touch of irony.

'No, I think I can manage to get away for a while,' said Charlie with a grin. 'These days everything is done via email and the internet, so I can work more or less from anywhere.'

Smithson stood up and placed his empty coffee cup on the tray, then shook hands with Suzanne and Charlie.

'Ladies, it's been great to meet you. I know I've given you a lot to think about, so I'm going to leave you in peace for now.' He opened the shiny leather attaché case he'd brought in with him and took out a slim folder. 'This is what I've been able to find out so far about Sunshine Supplements. Have a look at it and talk it through. Then give me a call; my number's in the folder. I'm here until the end of the week, so you've got a few days to think it over.'

As he reached the door, he paused and turned back with a grin. 'And, Charlie, Suzanne tells me you're a keen runner too. If you fancy going out for a run one day, you'll find me training in Hyde Park from five am each morning. Maybe I'll see you there?' And with a wave of his hand he was gone.

'Well, what do you think of that?' said Charlie. Then she held up a hand as her sister opened her mouth. 'No, don't answer yet; I'm going to put the kettle on again. I suspect this is going to be a rather long conversation.'

CHAPTER 3

'I'm sorry, Charlie, I just don't see what purpose I would serve by going out to Brazil with this guy. He's a fantasist—has to be.' Charlie watched as Suzanne paced up and down the office with her arms folded and wearing her 'serious, grown-up face'. 'A health supplement that changes people's moods, and then causes them to pick fights with people. It's like something out of *Dr Who* or an old B movie from the 1950s.'

'But Suzanne—'

'And the idea of me pretending to be a reporter; well, that's just preposterous! Who on earth would believe a story like that?'

'Someone who wants to believe it. Someone with an ego the size of a planet, who wants to be as rich as Donald Trump, and is happy to have some free publicity in a British national newspaper. Someone like this Nigel Atkinson in fact.'

'But I don't know anything about being a reporter!'

'Nonsense. You've been auditing factories for years, haven't you?'

'Yes, but—'

'And what do you do while you are auditing the

factory?'

'I ask questions and make notes.'

'And what do you do after you've finished auditing that factory?'

'I write up a report. A proper, scientific audit report, listing the strengths and weaknesses and making recommendations for improvement.'

'Precisely.' Charlie started ticking off on her fingers: 'You review the facts that you've collected. You summarise the facts in such a way that readers who are short of time can get the gist without having to read all the background. You produce a readable report. So it's not that different from a newspaper article, now is it? Besides, it's only a cover story. I don't suppose for one moment you'd have to deliver an article. It's not as though it's actually been commissioned, now is it?'

'Charlie, it's a stupid idea! And possibly illegal. It's certainly unethical.' Suzanne was being even more stubborn than usual and Charlie thought hard for something else to persuade her.

'Of course, we could always make it real by soliciting a commission in advance. I'm sure Francine could call in one of the favours she must be owed by some of the newspaper editors.'

'And that's another thing! I need to have a serious chat with Francine next time we meet. I know she thinks she's being helpful finding us work, but sending Damien over to see us with what has to be a wild goose chase is a bit much. And I don't know how she knew we were looking for new projects. I haven't seen her for ages.'

'Well, I might just have mentioned it when I phoned her last week.' Charlie felt herself going pink and smiled sheepishly at her sister.

'Charlie, how could you? She's our friend. You shouldn't lean on her like that.'

'Oh come on, sis; that's what friends are for.' Charlie gave a sigh and got to her feet, collecting the empty mugs and heading to the kitchen. At the door, she turned and raised an eyebrow. 'But you're right. It's a silly idea. We're going to be far too busy over the next few weeks to waste time in Brazil.' Suzanne looked at her in puzzlement. 'We're going to be looking for new, cheaper premises, packing this office up and moving. Or we might even be attending job interviews. Because, let's face it, Suzanne, if we don't get some more projects soon, The Jones Technical Partnership is finished, isn't it?' And with a bang, she disappeared into the kitchen.

The vigorous discussion—Charlie was fond of saying that the Jones sisters never fought—raged for the next few hours. Every time Suzanne came up with a reason NOT to take the job, Charlie came back at her with a counterargument. In the end, they talked themselves to a standstill and headed across the road to Sanjay's for takeaway curry which they carried back to Suzanne's flat. Charlie was at a loose end as her partner Annie was away on a course all week.

'Although why she needs to go all the way to York to learn more about being an estate agent, when there are more of them here in the capital than anywhere else in the country, I just don't understand,' she grumbled to Suzanne.

Secretly, Charlie was very proud of the success Annie was making for herself in the agency she'd joined two years ago. Already she was the senior salesperson and there was even talk of a partnership at some point in the future.

As the two women wiped the last traces of curry sauce off their plates with chunks of chapatti, Suzanne looked across at her sister.

'Charlie, why do you really want to go to Brazil? It can't just be about the money. I know you better than that.'

Charlie stared back at Suzanne and wondered what to say. How was her sister, who was already balking at the idea of crossing the Atlantic on what she saw as a wild goose chase, going to take to the idea that had been percolating through her brain ever since she'd heard Damien Bradley Smithson II say 'Brazil' that morning?

'I'll say just one word,' she said. 'Michael Hawkins.'

'That's two words,' said the pedant across the table from her, but Charlie could see she'd shocked her sister. 'Oh, Charlie, we haven't talked about him for months. What brings his name up now?'

'Come on, Suzanne, think! He went to Brazil! We have the chance to go to Brazil.'

'Brazil's a huge country, Charlie. And I thought you told us he flew to Rio?'

'He did. But there was also an ongoing internal flight on record, to São Paulo. He lives there, I'm sure of it. This gives us a chance to track him down. Prove who he is—maybe even get him back home to face trial.' Charlie stopped talking.

Suzanne was shaking her head again.

'Charlie, there are twenty million people or more living in São Paulo. How on earth are we going to be able to find one man—especially a man who's not keen on being found—among that lot? It's not like we can look him up in the telephone directory!'

'Actually, I think that's more or less exactly what we can do. You know this man; he's cool, he's arrogant, he thinks he's got away with everything. He's going to be hiding in plain sight. And you remember the sort of lifestyle he loved when he was here in England. He's going to be spending time with a certain class of people. I wouldn't be at all surprised if he isn't known to this Nigel Atkinson, or at least moves in the same circles.'

'But, even if we do find him, how are we going to deal with him? What are we going to do?'

'*We* won't be doing anything.' Charlie didn't want to push her advantage yet, but she sensed Suzanne was starting to weaken in her resolve not to take the job in

Brazil. 'You'll be there working for Damien, remember? I'll be there as your personal assistant, or whatever other title you want to give me. You'll be tied up looking around the Sunshine Supplements factory. I'll have time on my hands to sniff around and find out what I can.' She chuckled and rubbed her hands together. 'It will be just like the good old days in Zambia.'

Suzanne looked shocked and shuddered; and Charlie knew she'd gone too far, said the wrong thing. After all, it wasn't she who had been kidnapped and held prisoner in a hut in the jungle. She wasn't there when factory owner Kabwe confessed his involvement in a counterfeiting ring, before jumping to his death from her hotel balcony. Zambia had been far less pleasant for her sister than it had for her. In fact, Charlie suspected it was her experience in Zambia that made Suzanne much less willing to pursue Michael Hawkins than she herself was.

The two women decided to let the topic rest for the moment. Suzanne agreed to sleep on it and they could talk again in the morning. As Charlie said goodnight and headed to the bus-stop for the short journey to Elephant and Castle, she dared to hope her sister was coming around to her view.

The next day, Charlie was already at her desk when her sister arrived at nine o'clock. Suzanne insisted they went to work properly every weekday, even when there was nothing for them to do.

'A routine is important,' she'd insisted when they first talked about her leaving the European Medicines Agency and setting up the consultancy a year ago. 'If we're not working, we can be searching for work, pitching for projects or just keeping up to date with what's happening in the industry.'

'I couldn't sleep,' Charlie told Suzanne now. 'I never can when Annie's away. We've had a couple of emails, by the way.' Her sister's face had such a hopeful look, Charlie could almost hear her thoughts. If they could get some new projects, it would save them having to think again about the offer of work in Brazil. 'The project in Canada has gone to the American consortium, I'm afraid.'

'Well that was inevitable really.'

'But the other one is better news. We've got the project in Armenia. Apparently, the team's experience in the Former Soviet Union countries was just what they are looking for. But—'

'Well that's great news. That's only a short one at the moment, but it's the sort of project that can grow into a much bigger one. Look at the Belgian contract: a single day's audit turned into a lucrative ten-month job for several people.'

'Yes, and to think you almost turned that one down! But going back to Armenia, there's going to be a bit of a delay. They're waiting for the local project office to be set up and that's going to take several weeks, I'm afraid. They're asking if you can go out there for the kick-off meeting at the beginning of April.'

'April? But that's nearly three months away!'

'Precisely. Which means you have no excuse for not accepting the Brazilian trip, doesn't it?'

'Hmm, I thought we'd get back to that sooner or later.'

'Look, Suzanne.' Charlie thought she would have one final go at persuading her sister to accept the offer; 'at the very best, you visit this factory; find out it's all above board and put our client's mind at rest. Or you find out there's something dodgy going on and leave him to take it from there. Meanwhile I find Michael Hawkins, get the proof that he's Sir Fredrick Michaels—and we come home to England as heroes.'

'And the worst case scenario?'

'Well, it might all be a waste of time. You might not be able to get anywhere near Sunshine Supplements or Nigel Atkinson. I might not be able to track down Michael

Hawkins. Or I might track him down and find out he's a short-sighted, retired dentist from Halifax who just happened to be on a plane to Rio de Janeiro on the night Sir Fredrick Michaels disappeared. In which case we'll have had an all-expenses-paid trip to Latin America during their autumn, which is a lovely time of year. And we'll return home rested and slightly tanned, ready for you to head off to Armenia while I stay here and run the office.' By now, Suzanne was grinning and Charlie knew she'd won!

'I guess I'd better go and sort out my bikini, then, hadn't I?' said Suzanne.

Charlie let out a whoop.

'And I'll ring Damien and give him the good news,' she said.

'Make sure you ask him to push his friend for the results of the sample analysis. The more we know about this product, the better.'

'Will do.' Charlie picked up the receiver, then paused before dialling Damien's number. 'And you know the great thing about having a client with lots of money who doesn't mind spending it? Decent seats on the plane! Suzanne, I reckon this is going to be a memorable trip!'

CHAPTER 4

The sisters arrived at Heathrow Terminal 4 with plenty of time to spare on the Thursday evening. Suzanne's fear of getting stuck in traffic and missing a plane was so strong, she always allowed twice the necessary time for airport runs and although Charlie was normally mocking of what she called her sister's 'M25 syndrome', on this occasion, she raised no complaints.

As Charlie had predicted after their first meeting, their client had no quibbles about the cost of this trip—in fact he'd insisted they fly business class—and hadn't even complained much when they asked for seats on British Airways, rather than American Airlines.

Charlie seemed delighted at the opportunity to explore the facilities on offer in the lounge: lots of free food—and even a drinks cabinet. Suzanne smiled indulgently; she was much less surprised by all the goodies on offer than her sister, but it was certainly nice to be back in the place she'd lost touch with when she moved from the industry to the regulators, to become a 'poacher turned gamekeeper' as Charlie called it.

After a pleasant couple of hours sampling all the goodies, the word 'boarding' started flashing next to their flight number on the screens, and the pair headed for the departure gate. Once they were installed in their sleeper seats, Charlie started exploring once more.

'Look, Suzanne, it goes up and down at the touch of a button.'

'Yes, Charlie.'

'Wow, look at the films on offer! This is great, isn't it?'

'Yes, Charlie.'

'And as for this menu—oh boy, I'm going to enjoy this flight!'

'I'd never have guessed, Charlie.' But Suzanne was secretly delighted at her sister's pleasure and as the plane took off and turned westward towards the Atlantic, she settled down with a book, thinking she too was going to enjoy this bit of luxury, even if the project at the end of it was a little outside her comfort zone.

When they came into the arrivals hall at Guarulhos International Airport, Damien was waiting for them. They almost missed him, so intent were they on spotting 'the man with the buzzer'. Someone had warned them that the supposedly random way in which the green light over the exit gate turned red, signalling the need for a search of baggage by customs officials, was far from random. It was managed by one man with a control button who could change the colour at will.

'It will be the seemingly innocent-looking one with his hands behind his back,' Charlie had pronounced. But despite close examination of every official they passed, they were unable to spot a likely candidate, and the light stayed resolutely green as they passed under the archway.

'Although you were acting so suspiciously,' said Suzanne, 'I'm really surprised you didn't get a red light.' The two were giggling so much, they walked right past their client, who strolled up behind them and took each one by the elbow.

'Can I offer you a lift, ladies?' he drawled.

'Damien!' shrieked Charlie, throwing her arms around his neck and hugging him. Suzanne suspected the effects of one too many glasses of wine and a sleepless night watching movies might be catching up with her sister, but Damien didn't seem to mind, although he was a little pink around the gills as he turned to smile at her.

'Hello, Damien,' she said, offering him her hand. 'You'll have to excuse my sister—she's a little over-excited. Too many E numbers on the plane.'

Damien directed them to the front of the airport and then waved across to the line of hotel limos waiting for passengers.

'You really didn't have to meet us,' Suzanne said. 'We could have found the limo on our own.'

'Yes, I know,' he said, 'but it's a long flight, I thought you might be tired, and an airport arrivals hall can be such an unfriendly place without a familiar face.'

'Well, I'm delighted to see you,' said Charlie, settling back into the plush leather seating. 'And so is Suzanne, although my sister's too much of a reserved English Rose to admit it.'

Suzanne looked daggers at Charlie, then turned to Damien with a smile.

'Okay, boss,' she said, 'where do we start? Do you have a plan for getting me together with Nigel Atkinson?'

'No,' he said slowly, 'I think you're going to have to work on that yourselves.' She looked at him in alarm but he patted her arm before continuing. 'It's okay, I'm not going to desert you completely. But don't forget I've been talking about this company for a while, trying to get someone to believe my concerns. I think I'm probably on their undesirables list. Being seen with me is definitely not going to do your cause any good.'

'But, I can't just phone them out of the blue...'

'No, I'm not expecting you to do that, but we need to find a way you can meet up with our Nigel without raising his suspicions.'

'Well,' said Charlie, 'that sounds to me like a social occasion, rather than a business setting. Catch him off-duty, and off-guard, so to speak.'

Damien was nodding vigorously.

'My thought precisely. The marathon itself isn't until Sunday, but tomorrow there's a fun run and an afternoon of races for the kiddies. And in the evening, there's a reception—a sort of Meet the Sponsors session in the VIP marquee!'

'And by any chance...?'

'Yup, Sunshine Supplements is one of the sponsors. Nigel and his entourage will definitely be there.'

'And can you get us in?' Suzanne asked hopefully. Damien grinned and put his hand in his pocket. 'Well, it so happens, I have two passes for the VIP marquee right here. All the international competitors get the chance to apply for one—and it was easy to find someone over here on their own willing to sell me his. Oh, and here's some background reading on the race and the sponsors.'

As he handed the tickets and a thick glossy folder to Charlie, the car turned into a flower-lined drive and pulled up outside the hotel. Porters opened the doors, opened the boot, and whisked away their luggage, while a smiling doorman ushered them inside to check in. Charlie gazed up at the smoked-glass atrium, stretching through thirty or more floors; took in the piles of expensive-looking suitcases, and elegantly dressed guests; and gave a whistle.

'I'm guessing not all your opponents are staying in places like this,' she asked.

Damien nodded his head.

'You're right. The race starts and finishes at the university and most of the runners are staying nearer to the campus,' he said. 'In fact, although I've got a room here, I'm staying there some nights myself, with a few of the other Americans. Much better for morale and team spirit that way.' He stretched and gave a yawn. 'So, if you ladies will excuse me, I'm going to head back there. I had an early morning training session and there's another one booked for this evening. So I'm going to take a nap while I have the chance.'

He shook their hands, but before turning away, he paused. 'Remember, Suzanne, you're not going to be alone over here. If you're at all concerned at any point, just send me a signal—or text me if you don't know where I am. I may be hidden, but I'll be around most of the time.' Then with a wave, he strode off across the foyer and out into the sunshine.

'Oh dear,' said Suzanne staring after the disappearing figure, 'I'm not sure he's exactly what I would look for in a crisis.'

'What do you mean? Don't you trust him?'

'Oh, no, nothing like that. I think he's completely trustworthy and,' glancing around their luxurious surroundings, 'the sort of client I could definitely get used to. But let's face it; he's little more than skin and bone under those smart clothes of his. I'm not sure I'd want to rely on him if I was in trouble.'

'Oh, I don't know,' came the reply from a smiling Charlie. 'It never does to judge a book by its cover. I suspect there's a little more to Mr Damien Bradley Smithson II than meets the eye.'

She opened the folder and was casually flicking through the glossy marketing literature. Then she froze and gave a gasp.

'What is it, Charlie?' Suzanne asked. Her sister held out a sheet for her to see. It was the reprint of a newspaper article.

'It's a piece about the race and some of the big name competitors,' she said.

'Yes? And..?'

'Look at the name below this photograph.' She pointed to the picture of a striking-looking woman in running gear. 'Her name's Mercy Gove Hawkins.'

'Hawkins? It can't be the same one. It's not a good

photo, but she looks black to me.'

'But it's a start, isn't it, Suzanne? It's better than nothing.' Charlie rubbed her hands together. 'As Sherlock would say, the game's afoot.'

CHAPTER 5

'Well, well; Michael Hawkins and brawling runners all within the space of fifteen minutes! Who'd have thought it?' Charlie's words, against a background of children's races and a tannoy call for Fun Run entrants to go to the registration tent, broke into Suzanne's thoughts and dragged her back to the present. 'I could do with a drink. Do you reckon they've opened the champagne in the VIP lounge yet?'

'Oh, I doubt it,' said Suzanne glancing at her watch, 'it's only just gone eleven! But I wouldn't say no to a coffee if there's any going.'

'Come on, this is Brazil; of course there'll be coffee! But I'm still going to look for something a little stronger. I'll see you in a bit,' and Charlie went off in search of the refreshments tent while Suzanne headed for the sponsors' marquee.

It's highly unlikely Nigel Atkinson will be here this early, she thought, as she strolled across the grass, *but if Sunshine Supplements has any sort of marketing department, some of the minions should be setting up the displays, ready for when the punters arrive.*

It was a large marquee, covered with brightly-coloured

adverts for each of the championship's major sponsors. And there, right in the middle was the huge yellow logo of Sunshine Supplements. This looked like a good place to start.

Suzanne walked inside, helped herself to a coffee from the automatic machine and then casually glanced around to see what was going on. Along three sides of the tent, apart from where there were open flaps, long tables had been set up and teams of bright young things were putting up promotional displays, chattering all the time in a variety of languages, although Suzanne guessed Portuguese was the prominent one. She began strolling, sipping from her cup and glancing at each display in feigned interest. But as she approached the end of the tent and the one display she was really interested in, she got a surprise.

'Oh buggeration, now what am I going to do?' The words came from the mouth of a stunningly beautiful young woman with a head of red hair that would have done justice to any Pre-Raphaelite heroine. It was a surprise to hear the words spoken in English but even more so to hear them in a thick Belfast. Suzanne took a deep breath and stopped right by the table.

'You sound like you've got a problem. Can I do anything to help?'

The woman looked around, apparently startled by Suzanne's question. Then she smiled and shook her head,

'That's kind of you, but unless you travel with Scotch tape in your bag, I don't think so.' She pulled a face and put her hands on her hips before groaning loudly. 'I brought all the marketing stuff for the display but didn't bring anything to fix it up. And the office is halfway across the city. It would take ages to get there. I'm going to have to go and find me a shop somewhere, I guess.'

'This might help,' said Suzanne, fishing into her bag and pulling out an unopened pack of Blu Tack.' The woman looked at her in amazement and Suzanne felt compelled to explain. 'I saw it in the shop in Heathrow and thought it might be useful. It's got me out of all sorts of difficulties in the past.'

'You're a life-saver,' grinned the woman, taking the proffered pack and then holding out her hand. 'I'm Megan, by the way, PA to Nigel Atkinson. He's CEO of Sunshine Supplements. And you are?'

'Suzanne. Suzanne Jones.' The minute the words were out of her mouth, she realised her mistake. She'd agreed her cover story with Damien and Charlie the evening before and decided she would use a false name. Well, it was too late now; but at least she remembered the rest of the story. 'I'm a freelance sports journalist. I'm researching a story on athletes and nutrition. It's been commissioned by one of the red tops back home; but I'm hoping we can get it syndicated too.'

'Well, you've come to the right place,' said Megan. 'And my boss is going to want to talk to you. He really wants to make a splash over our new product.' She opened the packet and started pulling off tiny balls of Blu Tack. 'Look, let me get this display finished then we can go and get some lunch and you can tell me more about the story. Nigel's going to get here around five, so I'll introduce you to him later on.'

It was after six and the reception was in full swing, when Suzanne met up again with Megan, at the entrance to the marquee.

'There you are! I was wondering where you'd got to! Come and meet Nigel. I've told him all about you and he's looking forward to having a chat.'

Suzanne knew several of the local runners were being sponsored by Sunshine Supplements, so wasn't surprised to see Nigel Atkinson holding court to a group of admiring youngsters. He was a huge man, towering over the heads of most of his companions. His muscular arms strained against the material of his short-sleeved shirt. This was a man who spent many hours in the gym, by the look of it. He clutched a pint glass of water in one hand which he was waving to emphasise a point as they arrived. When he saw the two women approaching, he put down his drink and held his arms wide in welcome.

'Hello, Megan, baby, how're you doing?' His accent was pure New York; even Suzanne was able to recognise that, and was surprised, as Megan had told her Atkinson came from Florida originally. 'And this must be the reporter from the big newspaper in England.'

'Hey, Nigel, I've told you before, there's more to the United Kingdom than England!' Megan put her hands on her hips and emphasised her Northern Irish accent, but her boss just grinned at her and blew her a kiss.

'Chill out, Megan,' he said, 'I know there's more to our transatlantic cousins than England—but let's face it, London's where it's at!' Then turning to Suzanne, he held out his hand. 'Ms Jones, I'm delighted to meet you. I understand you want to interview me about our new baby?' Suzanne nodded her head and was about to go into her freelance reporter's act, but Atkinson didn't let her get a word in. 'Not today, honey,' he said, waving his hand dangerously close to her face, and causing her to take an involuntary step backwards. 'Today we're all off duty. We'll get together during the week and sort something out. Give Megan a ring on Monday morning; she's got my diary. Now, let's party.'

Atkinson called a waiter and gestured to Suzanne to help herself from the tray of drinks he was carrying. Then the boss of Sunshine Supplements turned back to his audience of seemingly adoring fans, his visitor from the United Kingdom apparently forgotten. Suzanne didn't mind. It gave her the chance to observe what was going on, see if she could pick up any tips about Nigel Atkinson that would help her in her role as a reporter when she finally sat down to interview him.

But his banter and overbearing personality soon

became wearisome. She had just decided to finish her drink and head back to Charlie and Damien, when her attention was drawn to a new arrival in the marquee.

When she first noticed him, the man was standing looking out across the sports field and all she could see was his back, which was bent and stooping. His iron grey hair cascaded down his back to well below his shoulders and was held in place by a beaded headband. *How quaint,* she thought, *like a throwback to the 1960s.* And then the man turned around and she was surprised to see a truly ancient-looking face, leathery from sun-tanning, and heavily wrinkled. There was something vaguely familiar about him, but Suzanne couldn't place him.

As she watched, Nigel Atkinson walked across with the same expansive smile he'd given her earlier and put his arm around the man's shoulders. He towered above him and had to bend to talk to him over the surrounding hubbub. Still smiling, Atkinson turned to face the view outside, his momentum carrying his companion with him. It looked for all the world like two old friends admiring the view, yet Suzanne got the distinct impression that wasn't what was happening at all. She edged closer to the entrance and was just in time to hear Atkinson hiss, '...shouldn't be here. You'll be recognised. Go home.' In one smooth movement he released the man, took his glass of wine away from him and gave him a push. The man stumbled slightly, righted himself and looked over his shoulder at Atkinson, before turning and shambling off into the night. Atkinson handed the second glass to a passing waiter and strolled back to his guests. But Suzanne thought she saw a fleeting look of fury on his face before he switched his smile back on.

CHAPTER 6

'You okay, sweetheart? You're very quiet.' Her father's voice broke into her thoughts, startling Mercy and making her almost drop the cup of coffee she was cradling in her hands as she stared out of the window. He must have seen her reaction, for he reached out and touched her lightly on the shoulder. 'Sorry, I didn't mean to frighten you.' She steeled herself not to flinch, adopting the dutiful daughter look she'd been practising for more than a year.

'It's fine, Tata; you didn't scare me. I just didn't hear you coming in.'

'Well, that's good, but is anything wrong? I don't like to see you like this.'

If only he knew what's really going on in my head, she thought, But how could he? He'd been her father for thirty-five years, but had only known her for such a short time. There was so much he wasn't aware of.

She wasn't quiet at all. Inside she was a seething mass of emotions: excitement, anticipation, and just a tiny touch of fear. Her first race as a veteran. She wanted this so badly; what if there was someone there who was even better than her?

When Hawkins disturbed her, she wasn't, as he

thought, just staring out of the window. In fact, although her eyes were apparently trained on the view outside, she was actually visualising the route for tomorrow's race, imagining what it would be like to take part, to the cheers of the local supporters and, hopefully, the respect of the visitors. So not quiet at all; apart from on the surface.

Now she turned away from the window and followed him across to the large white leather sofa in front of the empty fireplace. She curled her legs under her in the opposite corner and smiled at him.

'You were late in, last night. How did the dinner go?' she asked. Hawkins had invited her to accompany him to a dinner he was hosting for some Chilean business associates visiting Brazil, but she'd pleaded a headache and stayed at home. The last thing she needed was a heavy meal just before a race weekend. Her father grimaced and shrugged his shoulders.

'It was okay. The usual business dinner, too much food, far too many toasts. You didn't miss anything. Are you feeling better, by the way?'

'Yes, I'm fine. Just a bit of pre-competition nerves, I guess.' It didn't hurt for him to think her a little vulnerable. It made him even more solicitous than normal. Hawkins showed few emotions; but she suspected he felt guilty about abandoning her mother. Well, he must do. Otherwise, why would he have gone to so much trouble to find her and bring her over here to Brazil? And a little guilt did no-one any harm.

'You don't have to do this, you know.' His words pulled her out of her reverie once more.

'Pardon me?'

'This competition, tomorrow's race. You don't have to take part. If it's too much for you, you can always pull out.'

'Would you? If you were me, would you pull out?'

'But, honey, that's different. I'm a man. We have to do things all the time that we don't want to, that we're frightened of. It's what we do. But no-one's going to think any the less of you if you pull out. You've had a huge change in your life; it's bound to affect you somewhat. No-one would blame you!'

'No, I couldn't possibly. But it's fine. I don't know why I talked about nerves. I'm perfectly okay.'

He stared at her in silence, and she coolly held his gaze, determined not to show how his scrutiny disturbed her. Then he nodded and grinned at her.

'Okay, if you're sure.' Then he held up his finger. 'Wait a minute, I've just had a thought. How about if you throw the race?'

'I don't understand; what do you mean?' She was genuinely puzzled; it was a term she wasn't familiar with.

'Well, go ahead and compete from the start. There'll be loads of people milling around. Run for a kilometre or so, then when you get to one of the quiet streets, have a bit of a tumble. You will have competed, tried your best and can then retire gracefully, leaving the others to run the rest of the course.'

It was as though he'd punched her in the chest and for a few seconds she found it impossible to breathe, so hot was the anger surging through her. How could he suggest that? How could he think she would even consider such an action? She was going to compete and she was going to win. She stared into the fireplace for a moment, waiting for her own heat to die down. Then she stretched, uncurled herself and moved towards him, a warm smile plastered across her face. She bent to kiss his cheek. He took her hand and held it to his lips.

'You're very sweet,' she said, 'but you don't need to worry about me. I really am perfectly okay.' And she strolled out of the room, only allowing her simpering smile to slip once she was halfway up the stairs.

They had passed the 35 kilometre marker moments before. Mercy was leading the veteran women's field by nearly ten seconds and was beating all but a handful of the male veterans as well.

Then three things happened at once. A cat streaked across the road in front of her and she swerved to avoid the flying ball of orange fur. A voice in the crowd screamed, 'Lucky, no! Come back,' above a furious barking sound. She paused, momentarily, glancing in the direction of the shout, then her legs were bowled from under her as she collided with the large Alsatian running across the road in pursuit of its feline enemy.

Pushing aside the hands that reached out to help her, she pulled herself to her feet and checked there was no damage. Then she started running again. Several competitors had streamed past her as she lay on the ground and although she fought her way back, one runner at a time, there just wasn't quite enough of the race left.

Feeling the weight of the silver medal around her neck, Mercy gritted her teeth and applauded with everyone else as the new champion received the gold.

At dinner that night, Mercy displayed her usual calm exterior to the outside world, especially to her father, but inside a fire was raging, bubbling up and threatening to spill over at the slightest provocation. How could she have lost? She had trained so hard, practised every day; the gold medal should have been hers. That damn dog, running out like that at the wrong moment. Was it deliberate, she wondered, or just a mistimed, ill-fated accident?

But she blamed herself really. She shouldn't have been put off by a simple shout. In a crowd, there would always be someone making noise, coughing, laughing or talking too loudly. Athletes were trained to ignore distractions like this. She should have looked where she was going, then she could have avoided the dog. No, she had no-one to blame but herself. Although that didn't mean she wouldn't cheerfully strangle the young owner if she bumped into him in a dark alley.

Next time, it would be different. She was determined about that. She was not going to be beaten again. And the only consolation was she wouldn't have to wait a whole year before getting her revenge—and that was how she thought of it—revenge for the slight of being pushed into second place. There were marathons in lots of cities, all over South America, and other parts of the world as well. She would just have to pick her next target.

'Shall we start with champagne, sweetheart?' Her father's words pulled her out of her daydream with a start and she looked around, taking note of her surroundings for the first time. Usually, when they ate out, it was in one of the barbeque restaurants, complete with fire pit and waiters wandering around with joints of meat on giant skewers. But tonight, Michael Hawkins had decreed they would go somewhere different, somewhere special. 'After all,' he'd said, 'it's not every day my little girl is a medal winner, now is it?' And although Mercy had cringed at the idea of her father, several centimetres shorter than her, referring to her as little; and despite the fact that at thirty-five, it was many years since she had been considered a girl, she had readily agreed to his suggestion. From tomorrow, she was going to be on a strict training regime, including diet, but tonight she wanted to be treated, to take her mind off her humiliation, as she considered the silver medal to be.

'Yes, thank you, Tata. I would like that,' she said now. The waiter bowed and walked away across the polished, shining floor towards the bar. The restaurant, located on Rua Augusta, São Paulo's most exclusive shopping area, was small, discreet and, she assumed, very expensive. She'd never been anywhere like this when she was growing up—in fact, she was fairly sure there wasn't anywhere like this in Mozambique—but she'd quickly learned that Michael Hawkins liked to live the high life and to treat those around him whenever he got the chance. She'd fleetingly felt guilty about the people she'd left behind, but she'd pushed her conscience to the deepest recesses of her mind and learned to enjoy her newly acquired standard of living.

There were only a dozen tables in the room, separated by enough space to allow private conversations, but close enough to provide an intimate atmosphere. The table linen was crisp, white, with the discreet logo of the Michelin-starred chef in the centre. The cutlery and glasses sparkled from the extra polish they would no doubt have received just before being laid out; and the china was plain, white, but always with a slight twist in the design. The waiters were polite and friendly, but never intrusive. Mercy loved this place—and was grudgingly touched at the thought of her father for trying to celebrate a success even if she didn't see it as such.

It was only as they were finishing a delicate peach dessert, with melt-in-the-mouth meringues and a contrastingly tart lemon sorbet that Mercy realised her father had been very quiet throughout the evening. He'd been attentive to her needs as always; he'd shaken hands with a couple of acquaintances who stopped at their table on their way out; and he'd discussed each dish with her as it arrived—continuing her all-round education that had been an aim of his since she arrived in Brazil—but there was definitely something amiss. Now he placed his spoon on the empty plate and stared into space.

'Tata, is anything wrong?' she asked. There was no answer and she had to ask the question a second time before he gave a start and turned back to her. He reached over and patted her hand. As always the gesture put her teeth on edge and she resisted the urge to snatch her arm away.

'I'm sorry, Mercy, have I been neglecting you?'

'Not at all—it's been a wonderful evening—but you seemed distracted. I wondered if something was worrying you?'

He exhaled sharply and shook his head.

'Not really. It's just that I saw someone today in the crowd at the sports field. Just a face, for a moment that I'm sure I've seen before. Someone from the past, I think. I can't remember when or where. But somehow, I feel it's someone I'd rather not bump into.'

Mercy and Michael Hawkins had spoken very little so far about his time in Mozambique and the circumstances leading up to her birth to Grace Gove in the slums of Lourenço Marques. Mercy knew a little bit of the story—she'd heard it often enough from her mother when she'd had too much to drink. And that was a conversation she would make sure she and her father had one day soon—when she decided the time was right. But there was also a thirty-year gap that so far he'd failed to fill for her. Now she looked questioningly at him, wondering if he was going to let her into some of his secrets at last. But apparently not.

'I'm sure it's nothing to worry about. It's probably one of those doppelgängers we hear so much about.' He glanced around and beckoned to the waiter, making the internationally recognised sign for the bill. 'Right, let's get you home. If you really are starting training again straight away, you're going to need your beauty sleep.'

As they walked across the restaurant to the door and waited for the car to be brought around to the front, Mercy looked thoughtfully at her father. She wasn't sure, but when he said 'nothing to worry about' it sounded to her like he was trying to convince himself, rather than her.

PART II

CHAPTER 7

West Yorkshire, August 1955

I was fifteen when I ran away from home. I considered myself an orphan from then on.

It was ten years after the end of the war and Britain was starting, finally, to climb out of the mire and make something of itself. Rationing had finished. People were in work. It should have been a good time. But with my father, it was never going to be.

Stanley Hawkins was a miner from West Yorkshire. He was a real man's man; worked hard, earned his money, expected his dinner on the table when he got home—and woe betide my mother, Ethel, if it was late, or not cooked to perfection. We kids learnt to hide on a Friday night when he spent half the week's money in the pub on his way home from work. My mother was always there, waiting, when he came in—and had the bruises to show for it the next day. I never once heard her raise her voice to him or try to fight back. She was so weak, so pathetic!

The only thing my father really loved was his music. He played the trumpet in the local marching band and every Sunday throughout the summer we would go and watch him play in the park or at galas around the county. I would make sure I was at the front of the crowd when he first marched past, waving and cheering him on, then I would disappear and meet my mates until it was time to go home. But my mother and my sisters would stand and watch him every time, all afternoon, come rain or shine.

Then in 1950 there was an accident at the pit. I remember standing with my mother and the other women at the pit head for hours. There was a terrible silence hanging over the crowd, no-one uttered a word. And then they started bringing out the bodies. My mother was trembling and her mouth kept moving silently. I think she must have been praying. Such a silly woman, I thought. Can't she see this is the chance for us to get out from under his rule and start enjoying life? Everything is so much simpler for a child, isn't it?

My father was one of the last to be brought out. He was still alive, but his legs were crushed and one of them was hanging off. When they chopped it off just below the knee, I prayed he would die and leave us in peace, but the old bugger was stronger than all of us and he survived. For months there was peace in the house. Of course he shouted still, well sometimes anyway; but he was too weak to do anything else and my mother's bruises faded. Then one day he was well enough to get out of bed and it all started again. But now he was around the house during the day as well. And every Sunday we still had to go back to the park and watch the band play. My father would start out each time excited at the chance to see his old mates and listen to his beloved brass band—but it would always end up the same way. He would become morose and unhappy at having to stand in the crowd, but he couldn't walk without his crutches; couldn't march and play the trumpet at the same time. He would slope off to the pub with the rest of the musicians afterwards and come home hours later in a temper. And once again my mother would bear the brunt of his anger and frustration.

On my fifteenth birthday, my mother had a surprise for me. She'd saved some money out of her scant housekeeping and bought me a penknife. Well, it was more than just an ordinary penknife; it was a lock knife with a studded wooden handle. All day, I kept pulling it out of my pocket, flicking it open and pretending to slice through something. My father watched me and didn't say anything. Then he stomped off to the pub. And for once, I was still there when he returned.

'Oh look,' he sneered as soon as he came through the door, 'it's the bleedin' birthday boy. Still playing around with that toy knife of

yours, are you?' I ignored him, which seemed to make him even madder.

'Hey, I'm talking to you, boy,' he growled.

My mother cleared her throat nervously.

'Answer your father, Michael,' she whispered.

'Yes, answer your father, Michael,' he parroted in a high pitched voice, 'or you'll feel the back of my hand across that smug face of yours.'

'You wouldn't dare,' I said quietly. 'I'm as big as you now—and I've got all my limbs too!' I don't know what got into me. I'd never argued back at him before, but that day, it all got too much for me.

For an injured man on crutches, he could move a lot faster than I realised. With a roar of anger, he launched himself across the room and cannoned into me, knocking me down into an armchair. Leaning against the back, he raised one of his crutches and brought it down across my left arm which was stretched out trying to stop my fall. It didn't hurt too much, but the next one did—and the next—and the next. I heard my mother scream and beg him to stop, but he wasn't going to listen to her, now was he?

I curled into a ball on the chair and wrapped my left arm, numb as it was, around my head to protect myself. With my other hand, I pulled my knife out of my pocket and flicked it open. Then rolling to the edge of the seat, I dropped to the floor and slashed upwards, catching him on his good leg, just behind the knee. He went down like a rock face after an explosion and lay wailing on the floor beside me. My mother screamed again.

Jumping to my feet, I ran for the door, grabbing my coat from the hook on my way past. I was out of the house within seconds. It was the last time I clapped eyes on either of my parents. I had no idea how much damage I'd done with my knife—and I didn't care.

I spent that first night hiding under a hedge near the pit. I had friends I knew would be willing to take me in—but I also knew my father, or even the police, would look there first. In the morning, I crept into the back garden of the pit manager's cottage. The milkman had been earlier, leaving two pint bottles on the doorstep. I grabbed one and drank it straight down. There was an apple tree leaning against the back fence with a good crop of early fruit. It was tart, not really ready for eating, but my belly was so empty, I just gobbled one down, then reached up for a couple more to put in my pocket.

'Hey, get out of there, you little tyke,' came a shout from the upstairs window. The manager was just getting up ready for the early shift and by bad luck had been looking out of the window at the wrong moment. I jumped over the back fence and headed down the road before he had time to come downstairs and catch me.

I walked for the next week, sleeping in barns or bus shelters, stealing food where I could and foraging for fruit and vegetables the rest of the time. Seven days into my sixteenth year, I smelled salt in the air and from the top of a hill, looked down on the sea for the first time. I had reached Liverpool.

Like many waifs and strays, I headed for the waterfront. I wasn't the only child living rough in the city and I teamed up with a group of kids down by the docks. They showed me how to keep warm by wrapping myself in newspaper at night. They told me about the Seamen's Mercy Mission on Hanover Street, set up to help all sailors fallen on hard times, but also willing to help anyone in trouble. And they introduced me to Father Pat, a young clergyman in a tough seafront parish, who could always be relied upon to provide a penny for a cup of tea and a piece of toast, no questions asked.

'What are you going to do with your life?' he asked me one day as we sat on a bench on the docks, looking out at the seagulls squawking on the breeze. 'You're a smart lad; you don't belong out here on the streets.'

'God knows!' I said, shrugging my shoulders.

'Yes, son, I know He does,' was the gentle reply, 'but He's not going to make any moves for you. You're going to have to sort things out for yourself.'

I took my knife out of my pocket and started flipping it open and closed. It was the only thing I'd brought with me from my old life.

'Have you thought about emigrating?' he asked. 'Going off to another country, where there's more opportunities for a young lad like yourself.'

I stared at him in disbelief.

'Are you mad? How can I do that? I have no papers, no

passport, and no money.'

But he just laughed.

'Oh, I think we can get around that problem,' he said. 'Where do you fancy? How about America. The land of the free? Milkshakes, Frank Sinatra, Hollywood, motherhood and apple pie.'

'Sounds wonderful. But how would I get there?

'Don't worry about that, son; I'll sort it out,' he said. And I believed him. Why wouldn't I?

Father Pat took me to meet a friend of his; a grizzled old captain with a wall eye and breath that stank of fish and stale tobacco. He looked me up and down, then sniffed, cleared his throat and spat on the pavement.

'Ah well, he's a bit scrawny, but I guess he'll do all right!' he said. 'Tomorrow night, dock 9, eight o'clock.' And turning on his heel he stomped away down the lane towards the nearest pub. I felt a shiver of excitement and fear, mixed with cold, but that faded as Father Pat clapped me on the shoulder.

'I think he likes you! Now make sure you're not late tomorrow. The good captain doesn't tolerate poor timekeeping—and you don't get chances like this every day!'

I spent the last day with my little gang of mates down by the docks, chucking stones over the sea wall and watching the crowds embarking on the big ocean-going liner that was due to leave in the evening. One of the kids asked if this was the ship I was going to be on.

'I doubt it,' I said. 'Mine's on dock 9, over on the cargo side, not here among the passenger ships. But we're all going to the same place, so who knows? I may bump into some of these fine folks when I get to America.'

At first sight, the Prince Albert *wasn't much to look at—and she didn't get any better on second look either. She was much smaller than the liner; originally red and white but now so covered in rust that it was more orange and grey. Her deck was full of crates and odd shaped packages covered in rope netting. The captain was standing on deck chatting to a couple of scruffy looking sailors, who spoke with a strange accent, which I took to be American. They talked so fast, I could barely follow half of what they said.*

'Welcome on board, young man,' said the captain, giving me what I recognised, even in my innocence, as a mocking bow. The sailors grinned evilly at me and I decided I would keep out of their way as much as possible on the voyage.

Within a short while, the ropes were released, the anchor lifted and we pulled away from the jetty. I stood on deck until the lights of the harbour were just pinpricks in the distance. Then I turned away, wondering if I would ever see England again. Although at that point, I don't think I really cared.

The captain was standing at the hatchway leading down to the crew quarters and engine room. I gave him a grin as I walked towards him.

'How long will it take, Captain?' I asked, 'to get to America? When are we going to arrive?'

He stared at me, then gave one of his trademark spits.

'A bloody long time, boy. We're not going to America. Who told you that?' I looked around wildly, but the lights of the shore had finally disappeared and all I could see was the stars and a trace of moonlight on the wake of the boat behind us. 'We're headed for the Dark Continent, boy! Didn't your precious Father Pat tell you?'

'But I don't understand...'

'Well, that doesn't make no matter with me! We're bound for Cape Town. Got a few stops along the way, so we should be there in about six weeks. I told Father Pat I needed a strong lad to run errands, help in the kitchen and who knows what else—and he brought you to me.' I stared at him in disbelief. Then I started to tremble; with fear, with rage, with cold, or maybe a mix of all three. He reached across and grabbed me by my shoulders and gave me a shake. 'Snap out of it, boy, and get below. Cook needs help getting supper ready.'

That was one of the longest six weeks of my life. The captain was tough but fair; but the seven members of his crew were vile and took every opportunity to make my life a misery. If I did anything too slowly, I got a cuff around the head. If they thought I was being smart or cheeky, I got the back of their hands across my face. When we were in port, they locked me in one of the storage lockers. They made me eat last, and often there was very little food left.

And at night, I lay on my bunk in the darkness, waiting for the inevitable scrape of boot on metal and rough hands under the bedclothes as one or other of them forced themselves on me, quickly, brutally, silently. Many times I thought of twisting around and plunging my knife into one loathsome belly or another, or fantasised about slicing through their balls, so they could never do this to anyone else. But I was trapped on a small boat with a harsh crew and no-one else knew I was there, or cared. If I hurt one of them, I knew the others would have no compunction in throwing me overboard. And no-one would ever know the difference.

Then one morning, we reached land. I'd struggled up from sleep and forced myself on deck, wondering just how many more nights I could take. And in front of me at last was the sight I'd prayed so long for. A harbour, a growing township, and behind, a flat mountain, looking like some giant had sliced the top off with his knife. And as I stood looking out over the water and felt the African sun on my back for the very first time, I swore no-one would take advantage of me, ever again. My parents, Father Pat, the captain and crew of the Prince Albert. *I was done with all of them. And I was going to be the strong one from then on.*

CHAPTER 8

'Attention span of a grasshopper, our Nigel,' Megan whispered, creeping up on Suzanne as she was processing the scene she'd just observed and wondering just what the elderly man had done to upset Atkinson. 'Come on, let's get you some food.'

Suzanne was momentarily irritated, as she'd planned to slip quietly away, back to the hotel. But in the event, she decided to relax and let the following week take care of itself. Megan was good company; funny, scathing and totally lacking in respect for anyone. At least that's what she was like when she was off-duty.

When Suzanne phoned Sunshine Supplements first thing the following morning, Megan was back in professional mode, telling her Nigel Atkinson had cleared his diary for the day and was expecting her at ten-thirty am. She jumped in a taxi and just made it in time, to be met by a smiling Megan at the door of the huge glass building in the industrial municipality of Diadema, south-east of the city centre and some fifteen kilometres from her hotel.

After signing her in, Megan took Suzanne to her boss's office for coffee and an introductory talk. Suzanne and

Charlie had spent time the previous week working on the role she would adopt; and she slipped into it cautiously, holding out her hand to shake his.

'Mr Atkinson, it's so good of you to see me. I know you must be really busy, what with the new product and all.'

'Nigel, please!' he replied, 'You're not in stuffy old London town now, young lady. This is Latin America.' And waving aside her outstretched hand, he took hold of her shoulders and kissed her on both cheeks. 'And we don't shake hands over here either.'

Megan poured three cups of coffee and then joined them on easy chairs in a corner of the sumptuous room the CEO of Sunshine Supplements used as an office. The three of them chatted inconsequentially about the weekend race meeting and then Atkinson checked his Rolex and cleared his throat.

'Right, let's get started. How do you want to play this?'

'Well, I thought we'd start with some general questions about you, get to know the man behind Sunshine Supplements and then talk about the company and the products,' said Suzanne. 'Although,' and she gave a self-deprecating little laugh, 'you'll have to go easy on the scientific terms. I was never keen on chemistry at school.'

'Nigel, why don't you give Suzanne the factory tour first?' said Megan. 'That way, she'll have a better idea of what you're talking about.'

'Great suggestion.' He drained his coffee cup and jumped up. 'Are you going to join us, Megan?'

But she was already heading back to her desk.

'I've got a ton of work to catch up on after last week. I'll leave you to it and see you at lunchtime. I've booked us a table for two o'clock.'

From the street, the Sunshine Supplements building looked modern and state of the art. The glass-fronted building, although owned by Nigel Atkinson, housed not only his offices, but also a number of tenants, mostly medical professionals, judging by the list of names in the foyer. Atkinson told her that despite its industrial roots, Diadema was building quite a reputation for itself in the service sector, especially in the field of healthcare. The factory was an older, two-storey structure at the rear of the site, the two buildings connected by a covered walkway.

There was a suit of white factory clothing waiting for each of them in the visitors' changing room. Suzanne watched with interest as Atkinson donned the coat, buttoned it up carefully and put on the disposable hat. She copied his actions, all the time pretending this was completely new to her.

The supplement was a variation on the popular herbal tea drunk by so many people across the continent and was provisionally called Super Fit, although Megan had told her they were exploring the possibility of changing it to Super Maté. As a tea, it was classified as a foodstuff rather than a pharmaceutical. Suzanne had confirmed this through ANVISA, the Brazilian regulatory agency, before leaving the UK. So she was very interested to see it was being made in cleanroom conditions, just as one would make a tablet or a capsule. From other food factories she'd visited over the years, she knew this was highly unusual. Normally, producers went for the most basic facilities they could get away with. This was apparently not the case in Sunshine Supplements. She made a note to herself to explore this question at some point, but without alerting Atkinson to her knowledge of this technology.

Super Fit was in the form of dried leaves mixed with powdered granules, filled into gauze packets which were then sealed in paper and packed into boxes of ten.

'Oh, they look just like ordinary tea bags,' Suzanne said when they stood in the corridor looking into the packing hall. She had already 'ooh'd' and 'aah'd' her way around the manufacturing rooms, hoping to convince Atkinson she was seeing this sort of facility for the first time.

'Yes, I suppose they do to a lay person,' he said, smiling

at her in the way she remembered teachers smiling when she'd given the right answer in class. 'But they pack much more of a punch than that. Well, you saw that yesterday, didn't you? Some of 'our' runners did really well in the marathon.'

They continued walking and then entered an open area two storeys high, with racking reaching to the roof.

'I guess this would be the warehouse,' Suzanne said.

'Smart girl.'

Atkinson was obviously very proud of this part of the factory, and Suzanne could understand why. It was pretty much state of the art, with robotic controls and transport systems. He began spouting all sorts of statistics and Suzanne pretended to write them all down. But really, she was taking note of the chemicals she could see stored on the shelves. There were some standard ones she expected to find, like lactose and starch, both of which would have been used to make the granules. But there were others she was very surprised to see. *I need to go away and think about all this and do some research*, she thought. She cleared her throat.

'Tell me, Mr Atkinson.' He raised an eyebrow at her and she amended it. 'I mean, Nigel, did you have much difficulty with the authorities?'

'In what way?' he said, looking confused.

'Well, with health and safety. People are much more cagey about how this sort of product is made, aren't they?'

'No, no,' he waved his hand dismissively, 'this is a foodstuff, my dear, not a medicine. It's not subject to the same rules and regulations as other powders and potions produced for athletes and others.' He nodded his head and smiled at her. 'So everything went very well with the authorities, I'm pleased to say.'

Suzanne wasn't at all convinced by his performance, but decided this was the time to stop asking questions. She didn't want to raise his suspicions.

'Right, if you've seen enough,' he said, 'let's go back to my office and get started on the interview proper. We've got a bit of time left before lunch.'

As they walked back towards the passageway to the office block, they passed a locked door labelled *Private; No Entry*.

A door at the end of the corridor flew open and someone started walking towards them. His white coat was unbuttoned and flapped as he walked. His hat was sitting sideways on his head and completely failed to tame the thick mane of grey hair flowing past his shoulders. Suzanne recognised immediately the elderly man ejected from the marquee on Saturday night. He seemed to catch Atkinson's eye as they passed each other, but neither man spoke.

Again, Suzanne thought the man looked familiar, but she still couldn't put a name to the face. She paused and watched him continue on his way. The man's sprightly walk certainly belied his age. As she watched, he stopped at the locked door, pulled a key from his pocket, and let himself in. She heard the key turn once more from the other side of the door.

'That looks mysterious. What's in there?' Suzanne asked, but Atkinson was striding ahead of her and didn't seem to hear her question. *Or if he did,* Suzanne thought, *it doesn't look like he's going to answer me.*

CHAPTER 9

Charlie was delighted that her instincts had been proved to be correct. There was indeed a connection between Mercy and Michael Hawkins. So while Suzanne pushed forward with the investigation into Sunshine Supplements, she decided it was time to make contact with the runner, to see if there was any way she could reach her quarry through her. She'd noticed a name on the back of the girl's tracksuit: São Paulo Runners; that's where she would start. A chat with the concierge at the hotel quickly gained her the address and advice on how to get there. Her taxi pulled up to the gates just after ten am.

But she was out of luck. When she arrived, the gate was open, but the clubhouse was locked and there was no-one around.

'Well, what did you expect?' she chided herself. 'It's Monday morning; most people will be at work.' She checked the clubhouse hours on the door and made a note to come back later in the day. As she turned away and walked down the steps, she realised she should have checked the place out before letting the taxi go. What was the chance of picking up another cab on the street?

The sound of running feet made her turn, as a lithe but

muscular man raced across the grass from the rear of the site, slowing as he approached her.

'If you're hoping to join, I'm afraid you'll have to come back,' he said. 'The secretary doesn't come in until after lunchtime. There's usually no-one else around in the mornings.'

She grinned at him, deciding to go along with his assumption for the moment.

'Yes, I realise I was being a bit optimistic,' she said, 'but I was so keen to sign up. Looks like I've had a wasted journey.'

'Tell you what. Why don't you hang on for a moment while I freshen up and then I'll buy you coffee? So you won't have completely wasted your time.'

'Oh, no, I couldn't bother you.' She knew that, after her experience in Zambia, Suzanne would have kittens at the idea of her going anywhere with a strange man connected, even remotely, to Michael Hawkins. But her refusal didn't put him off.

'No, you wouldn't be bothering me. I always go across the road for breakfast after my run,' and he nodded towards a café on the other side of the busy road. There were tables and chairs set up under the trees, and quite a few people were already taking refreshments there. 'And we can sit outside in the crowd, so you will be quite safe,' he went on with a smile, as though reading her mind.

'Okay, well if you're sure I'm not putting you out,' she said, thinking to herself that Suzanne need never know, 'then I'd love to.' He nodded and raised his hand to indicate he would be just five minutes, before jogging away behind the back of the clubhouse.

She perched herself on a wall under a huge tree and stared into the distance. But it wasn't the flowing traffic she saw.

It was a different country, on a different continent. Some ten years before. Her team was holed up in a remote farmhouse waiting for nightfall and their chance to escape the local militia who were searching for them. Most of the others were crashed out, trying to grab some sleep before the night's hike. Charlie rarely slept during an operation, and she had volunteered to stay on guard. The two young aid workers they'd come to rescue sat alongside her; too wound up to sleep and unwilling to believe they were really going home. The British nurse had talked for hours, telling her about their ordeal and how they'd coped. The young Brazilian by her side had said very little, just a word or two of confirmation now and then. But his smile told her their rescue had been worthwhile.

He'd been much thinner then, his hair had been long and dirty. But today, she'd recognised his smile as soon as she'd seen him. In those days, her hair was closely shorn and bright orange. She'd been wearing army fatigues. She'd looked nothing then like she did now. And she hoped he wouldn't recognise her. This was a complication she could do without.

In a little over four minutes, he was back, showered and dressed in jeans and a brilliant-white vest. *My, you're keen*, she thought as the two strolled towards the road.

'Felix, by the way,' he said. 'My name's Felix.'

'And I'm Rose,' she replied, effortlessly slipping into the role she and Suzanne had worked up.

'Such a wonderfully English name for a beautiful English lady,' he said, taking her hand and settling her at a table. She looked at him closely to see if he was mocking her, but it was apparent from his expression he was perfectly sincere. Once he'd ordered coffee for two of them and breakfast for himself, he turned towards her, one foot hooked casually across the other knee. 'So tell me about yourself. Are you living here?'

'Oh, no, I'm only visiting for a short while,' she said, 'but I want to keep in shape, and I don't know the city well enough to run around the streets on my own. So I thought I'd see if I could join temporarily.'

'Very wise,' he replied, 'the streets of São Paulo are not that safe, even in the daytime—not to mention the unhealthy level of pollution from all this traffic.' He pointed to the cars racing past. 'I'm sure the club will be able to accommodate you. So you're another runner?' Charlie nodded. 'Maybe we can run together sometimes.'

'Oh, I'm only a beginner really; I'm sure you won't want to be held back by me. You're obviously a professional.'

She could see him beginning to preen. This was way too easy.

'Oh, I wouldn't say I'm a professional; I just dabble really. I'm at the university.'

'What, a professor?' She knew he was too old to be a student, and she thought she'd flatter his ego a tad more.

'No, no, nothing so grand. I'm a post-doc in the English department. I tend to have free periods in the mornings, which is how I manage to fit in a run.'

Charlie realised she might have struck lucky after all, even with the clubhouse being closed.

'And were you running in the marathon yesterday?'

'No, I'm not into long distance running; but I was there of course. Pity I didn't meet you sooner; we could have gone together.'

She decided to ignore that but see if she could get the subject around to Mercy.

'There were some brilliant performances, weren't there? My sister and I had a great spot just by the finish. Some of the times were impressive, especially the women.'

'And what did you think of Mercy, our new star?'

Bingo! thought Charlie. But she looked at him with her head on one side, pretending ignorance of the name.

'Not sure; which one was she?'

'Oh, you couldn't miss her. The statuesque African woman.'

'Right, yes, I did notice her; came second in the women's veteran class, didn't she?'

'Yes,' he laughed, 'and wasn't she mad about that! She's a sore loser, is our Mercy. Apparently she had a bit of a tumble just before the finish and lost her lead.'

'What's her background?'

'Not sure, really. She arrived here some time last year, I think. She runs on the track most mornings and then has lunch in the clubhouse, but she keeps herself to herself. But I do know it's not just running she excels at. She's a crack shot with the pistol. And I hear she's a bit of a linguist too. She's certainly fluent in both English and Portuguese, and she can speak at least one other language—er, Russian, I think.' He stirred his coffee as he went on. 'Anyway, enough of that. Where are you staying? I'd love to take you out to dinner one evening; get to know you better.'

The man was still flirting with her! Obviously gaydar hadn't reached this side of the Atlantic. Charlie smiled shyly up at him.

'That's so kind of you; and in other circumstances, I'd love to. But I have a partner back home; and it wouldn't be fair...' Then she drained her cup and stood up. 'Look, thanks so much for the coffee. But I must get back now; I've got a ton of notes to write up.' His look of disappointment quickly gave way to his beaming smile.

'He's a very lucky man, this partner of yours. It was a pleasure to meet you, Rose.' And as she walked away she heard him call after her. 'And don't forget about that run; let's do it one day soon. I'm always here around nine.'

CHAPTER 10

Cape Town, October 1955

There was much confusion, noise and bustle as we docked. The captain was on the bridge manoeuvring the Prince Albert *into its place between two other equally disreputable looking vessels, one a fishing trawler and the other another cargo ship. His crew was busy attending to their duties. Once the gangplank was in place, I waited until the deck was clear, then scurried down to the jetty and raced towards a huge stack of pallets against the side of a warehouse.*

It was only a short distance in reality, but it felt like a marathon by the time I got there. I stood, bent over, with my hands on my knees, panting, until I could breathe normally once more. Then I straightened and peered around the side of the stack, back towards my former home. There was no-one in sight; no hue and cry. It looked as though my disappearance had not yet been noticed. Or maybe they just didn't care. Either way, I was free. I was never going to let myself be used by those dreadful men again. But if I ever got the chance, I would get my own back on them; that much I knew. I took a deep breath, checked the empty deck one final time and slipped off to start my new life.

Sensing I would be safer in a crowd than in a deserted place, I headed for the passenger terminal, where an oceangoing liner had recently docked. People were pouring down the gangplank, meeting friends and relations on the jetty, streaming towards cars and taxis. I stopped, looking around, wondering where I should go. My stomach was rumbling; it had been a long time since the watery stew of the previous night. I had a few coins in my pocket, left over from the returns on empty bottles we'd scavenged back in Liverpool and I wondered if I'd be able to use them here in this strange land.

'Boy, hey, you boy! Don't just stand there. Give me a hand!' I spun on my heel as something hit me on the back of the leg. A very small man with a very large suitcase was standing behind me puffing and blowing. The case had hit me as he dropped it to the floor. 'Come on, boy,' he went on, pulling out a handkerchief and mopping the sweat from his brow, 'give me a hand. There's a shilling in it for you.'

He spoke in the same strange accent as the sailors, rather like American but not quite. But his words were clear enough. Shrugging, I picked up his suitcase and smiled at him.

'Sure thing, mister; where to?'

'This way; follow me,' he replied, waddling off in the direction of the taxi rank. He was a fussy little fellow, who took his time choosing the right car. The first one was too small; the second one was too dirty. But the third one satisfied him and I gave the case to the driver. I'd seen a few black men on the docks in Liverpool before we'd left, but this was the first one I ever spoke to. He grinned at me and winked. The owner paused as he reached for the door handle, putting his hand in his pocket and pulling out a silver coin.

'Here you are, boy,' he said, thrusting the coin into my outstretched hand. 'Much obliged to you!' Then climbing into the taxi, he settled himself in the back seat and closed his eyes.

I stared at the coin in my hand. It looked just like the ones back home, with the young queen's profile on the front. I had no idea how long it would last out here, but I hoped it would be enough to buy me some breakfast.

I wandered out onto the street and looked for a café. There was one directly opposite that looked perfect. It was just a little run down, open even at this early hour, and with a mixture of customers; some well-dressed, but most, like me, showing the signs of a long journey and a hard life. I pushed the door open and went in.

Taking a seat near the window, I watched closely, both inside the building and out. Outside, I kept an eye out for the crew of the

Prince Albert. *I guessed they would be tied up for hours unloading their cargo, but didn't want to risk one of them finding me and dragging me back to the ship. But I also watched the customers coming in, to see how this place worked. After a few minutes, it became clear no-one was going to come and see what I wanted; I had to go to the counter to order. I strolled across and waited my turn in the short queue.*

There was a board on the wall behind the counter with the menu and prices. I was pleased to see I could buy a decent meal and still have change left out of my shilling. When my turn came, I ordered a cooked breakfast and tea; and ate better than I had certainly for six weeks and, in fact, for far longer than that.

As I ate, I pondered my next move. It was imperative to get away from the docks. The more distance I could put between myself and the crew of the Prince Albert *the better. I needed somewhere to stay and some way of earning money. But if my experience so far was anything to go by, the money side of things wasn't going to be too difficult. Maybe Father Pat had done me a favour after all. I was never going to forgive that Bible basher for setting me up like he did, but it looked like South Africa might just be a reasonable alternative to America.*

Outside on the street once more, I turned my back on the sea and started walking towards the city proper. It was still early, a little after nine o'clock and the shops were just starting to open, but the sun was already beating down on the pavements. In the distance, the flat top of the mountain shimmered in a heat haze.

The citizens of Cape Town were a varied lot. There were white folks, mostly poor looking ones in this part of the city; so I felt right at home and didn't worry that I would be told off for being where I shouldn't be. There were brown skinned, exotic looking people; the women in brightly coloured saris or cotton trousers and tunics, the men in light suits, open necked. I don't think I saw a necktie once during that first walk through the city. But by far the most numerous were the blacks. They crowded the streets, shopping for food, stopping to chat, laughing and joking. But only to each other. The white folks talked among themselves; as did the Asians; and as did the blacks. It was a way of life that would last for another thirty years, and one I found difficult to get used to, although it didn't necessarily hold with me and the group I got to work and live with.

After walking for half a mile or so, I saw a sign that brought me up suddenly and the answer was so obvious, I had to laugh. I was standing outside the main railway station on the corner of Alderley Street. This was another place where people came and went all day long. Where heavy bags needed to be carried. And where the people owning those bags were willing to pay a little for the privilege of not having to carry them themselves. I had found my first objective.

I slipped through the doors in the imposing stone-clad frontage and took up a position at the back of the concourse, watching everything that went on. Taxis and other cars stopped outside the station and passengers walked to the ticket office to pay their fare, then across the concourse, under the massive glass archway at the other end of the building and down the steps to the platforms lined up across the station, with a ticket barrier stretching along one end. There was a small seating area on the concourse for anyone who had arrived too early to go onto the platform. Many of the people using this area looked quite down at heel and I doubted they would be willing to spend money on someone else carrying their bags.

Then I spotted a discreet door near to the ticket office, with a sign indicating it to be the first class lounge. Now there was a place where people with money would congregate. I sauntered across the concourse, taking up a position just opposite the doorway. Almost immediately, it swung open and a young couple came out; he dressed in morning suit and cravat; she in silks with a fox fur around her neck, despite the heat. I smiled at the woman, guessing she would be an easier catch than the man.

'Carry your bag, lady?' I said, bowing slightly. She smiled back and although the man went to walk straight past me, she pulled on his arm to stop him.

'Come on, Johnny, don't be a bore. Let the boy carry the cases.'

I picked up the two bags he dropped and followed the couple across the concourse, down the steps and through the barrier of platform 7. They were heading up north to Johannesburg, although judging by the size of their cases, they could well have been travelling much further afield. Johnny showed their tickets to the inspector on the barrier, but he just waved me through after them. And as easy as that, I was in. We stopped at the first class carriage, I took the cases into their compartment and stowed them on the luggage racks above the seats. Johnny patted his pockets, pretending to look for some coins, but his companion laughed at him and pushed two shillings into my hand.

'It's alright, Johnny, I've sorted it,' she said.

I flashed her another smile, sketched an ironic salute to her miserly companion and jumped off the train as the whistle blew and stewards started banging the doors shut. I watched the train depart before strolling back to the concourse and taking up a position outside the first class lounge once more.

For the rest of the day, I did a steady trade. Sometimes I picked up a few coppers; sometimes a shilling or even more. By the end of the day, I had a pocket full of change and was beginning to think about finding somewhere to stay for the night. But as I walked off the platform, someone grabbed my arm and pulled me into a corner behind a trolley loaded with luggage.

'We want a word with you, boy,' said the large youth holding my arm. I glanced around and realised we were not alone. There were several others crowding behind us or hidden in the shadows. 'Who are you and what gives you the right to pinch our business?'

I stared at them for a few moments, my heart thudding. Surely not. I was tired and I'd worked hard for the cash I'd earned today. I couldn't lose it all at the last minute. I swallowed and held out my hand.

'Hawkins,' I said, 'Michael Hawkins. Very pleased to meet you.' My captor looked nonplussed at this gesture and didn't react; but someone behind me repeated my words in an exaggerated Yorkshire accent and one or two of the others chuckled. I needed to do something quickly, or this was going to end very badly. 'I'm glad to meet you all. I need some advice on where I can find a bed for the night.'

'That's all very well; but you can't just dive in here and pinch our trade,' my captor said. I smiled at him, trying to show a confidence I didn't really feel.

'I'm sorry if that's what you think I've been doing, but I can

assure you it's not how it looks.' He didn't look at all convinced, but I felt his hold on me slacken slightly and I took my chance. Twisting sideways and using his grip against him, I pulled his arm behind him and backed us against the wall so we were protected from that side. At the same time, I whipped my knife out of my pocket, flicked the blade out and jabbed it against his neck. There was a growl from some of the others in the crowd, but I pushed the point of the knife into his neck just enough to break the skin, and a thin trickle of blood appeared below the blade. He shrieked and everyone else froze.

'Right,' I said, 'now everyone calm down and we'll talk about this in a civilised manner. Agreed?' There was a silence and I pushed the knife just a little harder into his neck. 'I said, do you agree?' I asked quietly.

He nodded, then when I opened my eyes wide in question, he swallowed and said in a high-pitched voice, 'Back off everyone. We'll listen to what he has to say.'

My captor's name was Enoch. He was African, a few months younger than me, although taller and stronger. He was kind-hearted, saw the rest of the group of kids as his responsibility, but didn't really want to hurt anyone. Over the next few months, we grew to be good friends. Once I'd told my story, they accepted me into their number and helped me find somewhere to stay. It was small, not particularly clean, and I shared it with two of the others, but it was dry and safe. It would do for now.

They were impressed with my tactic of stalking the first class passengers. They'd been used to working the platforms for the arriving passengers. They hadn't thought of starting at the other end of the chain with the departing ones. Together, Enoch and I worked out a rota which gave everyone a turn at the different places on the station.

They'd been sharing their tips before I arrived and I agreed to throw mine into the pot as well. At least some of them went into the pot. The kids never realised just how much I was earning through carrying cases and running other errands for the wealthy travellers, and although I think Enoch might have suspected I wasn't being completely honest with them, he never said anything. Maybe he too was keeping a little on the side for himself. But I would never find out.

Eight months later, Enoch's family decided to move back to the countryside from where they'd originally arrived to make their living, and we never saw him again. But by then, I was the acknowledged leader of the railway porters and life was starting to look up. I had a place to live, somewhere to work, and friends who trusted me and would look out for me. I was a few weeks short of my sixteenth birthday.

CHAPTER 11

When Charlie strolled into the now open clubhouse, it was nearly lunchtime and the place was packed. The club was on the edge of a busy suburb and it looked like quite a few of the staff from the local businesses were members.

As she queued at the drinks counter, she glanced around her. There was a real mix of ages and nationalities in the place and her brief concern that she might stand out as a stranger was soon allayed. Having bought herself a black coffee, she took a seat near the window, where she could observe both the crowd at the counter and the people wandering around outside. She settled herself down, expecting to have a long wait, or even to be out of luck altogether. *I'll just keep coming back until I see her*, she thought. But someone somewhere must have been looking down on her and showering her with good fortune, because less than ten minutes later, she spied Mercy Gove Hawkins arriving.

Mercy's height and athleticism were emphasised by today's outfit. She wore black leather trousers and a jacket, and carried a motor cycle helmet. She was alone and didn't acknowledge any of the people milling around her. Charlie realised she'd not seen her talking to anyone other than

Hawkins during the race meeting either. Maybe the girl had difficulty making friends. Or maybe she had no wish to mix. Would this make Charlie's job easier or harder, she wondered.

After Mercy bought her lunch, she stood at the edge of the crowd, looking around for somewhere to sit. *Walk this way*, thought Charlie, *walk this way*. And once again, Charlie's luck held. Mercy started moving towards the window, where a small table had just become free. As she passed by, Charlie stood up suddenly, stepping into the other woman's path and 'accidentally' nudging her elbow.

'Oh, I'm so sorry,' she said, 'how clumsy of me. I hope I didn't spill your drink.' Mercy smiled thinly and shook her head.

'No, it's fine,' she replied, then tutted in exasperation as a couple grabbed the table she was heading for.

'Crowded, isn't it?' said Charlie. 'Look, why not sit here,' as she indicated her own table. 'There's plenty of room—and I did make you lose the other table, after all.' Mercy looked at her as though considering whether she wanted to share space with this clumsy stranger, then shrugged elegantly.

'Okay, thanks,' she said and settled herself across the table from Charlie who resumed her seat.

'I'm Rose,' she said, 'Rose Fitzpatrick.'

'Mercy Gove Hawkins,' was the cool reply. She didn't seem keen to start up a conversation and stared over Charlie's shoulder out of the window as she began eating her salad. This was going to be a tough nut to crack. Just as Charlie was about to have another go, maybe talk about yesterday's marathon, her phone rang. At least, she thought it was her phone, but as it was at the bottom of her rucksack, she wasn't sure.

She stuck her hand into the bag and started rummaging around. But there was so much rubbish in there, she couldn't find her phone. So she upended the lot onto the table, taking care to avoid Mercy's tray.

By the time she'd found the phone, it had stopped ringing. The display showed *Damien* and she wondered why he was trying to phone her. Was it just a casual call about lunch, or more serious? Ever since Suzanne's kidnapping in Africa, Charlie was wary of unexpected phone calls. Should she ring him back?

But before she could hit redial, she glanced across at Mercy and what she saw made her freeze. Among the assorted junk she'd tipped from her bag was her bunch of keys; keys to the flat back in south London, their office on the Thames Embankment, and a couple of odd ones she'd collected over the years and could no longer remember what they opened. The whole lot was held together with a brassy enamelled keyring in the shape of Africa, which she'd found in a street market in Zambia two years before. A keyring which Mercy had picked up and was stroking gently. As Charlie caught the other woman's eye, she realised there were unshed tears in their deep brown depths.

'I bought that in Zambia; beautiful isn't it?' she said softly and was rewarded when Mercy's face lit up.

'You've been to Africa?'

'Yes, a couple of years back; Zambia and Kenya.' She didn't think it was the right time to explain why she'd been there—but there was no need.

'I miss it so much,' said Mercy. 'I love it here, it's a wonderful country and everyone is really friendly, but it's not Mozambique. It's not home. Does that sound silly?'

'Not at all. It doesn't matter where you were brought up, and where you end up, there will always be a part of you that yearns for home.'

And just like that, the barrier was gone and Charlie found herself chatting away to Mercy—a very different person from the cool, aloof one who had first sat at the table. They talked about Mercy's home in Mozambique, about the weather, the people and the music. Charlie introduced herself as an author visiting Brazil to carry out research for her next book. She didn't have to explain why she'd been in Africa; she merely mentioned she'd been working and Mercy accepted it without question.

'So what brings you over to Brazil?' asked Charlie when they'd exhausted for the moment their conversation about the wonders of Africa.

'I've come to live with my father,' she said. 'My mother died when I was a child and I was all alone. Friends took me in and looked after me, but it's not the same as having family, is it? Then out of the blue, my father came looking for me. I didn't believe it at first; my mother told me he'd died before I was born, but then I saw the marriage certificate and other papers to prove who he was, so I thought I would come over here. What did I have to lose?'

As the woman talked about the death of her mother and the reappearance of her father, the light went out of her eyes and she seemed to withdraw into herself once more.

'So is your father from Mozambique originally?' Charlie asked. Mercy shook her head.

'No, he's British. My father's name is Michael Hawkins. I don't really know what he was doing in Mozambique. I've asked him, but he doesn't want to talk about it.'

Charlie surmised all was not well in the Hawkins household. Was this the opportunity she needed to get a hold over their old enemy? But, she decided that would be for another day. She didn't want to raise Mercy's suspicions by asking too many questions today. She looked at her watch and jumped up.

'Is that the time? I have to go. I've got an appointment to see the secretary, arrange my temporary membership.' She reached over and shook the other girl's hand. 'It's been good chatting to you, Mercy Gove Hawkins. Maybe I'll see you in here again; I'm going to be around for the next few weeks.'

'Yes, I'd like that,' said Mercy, smiling. Charlie turned on her heel and walked away, her mind buzzing with possibilities for the next step.

CHAPTER 12

As the sun went down over the tree-lined tennis courts, Suzanne, Charlie and Damien sat on the terrace sipping their drinks and catching up on the day's events. Suzanne put down her orange juice and looked across at their client.

'Well, I have to admit, after spending the day with Mr Nigel Atkinson, I'm beginning to think your suspicions about Sunshine Supplements' new wonder product might be well-founded.'

'He didn't rumble you, did he, sis?' Charlie said anxiously.

'No, nothing like that. In fact he was charm itself.'

'That bad, eh?' The sisters exchanged brief smiles, then Suzanne turned back to Damien.

'I can't really put my finger on it, and I certainly don't have any evidence yet, but I'm sure he's hiding something.' She went on to describe the locked room, and the way in which Atkinson avoided her question about its purpose. She listed some of the chemicals she'd seen in the warehouse, chemicals she wouldn't have expected to find in a food supplement factory. And she described the elderly man from Saturday night, a man she was sure she'd seen before.

'I couldn't show too much interest in any of this. After all, I'm supposed to be a freelance hack, not a pharmaceuticals expert,' she concluded. 'But I'm having lunch with him tomorrow and we're starting the interview proper, so maybe I can steer the conversation in the right direction then.'

'Well, at least you don't think I've dragged you all this way on a wild goose chase,' said Damien. 'And I got an email today from my friend back home; the one who's a chemistry post-doc.'

'The analysis of Super Fit?' asked Suzanne.

'Yep. Although I'm not sure it's much help to us. All he found was a couple of vitamins, caffeine and the *yerba maté* herbs.' Damien drained his glass and stood up. 'Right, ladies, I'm meeting some of the other US runners for dinner. I would invite you, but I don't think it's going to be the sort of evening you would enjoy.'

'You'll be letting off steam, will you?' grinned Charlie. 'Just my sort of evening.'

But Damien was adamant.

'No, I really think you guys would be better off eating elsewhere tonight. Besides, we don't want to risk anyone from Sunshine Supplements seeing us together and getting suspicious. See you in the morning!' And with a wave of his hand, he strode off across the foyer towards the noisy sports bar.

'Well, looks like it's just you and me, Suzanne,' said Charlie. 'Still, it will give me a chance to tell you how I got on today. And we can do some more work on your questions for tomorrow's interview. Where do you fancy eating?'

After another chat with Charlie's new best friend on the concierge desk, they jumped in a taxi and gave the driver the address of the best *comida gaucha* restaurant in town.

'I fancy playing the carnivore this evening,' Charlie said. 'A spot of Brazilian barbeque will go down just fine.'

Suzanne unwound sufficiently to let her sister persuade her to try the Brazilian cocktail, *caipirinha.* 'Although I'm definitely sticking at one,' she said. 'Something tells me I'm going to need a very clear head when I'm dealing with Mr Atkinson.'

As they sat sipping their drinks, they reminisced about their trip to Africa and, in particular, their visit to the barbeque restaurant on the outskirts of Nairobi.

'Well, this one's just as noisy as Game Park,' said Charlie. 'And the joints of meat on swords look just as big, although I doubt if we're going to get any giraffe or bison steaks here today.'

'I think we need to try some of the meat before we decide which is the best,' Suzanne replied. At that moment, the doors from the kitchens burst open and one of the waiters bustled through pushing a huge wooden trolley in front of him to a round of applause from nearby tables. On top of the trolley sat a whole roast pig, complete with thick, crispy crackling.

'Okay,' said Charlie waving over a passing waiter, 'I guess you're right. Let's eat. But' she went on, gesturing the passing trolley, 'I suspect it's game, set and match to Brazil, if that pork is anything to go by!'

And so it turned out. After eating their fill of chicken, beef and the wonderful pork, while working on tactics for the next day, they agreed their current location just about pipped Game Park to the post.

'But, talking of Africa,' said Charlie, as they finally stopped eating and decided to take a break before hitting the sweet trolley, 'I've had an interesting time today as well.' She brought Suzanne up to date on her visit to the running club, mentioned briefly her intention to return and go running with Felix, shrugged off her sister's concerns about her running with a strange man in a strange city, and grabbed her attention fully when she talked about her lunchtime meeting with Mercy.

'So her name isn't just a coincidence?' asked Suzanne.

'And that really was Michael Hawkins we saw with her the other day?'

'That's right, and better still, she's his daughter, so we now have a direct link back to him. Mercy puts on the appearance of being strong and independent, but if you could have watched her stroking my little keyring this morning, you'd have seen a different side to her altogether. I reckon Mercy's lonely. And that being said, she's going to welcome the chance to chat with someone who knows her home continent, if not her home country.'

'So, what's the next move?'

'Well, I said I'd probably see her again, and she looked pleased at the prospect. So I thought I'd pop back there tomorrow lunchtime, see if I can bump into her,' she used her fingers to mime speech marks in the air, 'and maybe find out a bit more about the set-up with her father. I got the distinct impression it's not all sweetness and light on the home front. Maybe Mercy's regretting leaving Africa and coming to live with a father she'd never met, here in Brazil.'

'I do hope you know what you're doing, Charlie,' said Suzanne. 'Remember what happened to me when I got too close to Hawkins' operation. We don't want you getting caught up in anything dangerous.'

'I reckon it's a bit too late for that,' muttered Charlie, 'and it's not as though this is the first time.' But seeing her sister's anxious look, she patted her arm. 'Don't worry, Suzanne, I'll take care. It would never do for another Jones sister to get kidnapped, now would it?'

'Don't even joke about it,' Suzanne said, suppressing a shudder. Charlie put on her most reassuring look and directed it at her sister.

'You really don't have to worry, Suzanne. I'm only going to chat to Mercy; it's not as though I'm going to visit her at home, now is it?' *At least, not straight away*, she thought, but kept that to herself. 'After all, Hawkins has never met me—and probably doesn't even know Suzanne

Jones has a sister. He certainly can't know she's here in Brazil, looking to bring him down. He probably won't have thought about you for ages.' She looked around the restaurant and waved over the waiter once more. 'And anyway, I didn't give Mercy my real name. So would you care to join Ms Rose Fitzpatrick in sampling something from that sweet trolley? It would be such a pity to visit this famous restaurant and not try out everything it has to offer!'

CHAPTER 13

Cape Town, October 1956

For the next year, I was as happy as I'd ever been. My parents, especially my father, were half a world away; I had never run into the captain or crew members of the Prince Albert, *and no-one tried to push me around. I had money in my pocket; not a fortune, granted, but enough to keep a roof over my head and food in my belly. The punters, or the passengers to give them their correct title, could be awkward on occasion, but a smile and a servile attitude was usually enough to charm a tip of some kind out of them. And if there was an occasional miserable old bugger to contend with, there were plenty of softer ones, usually the women, to make up for them*

But gradually, I began to want something more. I looked around at my little gang of porters and realised as I grew older, they stayed the same age, or got even younger. Some, like Enoch, drifted off to the countryside with their families. Others got pulled into the gangs in the townships that were growing up around the city as a result of the segregation laws; they found other more dangerous, but more lucrative, lines of work. Some just disappeared altogether. And there were always other youngsters ready to take their place.

At this rate, I was going to end up so much older than them, I would lose their respect—and inevitably, someone would come along who would be stronger than me and take over, just as I had from Enoch when I first arrived. I needed to find a way out before I was pushed out. And to do that, I needed to improve my level of education.

Frank was an old black man who sold newspapers in front of the station. He must have been in his sixties at least. That's no age these days, but to us kids, he was ancient. He had a kind smile and was always ready for a chat on a quiet day. And when he wasn't chatting to us or passing the time of day with one of his customers, he always had his head in a book.

Now, I could read and write pretty well. I'd loved going to school back home in Yorkshire, not only because it kept me out of the house and away from the old man's line of sight, but also because I'd found one or two of the teachers inspiring. Of course, I couldn't put that into words as a kid, but that's what it was. But when I looked at the books Frank was reading, they were ones I'd never heard of. So one day I asked him to tell me about them. He chuckled.

'Well, lad, I don't reckon there's much I can learn you,' he said. 'All I do is read these 'ere stories and imagine I'm one of the characters in them.'

From then on, whenever I had a chance, I sat with Frank and we talked about what he called 'great literature'. Some of the books we discussed were ones I knew of from home, such as Moby Dick, Treasure Island *and* The Water Babies. *But he also read books from Africa, by authors I'd never heard of, such as Thomas Mofolo and Naguib Mahfouz. After a while, he started loaning me books and I would devour them at night, back in my digs. When I returned them, we would discuss the characters, their motivation and whether we thought the story had turned out as it should or not. Then one day, Frank told me he'd had an idea.*

'You know, young Michael, this book reading is all well and good, but if you want to be educated and get a proper job, then you need to do more than fill your head with stories.' He looked at me over the top of his glasses, held together as usual by a bit of sticky tape, and blew out his cheeks. 'We need to get you some proper learning. Words is all very well, but I reckon it's numbers that make the world go around.'

I'd told Frank I wanted a job in an office, like some of the young men and women I saw arriving on the train each morning from the suburbs and returning home each evening. And he was right. My numbering wasn't good, and I knew most office jobs involved figures or sums of some kind.

The following Sunday, Frank was waiting for me outside the station at the end of the afternoon. We'd had a busy day, my feet were aching and I just wanted to get some supper and go to sleep, but he grabbed my arm and pulled me along the road with him.

'Oh no you don't, lad,' he said. 'I've fixed up a meeting for you and you're going to come with me.' He wouldn't tell me where we were going, but I didn't have long to wait. We stopped outside an old building from which I could hear singing. Hymn singing. My stomach lurched and I pulled away from Frank. My last encounter with the church had ended disastrously and I wasn't going to risk meeting up with another Father Pat.

'It's alright,' said Frank with a laugh when I told him in no uncertain terms what I thought of the church and clergymen in general. 'This one's not like any other pastor or priest you'll ever meet.' He persuaded me to wait with him for a while and I have to admit it was pleasant sitting in the sunshine listening to the soaring voices coming through the windows. Shortly afterwards, with a final 'Amen', it was all over and a crowd started streaming out of the doors. Most of the congregation was black, but I was surprised to see a sprinkling of coloured folks and even the occasional white face. And the whitest of them all was the preacher, who came down the steps at a gallop and grabbed Frank's hand, pumping it up and down.

'Frank, we missed your baritone in the choir today. Is this the young friend you've been telling me about?'

'Yes, Reverend, this 'ere's young Michael. I reckon he needs some advice. Michael, this is Reverend Joe Marks.'

'Well, how about you folks come and join Amelia and me for supper and we can talk about it,' he said. He pointed to a small house around the back of the church and Frank and I walked with him.

Amelia Marks was a slight woman, little more than a girl really, with coffee coloured skin that spoke of mixed parentage. That in itself must have caused her problems in the South Africa of the 1950s, but her marriage to a white man was even more courageous. Yet she and

Joe were the happiest couple I ever met. They never talked about the inevitable problems they experienced and were always ready with a helping hand for anyone that turned to them for support. They were the most Christian people you could meet and I sometimes wonder what they would think if they knew how I turned out.

That first evening, after a wonderful meal of chicken stew and dumplings, Joe lit his pipe and we sat in front of the fire while I told them my story, how I'd got to where I was now, and where I wanted to go from then on.

'Well, young man,' said Joe as my tale came to an end and my words dried up, 'you certainly seem to have gone through some rough times.' Amelia said nothing, but put her hand on my arm and smiled at me, her eyes warm and comforting. 'I'm sure we'll be able to find you a position at some point,' Joe went on, 'but Frank's right; you need some more schooling first.'

Amelia cleared her throat.

'I used to teach maths before I gave up work to look after the twins,' she said. 'I could help to start with.'

And from then on, I had supper with the Marks family—Joe, Amelia and their four-year-old sons, Peter and Paul—at least once a week. After supper, Joe would put the boys to bed while Amelia and I pored over maths books and I puzzled my way through the homework she set me. We discovered I had an aptitude for numbers which had lain undiscovered during my schooldays and I began to outstrip her knowledge. We also talked a lot about economics and how businesses ran. It was to be the basis, although I didn't realise it, for much of the rest of my life.

One evening about thirteen months after I first met her, Amelia pushed back from the table where we were working our way through an old exam paper, and pulled her hair out of her eyes with one hand. She kept looking at me, but it was to Joe she spoke.

'Well, that's me done.' She pointed to me. 'He's outgrown my knowledge of maths and economics. I can't help him any more. We need to find him another tutor.'

'Or get him into the night school,' replied Joe. 'I'm sure he's ready for that now.'

'Hey, guys, I'm here in the room. You can talk to me, not about

me,' I said with a laugh. But I was pleased they thought I was good enough to go to night school. Amelia did some more coaching, this time in exam technique, and a few weeks later, Joe took me to meet the administrator for the local college. And two weeks after that, Joe, Amelia, the boys, Frank and I celebrated with ice-cream sundaes when I heard I was to enrol in the maths class in the local college, starting the following term.

For the next year, I worked diligently on my maths, often studying my books or doing my homework in the quiet moments at the station. I passed the course successfully; not top of the class, but a respectable fifth. And the tutor suggested I enrol the following term for the two-year business studies course. I was on my way towards a better job, outside the twilight zone of railway portering.

CHAPTER 14

Once she'd finished her lunch, Mercy had jumped on her bike and headed out of the city. She didn't really want to return yet to the luxury compound her father desperately wanted her to think of as home. As she sailed along the highway and out into the rural roads outside São Paulo, she found herself musing on the British woman she'd met over lunch. Rose; what an appropriate name. But she rather got the impression there was a bit of a rebel behind that calm façade, and that Rose would not be at all offended at being considered as such. She'd given out a couple of subtle signs she might be more interested in women than men, and although Mercy was no stranger to relationships with men, she was equally at ease with members of her own sex. No, she realised, she wouldn't be at all unhappy to see this new acquaintance again. She found herself looking forward to their next meeting.

Her father's Mercedes was parked in the driveway when she finally reached home and Mercy gave a wave to Max, the chauffeur-cum-bodyguard who was polishing the bonnet, bulging muscles glistening with sweat in the early evening sunshine. She went around to the rear of the villa, hoping to climb the back staircase and reach the sanctuary of her bedroom unnoticed, but as she crossed the kitchen, Michael Hawkins must have heard her footstep, light as it was.

'Mercy, is that you? Come on in for a minute; I want to talk to you.'

She changed direction and headed for the airy room her father called his study. He was reading at the large mahogany desk. He'd told her it was modelled on the one in the White House, gifted by Queen Victoria to whoever was the president at the time—she never could remember. Hawkins put his papers down as she came in and stood up. Then, as she'd anticipated, his welcoming smile turned to a frown of disapproval when he saw her outfit.

'Mercy, I thought I told you I don't like you riding around on that motorcycle. It's not safe for a woman on her own in this city. I don't know why you can't take the car.'

'Yes, I know, Tata,' she said, tacking a smile on her face, 'but you know what the traffic's like in the centre during rush hour. I'd never get anywhere on time if I relied on Max driving me there.' She looked at him with what she hoped was a winsome look on her face. 'I'll be very careful; I promise. I'm a good driver—and I used to ride all over the place before I came here.'

'Well, you're a grown woman, so I can't tell you what to do,' he said, 'but I really don't want you to ride around at night. If I stop nagging you about using the bike during the day, will you at least agree to use the car in the evenings?'

'Okay, deal,' she said, although she knew there was no chance she was going to keep this promise. Apart from anything else, he often used the car himself in the evenings; but she guessed there was no harm in pretending. She spat on her hand and held it out to shake her father's hand—a method of sealing deals that she'd seen in old movies. But he grabbed her arm and pulled her towards him, enveloping her in a bear hug.

'That's my girl,' he said. 'I've only just found you; I don't want to lose you again.' She returned his hug briefly, although she growled internally at his naivety in believing she would be that submissive. Maybe she should suggest they get a second car just for her. But then, he'd no doubt want to employ a driver for her; and the last thing she wanted was any more spies for her father following her around and knowing her business.

As she disentangled herself from her father's embrace, she noticed he was wearing evening dress. He was always smartly dressed, but a dinner jacket and bowtie was unusual, even for him.

'Looking smart, Tata! You're obviously on your way out?'

'Yes, that's why I called you in. I'm going to a meeting; and it'll run on into dinner. I'll be back quite late. Can you look after yourself tonight?' She was amused that after all these months, he still thought it was his duty to entertain her and made a point of their having dinner together whenever possible.

'Yes, of course I can,' she replied. 'But would you like me to come with you? It won't take long for me to change.' On a number of occasions, Hawkins had used Mercy as his partner at formal dinners. He described himself as a widower and Mercy assumed this was in deference to her mother. She wasn't interested in any other wives he'd had in the years since he left Africa. She only had one mother and she was happy at anything that showed respect to her memory.

Now, Hawkins was shaking his head, although it appeared to be with regret.

'No, sweetheart; not on this occasion. It's an all-male gathering, and our host, in his wisdom, has decreed we should meet in *Il Paradiso*.' She shrugged; she'd never heard of the place. He went on: 'It's down in the centre of the city; calls itself a club but to be frank, it's nothing more than a high-class strip joint.'

'Not your sort of place, then?'

'Not at all—and certainly not somewhere I would want to take my daughter, even if we were allowed to take partners with us.'

'Rough?'

'Not rough, as such, but let's just say the only women in there are working rather than relaxing. Most of the strippers are on the game, and half the waitresses too. Not the sort of women I would want you to associate with.' He walked over to his desk, picked up some papers and pushed them into his pocket. 'Right, I'd better get going or I'm going to be late. Don't wait up for me!' He blew a kiss in her direction as he walked past and headed for the door.

As she stood at the window, watching her father climb into the car and drive away, she thought once more about her mother—his legal wife—who'd been forced to make a living as a prostitute in order to keep them fed. He seemed to have conveniently forgotten about this, or that his actions had put her in that position. He may not have known about his daughter's existence, but he certainly knew what he was doing when he abandoned her mother in Mozambique all those years ago. Mercy found her previous burst of warmth at her father's concern fading away to be replaced, as so often, by a strong desire for revenge, not just for herself, but more importantly, for her mother.

CHAPTER 15

Suzanne arrived at the offices of Sunshine Supplements at just before one pm. Nigel Atkinson had suggested they have lunch first and then settle down in his office to do the formal part of the interview. It was Megan's day off and Suzanne didn't recognise the young woman who met her in the foyer and handed her a temporary security pass. Unlike Megan, this woman was Brazilian, and although her English was faultless, with only a hint of an accent, she was much less friendly than her Irish colleague and also seemed to be avoiding Suzanne's eyes. When they reached the fifteenth floor, she pointed to a squashy leather sofa in the foyer.

'I will tell Mr Atkinson you are here. He will call you when he's ready.' And turning on her heel, she left Suzanne alone.

The office walls were all glass and from her position, she could see into Atkinson's office. He was on the telephone and didn't look like the cheerful, smiling charmer she'd met previously. At one point, he glanced through the glass in her direction and Suzanne smiled and gave him a little wave. But to her surprise, he returned neither the wave nor the smile. Instead, he picked up a remote control from his desk and pointed it at the wall. Immediately the glass turned opaque and he was hidden from her view. *How strange*, she thought. *I wonder what that's all about?*

She didn't have long to wait to find out. She heard the phone being slammed down just seconds before the office door was yanked open to reveal a definitely unsmiling and unhappy-looking Nigel Atkinson. Suzanne was starting to get a bad feeling about this. He gestured wordlessly for her to come into the office. As she walked towards the area of easy chairs they had used before, Atkinson slammed the door shut and returned to stand behind his desk. Suzanne adjusted her direction and stood in front of him, feeling just a little like a naughty schoolgirl in front of the head teacher.

'Are you well, Suzanne?' he asked.

'Yes thanks, Nigel, I'm fine.'

'And how's the story going?'

'Not too bad. I'm looking forward to talking to you about Sunshine Supplements this afternoon. That's going to give me lots of good material.'

'Really? I find that very interesting.' He sat down and gave a sigh. 'You know, I was really getting to like you, Suzanne.' She said nothing, just looked at him enquiringly. Something was obviously bugging him, and if she waited, no doubt it would come out. And sure enough, after a short silence, he carried on. 'I bumped into an old friend of mine last night at a meeting. Chap by the name of Bertram, Clifford Bertram, but everyone who knows him calls him Bertie. Do *you* know him, Suzanne?'

'No, don't think I've heard of him. Should I have?'

'Well, I'm surprised that a journalist of your calibre doesn't know his name. He was one of the lead foreign correspondents for the *Daily Mail* for many years.'

'Oh.'

'And even though he's retired, he's still quite an influential figure in Fleet Street—or whatever you call the

English newspaper world these days.'

'Seems strange, doesn't it?' said Suzanne, although her heart was sinking and she was beginning to wonder how long she could keep this up.

'Yes, it does. And do you know what's even stranger? He's never heard of a freelance journalist by the name of Suzanne Jones either.'

'Well no, Nigel, that's hardly surprising; I'm not that well-known—'

'—Oh come off it, Suzanne. You can stop pretending!'

'I don't know what you mean!'

'My dear girl, how difficult do you think it was to find you? I did a little searching on the internet and made a couple of phone calls to friends back in London. Bertie's never heard of a freelancer called Suzanne Jones, because there is no freelancer called Suzanne Jones—at least not in the newspaper industry.' He was talking more quietly now, as though he had reined in his temper. Somehow, that seemed all the more chilling to Suzanne. She just knew what was coming next

'But of course, there *is* a Suzanne Jones in the consulting world, isn't there? Owner of Jones Technical Partnership, a pharmaceutical consultancy company. And I must say, you're very highly thought of in that world. Apparently you were the star in some operation to bring down a counterfeiting gang in Africa a couple of years back.'

Suzanne's legs were suddenly incapable of supporting her any longer and she collapsed into the chair unbidden.

'So, the question I'm asking myself, Ms Jones,' he went on, the sudden formality even more chilling, 'is just what is a pharmaceutical consultant doing visiting my company under false pretences?'

'I was asked to take a look at your new supplement, Super Fit,' Suzanne said, suddenly relieved that all the lying was over for better or for worse.

'Asked? By whom?'

'Oh, I can't tell you that. It would be breaking client confidentiality.'

'So it's okay to lie your way in here and waste my time on the pretext of an interview that would never get published, but your conscience forbids you from telling me who you are working for?'

She stared at him, unable to think of anything to say, but mentally cursing Damien and Charlie for talking her into this ludicrous situation against her better judgement. Atkinson carried on.

'Look, I told you yesterday, this is a food supplement, nothing more. It's not covered by any pharmaceutical regulations, it's not controlled by the health authorities and there's nothing to investigate.' Suddenly, his temper was back and he jumped up. 'I've had enough of this. I want you out of my office now!' He strode to the door, yanked it open and pointed outside.

Suzanne picked up her bag and what was left of her dignity and headed out of the door. She couldn't wait to get out of there. But as she walked across the hallway to the elevator under the eyes of the three secretaries who were not even pretending to do anything but watch her exit, Atkinson called after her.

'Ms Jones, you're lucky I'm not calling the police. But if I so much as hear your name again, or see you anywhere near here, I will do just that.' And he slammed his door closed; the echo of the bang reverberated through her head all the way down to the ground floor and out onto the street.

Suzanne looked at her watch. Although it had seemed like a very long time, she'd been in the building for barely twenty minutes. But in that short time the sunshine had been replaced by lowering clouds. As she stood on the pavement taking deep breaths and trying to recover her equanimity, large warm drops of rain started falling all around her. She quickly stuck out a hand and stopped a passing taxi. She needed to get away from here, back to the hotel, and to talk to Damien and Charlie. Was the job over? Should they just give up and head home? Two days ago, she would have thought so, but having seen the locked room, the furtive behaviour of the elderly man, and the shifty way in which Atkinson had avoided her questions, she just wasn't so sure.

CHAPTER 16

Cape Town, October 1960

As my education programme progressed, I was able to earn some extra money working with Amelia. She'd set up an unofficial school within the township and I taught some of the classes, especially the older children who wanted to learn more about their numbers. And although we were working in the township, not everyone we came across was hard up. It's a common misconception that all the blacks were poor, when in fact, many of the families had quite a bit of money. They just couldn't spend it in the same places as the whites. And although the blacks were barred from the white establishments, the reverse wasn't true. White faces were rare, but not unheard of in the black areas.

And of course there were the coloureds and the Asians. Neither one thing nor the other, they lived between the two halves of society, often running shops and factories. So they too had money; money they were happy to spend on the education of their children.

As I did well in my studies, I also had the opportunity to help with some of the basic classes in the college too. I particularly enjoyed working with the adults: seeing their looks of amazement and joy when they finally managed to decipher the headline on a newspaper or a leaflet they'd picked up at church was reward in itself.

I carried on working as a porter at the railway station as well. Not every day, and not all day long. I was more of an overseer, really, keeping an eye on the gang of kids. The faces changed on a regular basis but in other ways everything remained the same. I'd introduced a system where each kid paid me a small retainer once a week to rent their space on the platform. It meant I got my money even if it was a quiet week; but as they got to keep all the tips themselves, they were mostly happy with the arrangement.

Every so often, I would do a shift myself, just to keep my hand in, as it were. And it was during one of those shifts, some five years after I'd first arrived in Cape Town, that my life took another drastic turn.

The Durban train had just pulled in and its passengers were spilling out onto the platform. I'd positioned myself opposite the door to the first class carriage nearest the ticket barrier when my eye was drawn to a man who appeared in the doorway. Dressed in a scruffy tie dyed caftan and wearing a large panama hat with a leopard skin print around the crown, he stood out from the crowd, not only because he towered head and shoulders above most of the other passengers, but because he had a very loud voice and an even louder laugh. As he came down the steps, he glanced back over his shoulder at someone who spoke to him, laughed at what was said, missed his footing and came suddenly down onto the platform, grabbing for the rail to break his fall. His hat flew off his head and the bag in his hand, a battered old thing that looked a bit like a tool box, fell from his grasp and ended up sliding across the platform to stop at my feet. The man let out an oath and jumped to his feet, dusting himself off and looking around for his belongings. One of the other kids, who had been shadowing me to pick up some tips, grabbed the hat, hit it on his leg to expel any dust and handed it back with a little bow.

I bent down to pick up the box. But in the fall, the catch had become unlatched and as I pulled on the handle, the lid came open, scattering the contents, which looked like small pieces of bone, across the platform under the feet of the advancing passengers.

'My samples!' the man yelled, jumping forward and holding his arms wide. 'Stop walking, now! You will damage my samples.' People all around us stopped dead, compelled by the urgency and authority in the man's voice. He looked across at me. 'Don't just stand there, imbecile,' he yelled, 'pick them up—but carefully. Some

of them are very rare.'

Well, I wasn't at all sure about being called an imbecile, but there was something about his voice that just couldn't be denied and before I could stop myself, I was down on the ground scrabbling in the dust to pick up the little pieces of bone, which I pushed back into the box.

'Gently, gently, man,' he cried at me, 'those are delicate samples. Some of them are thousands of years old.'

Yeah, right, *I thought, but I slowed down anyway and laid each piece carefully on top of the previous one.* There'd better be a good tip in all of this.

By the time I'd finished picking up the spillage, the other kid had helped the man carry his luggage off the train and had piled it up on a trolley. Five bags! This was a guy who didn't believe in travelling light. I went to put the box on top of the pile, but he stopped me with an outstretched arm.

'No, you carry that one to the car for me,' he said, 'I don't want to risk it falling off and spilling out again.'

We must have looked a strange procession: the young black kid pushing a trolley and peering around the luggage piled way above his head; me behind him, carrying the prissy little box; and the big guy in the caftan chivvying us along, like an over-sized sheep dog.

When we got to the taxi rank, our customer marched straight to the front of the queue and commandeered the first vehicle in line. People watched open-mouthed as he ordered the driver around, made sure his cases were properly stowed and then settled himself on the back seat. He reached out and took the box from me, pushing a folded note into my hand in return.

'Mount Nelson,' I heard him say as the car drove away. I stared after him as his car disappeared into the distance. Mount Nelson! That was one of the best hotels in town—and certainly the most expensive. Our customer might be scruffy and unshaven, he might have the manners of a pig, but he certainly wasn't short of a bob or two. And then I looked down at the paper clutched in my hand. They say the richest people are the meanest—and here was something to prove it. The piece of paper staring up at me was not, as I'd hoped, a pound note, but a tattered flyer, advertising the services of Mr Stefano

Nicovic Mladov, archaeologist, fossil hunter and lecturer. Almost against my will, I began to laugh.

'There you are, sonny, there's a lesson for you,' I said, clapping my young shadow on his shoulder. 'Not all the likely tips come to pass.' I showed him my empty hands. 'Nothing doing this time, I'm afraid. But there will be plenty of other opportunities.' I sent him over to my favourite spot, outside the first class lounge, and told him to wait for the next kindly old lady to come out. Then I strolled back to the platform to see how the others were getting on.

As I approached the place where I'd first seen Mladov, a white glint caught my eye under a trolley at the back of the platform. Bending down, I spied one of the pieces of bone—or should I say fossil—which had got missed in the crush earlier on. I wondered if he would miss it. Then I wondered if it was worth anything. I stared at it speculatively, before pushing it into my pocket and carrying on with my stroll around my 'territory'.

By about four o'clock, I'd had enough and decided to knock off for the day. The kids had paid their weekly dues and I had a pocket full of change, but it was a nice evening and I wanted to stretch my legs and get some fresh air after the fumes of the station. So I decided to walk south, away from the sea, towards the Table Mountain—and almost without realising it, I found myself standing on Orange Street gazing at the drive leading up to the Mount Nelson Hotel. I'd never been inside, and doubted whether I would ever be able to stay there, but the fact my mysterious customer was a guest seemed to work as a magnet.

I didn't think I would have much luck getting through the door, even though I was wearing my working suit: the best one I could afford. I'd found the smarter I looked, the larger the tips that came my way. But one of my old porters, a young boy called Sammie, had recently got a job there as bell boy, so I knew a little about the place.

There was a pathway running around the side of the hotel, into the palm tree filled gardens. I waited to make sure no-one was watching me, and then slipped down there and into the shrubbery. I'm not sure what I thought I could achieve by trespassing in this way; it was an impulse move, really.

And in the strange way that thinking about something can

sometimes cause it to appear, I turned a corner and there was the subject of my thoughts, sitting on a bench, staring across the gardens. I stopped dead under a tree, unwilling to disturb him, and not at all sure how he would take to my following him there.

'I can hear you breathing,' he said in a low voice, turning towards me and fixing his hawk-like eyes on me, 'you might as well show yourself.' So I walked forward, reluctantly, but drawn by a strange compulsion. He looked me up and down, apparently puzzled for a moment and then his face cleared and he laughed. 'Of course, you're the boy from the station. Although you're not really a boy, at all, are you? How old are you?'

'I'm twenty, sir,' I muttered.

'Yes, I thought you were a bit old to be part of the station crew. What are you, their minder?' then he paused and closed one eye knowingly, 'or maybe their pimp?' He barked out another laugh. 'That's it, isn't it? You're running the racket down there.'

I didn't reply, just stared at him, feeling myself go red. But he moved across to make room on the bench.

'It's alright, son, I'm not criticising you. I'm a great admirer of enterprise.' He patted the place next to him. 'Come on, sit down and tell me about yourself; and why you're skulking around in the garden of the most exclusive hotel in Cape Town.'

I came to, as though from a trance, shook myself and sat down on the bench. Putting my hand into my pocket, I pulled out the fossil I'd found under the trolley on the platform. I cleared my throat.

'I found this after you left. I thought it might be valuable...' My voice died away as he reached out and took the thing out of my hand and turned it over and over.

'Valuable, no; it's a fairly common piece. But its return is important to me, nevertheless.' He smiled and popped the fossil into his pocket. 'And you certainly deserve a reward for bringing it back to me.' He glanced at his wrist, where he wore a pink plastic child's watch with a picture of Mickey Mouse on the face. 'It's getting close to supper time. How about you come and eat with me this evening and I'll tell you its story.' He paused, and then went on: 'that's if you've not got anything else planned for this evening.'

As it happened, I was scheduled to go with Amelia to the school, to tutor a class in mathematics. But although my head told me I should decline his offer and leave, my heart was pounding and telling me I should not turn away this opportunity. So I just shrugged.

'No, nothing planned. Supper sounds great.'

My companion, who insisted I call him Stefano, suggested we eat in the terrace café. That way, he didn't need to get changed before the meal, and I wouldn't feel out of place in my daily work clothes. In 1960, we were in a transition period; many people still dressed for dinner, although dress suits were far less common. But there was a growing number who preferred an alternative lifestyle and a less formal approach to everyday living. And Stefano Mladov seemed to be one such person.

As we ate, Stefano told me about his fossil hunting trips on behalf of a university back in the Soviet Union, where he came from. The one I had found was a particularly fine example of Astropecten pontoporseus *he'd found in Simon's Bay, on the Cape of Good Hope. He'd just returned from a short visit to Durban, but before that he'd been in the Cape Town area for several weeks. At that news, I looked around at the hotel and pursed my lips, but he laughed and shook his head.*

'No, I couldn't afford this place for a long trip like that. Not on the fee the university's paying me. But that project's coming to an end. I've got the last lot of samples to parcel up and send off to Kiev and that's finished.

'And now I've got a totally different project starting up, and for that one I needed to put on a good show.' He pulled out a pipe, made a great point of packing it carefully with tobacco and lit it, inhaling deeply and then blowing out a string of perfect smoke rings. Then he pointed the pipe at me and smiled again. 'You know, I like you, young Michael. And I could do with some help on this new project. We may have only just met, but I'm a pretty good judge of character. You could be exactly the person I'm looking for.'

CHAPTER 17

Suzanne was sitting on the terrace finishing her late lunch when Damien and Charlie strolled out into the sunshine. She'd stopped shaking and the food had restored some of her calm, but she was still shocked by the power of Atkinson's anger. She took a deep breath, staring at her plate rather than meeting their eyes.

'I didn't expect to see you here,' said Damien. 'We thought you'd still be interviewing friend Nigel.'

'Or still stuffing your face at the fancy restaurant he promised to take you to, more like,' chimed in Charlie with a grin. But her smile faded as Suzanne looked up at her. 'Suzanne, what's wrong? What's happened?' She dropped into the chair and took Suzanne's hand.

'He knows,' Suzanne said in a voice with a break in it, then clearing her throat, she tried again. 'Nigel Atkinson knows who I am. He's got a friend in the press and he made some calls...'

'What did he do? He didn't hurt you, did he?' asked Damien. Suzanne was quick to reassure them.

'No, nothing like that; it's not his style. But he was very angry. He yelled at me and then threw me out of his office. It was so bloody embarrassing!'

There was a long pause, as the three conspirators stared across the gardens and pondered their next move. Finally, Damien gave a sigh.

'Well, I guess that's it.' He stood and walked backwards and forwards in front of them. 'I'm so sorry I put you in this position, Suzanne. I don't know what I was thinking of; but I was so convinced Lulana was being harmed by that damn supplement, I just wanted to get some justice for her.' His shoulders slumped and he sat down again. 'I guess now, we'll never know.'

But Suzanne wasn't prepared to give in that easily. Her run-in with Atkinson had made her more determined, rather than less, to find out the true story of the strange goings on in the world of running.

'Oh, I wouldn't say that,' she said. 'We'll just have to take a different approach to things.' Damien looked at her in surprise.

'You mean you're willing to carry on?'

'Absolutely! After all, if he had nothing to hide, why did he react so badly to my presence?'

'Er, maybe the fact that you were there under false pretences and virtually accused him of dealing in dangerous drugs?' murmured Charlie. But Suzanne threw her a grin and shook her head.

'No, I think it's more than that. And I still want to know what's in that locked room.'

The call came in not long before midnight. Suzanne was settling down to read before sleep, and put her book down with reluctance. *What does Charlie want at this time of night?* she wondered. But it wasn't her sister's voice at the other end.

'Miss Jones?' The caller was male and his voice sounded like it could make rock splinter just by telling it to: 'Miss Suzanne Jones?'

'Yes, this is Suzanne Jones. What can I do for you?'

'Miss Jones, you've been poking your nose where it's not wanted. People are not happy!'

'People? What people? This is ridiculous.'

'Not ridiculous. Very serious. You need to stop asking questions. Or people will suffer. You will suffer.'

'Now look here. I don't know who you are—' but the dialling tone in her ear told her she was talking to thin air.

Telling her companions about the call over breakfast, she felt as indignant as she had the night before, although secretly she trembled slightly at the thought of what the voice had suggested.

The three bounced around ideas for the next hour or so. The rest of the tables had emptied and the sun was halfway to its zenith when Charlie came up with her bombshell.

'You know, sis, I think it's probably time for you to go home!' Suzanne felt a surge of frustration and, from the look on his face, Damien was more than a little surprised.

'What on earth are you talking about, Charlie?' Suzanne said through gritted teeth. 'Haven't you been listening to anything I've been saying? We're pretty sure Nigel Atkinson is dirty; and the fact that I've been threatened proves we must be on to something. And if he is dirty, he mustn't get away with it. How can we possibly give up and go home now?'

'Yes, I understand all that,' said her sister patiently, 'but I don't think you were listening. I didn't say *we* should go home. I said *you* should go home.' Suzanne didn't believe what she was hearing, but Charlie held up her hand and started ticking things off on her fingers. 'Firstly, your cover is blown. Atkinson knows who you are and what you're looking for. He's going to be on the lookout for you at every turn.' Damien nodded at this, although Suzanne glared at him and he didn't open his mouth.

Charlie went on: 'Secondly, you have a huge network of

contacts back in Europe. Couldn't you call in some favours and find out what's going on by some back doors? Thirdly, Damien has told us the incidents associated with Super Fit have been observed not just here and in the States, but in Europe too. You'd be able to set up interviews much more easily over there, than here where Atkinson will be watching out for you.' By now, Damien was nodding hard and even Suzanne was beginning to think that maybe her sister had a point; well, several actually.

'I suppose you could be right...'

'Of course I'm right. And I'll be a lot happier if we can get you safely out of the country,' Charlie finished and sat back, smiling at her sister.

'Do you really think so?' said Damien, 'After all, Atkinson doesn't strike me as the violent type—' but Charlie rounded on him fiercely.

'Trust me, Damien. I know what I'm talking about. The quiet ones are often the most deadly. And even if our Nigel is above a spot of assault and battery, I suspect he has lots of friends who have fewer scruples. Including one with a habit of making late-night threats.' Damian stared at her in silence.

She suspected Charlie still hadn't told her the full story about what happened after she left the army in disgrace all those years ago, but Suzanne knew enough of her sister's past to take her comments at face value. She sighed and looked around the beautiful surroundings.

'I guess you're right, Charlie. What a pity. I was just getting used to the life here.'

'I'll book two more tickets on tomorrow night's flight to Dallas with me,' said Damien. 'You guys can fly back to the UK from there.' Then he looked in surprise at Charlie who was pulling a face.

'Now you're not listening to me, Damien,' she said. 'Suzanne needs to go home, and you've got to go back to college. Plus, Atkinson would probably be able to link you two together quite easily. And you can make contact with some of the affected athletes in the States. But I'm staying put for the moment.' Her two companions looked at her in surprise. 'He doesn't know me; he's never met me. I think I can probably do more good if I hang on here for a while.' She looked at Damien with a wry look on her face. 'That's if you're happy to keep paying the bills for the moment, Mr Client?'

Suzanne wasn't completely convinced by Charlie's arguments for staying and strongly suspected it was more to do with her desire to continue investigating Michael Hawkins, rather than Nigel Atkinson.

'Okay, Charlie, I'll do what you suggest. But, on one condition.' Charlie looked puzzled, but gestured that her sister should continue. 'We're going to level with Damien and tell him exactly why we, or should I say you, were so keen to take his commission.'

But Damien had a surprise for both of them.

'I suppose you're talking about Michael Hawkins?' He burst out laughing. 'Oh, if you guys could only see your faces!' Then he became serious again. 'I know about Banda; I know about Sir Fredrick Michaels and I know you don't believe he's dead.'

Suzanne and Charlie stared at each other—and then, just as they had in their first meeting with Damien, they came to the same conclusion at the same moment:

'Francine!' they both mouthed.

'Spot on,' Damien said, nodding his head. 'Francine listened to my story about Sunshine Supplements, heard the word 'Brazil' and realised it was an ideal opportunity for you to continue your investigations. So, yes, Charlie, I'm happy to continue paying the bills. And if we can bring down two bad guys instead of one, so much the better.'

CHAPTER 18

The rest of the day was taken up with making travel arrangements and plotting their next moves, both on the Sunshine Supplements job and the Michael Hawkins investigation. And although Charlie didn't go to the airport to see her companions off the following day, by the time they'd left, it was well past lunchtime. So it wasn't until the end of the week that she found herself sitting once more in the bar of São Paulo Runners Club, scanning the crowds for a familiar face. And she didn't have long to wait.

She spotted the tall African woman as soon as she entered the room. Head and shoulders above most of the others, she caused a ripple of interest wherever she went. But once again, Charlie observed, the interest was reserved, rather than friendly, and Mercy didn't seem to have any friends among the people milling around her.

Mercy bought her lunch and then stood scanning the room. Charlie had the distinct impression she was looking with purpose, rather than aimlessly searching for a table. And this suspicion was confirmed by the smile that lit up the other woman's face when she spotted her. She headed through the crowd, straight for her table.

'Hello, Rose, how are you? I was hoping I would see

you. Where have you been?'

'Sorry, I've not been able to get over here for a few days,' she replied. 'I was up to my eyes in research. I'm just having some lunch then I've got to get back to work,' she said with a grin. 'Are you going to join me?'

Mercy sat down and started eating her salad. She seemed to be much more relaxed than the first time they'd spoken. And afterwards Charlie had difficulty remembering what they talked about. They chatted, as any friends do, about this and that; inconsequential things, the sort of conversation Charlie was not used to having. After about half an hour she stood, brushed the crumbs off her jeans and smiled at Mercy.

'Well, time to get back to work, I guess,' she said. 'This has been fun. See you again soon.' And as before, she walked away, feeling the other woman's eyes boring into her back as she went.

Charlie returned to the bar daily the following week. She made a point of being there before Mercy arrived each day and always left before her, citing a visit to the library, a meeting or other research. And in between, she carried on the investigation into Nigel Atkinson.

And finally her work paid off. As she was about to leave on the Wednesday afternoon, Mercy caught hold of her wrist.

'Have you ever been to Iguaçu?' she asked.

'The waterfall?' replied Charlie.

Mercy laughed.

'Well, I think it's a little more than just a waterfall, but yes, that's the place. Have you seen it?'

'On screen yes; looks impressive, but I've never been there. Why do you ask?'

Mercy bit her lip and smiled shyly at her.

'My father's got a business meeting there at the weekend. He's flying down in a private jet and suggested I go with him. I'd love to see it, but that sort of thing's no fun on your own—and he's going to be too busy to do any sightseeing. I wondered if you'd like to come with us and keep me company?' Charlie paused before replying and the other woman pulled her hand away, a rueful expression on her face. 'Sorry, sorry, it was a silly idea. You hardly know me...'

'Mercy, it's not that,' Charlie replied, sitting down at the table once again. 'I'd love to come with you—and seeing something of this country would be wonderful too. It's just that I don't have much money, being a writer on a study trip and that—' She broke off as Mercy grabbed her hand once more.

'You don't need any money, silly. You'll be my guest. My father suggested I bring a friend so he'll be fine about it. We'll fly down on Saturday morning, stay overnight in the Hotel das Cataratas and come back after lunch on Sunday.'

'Well, in that case,' said Charlie, squeezing her hand, 'I'd be delighted.' Then looking at her watch, she said, 'but I really do have to rush now. I'll see you tomorrow.' Mercy stood and took Charlie by the shoulders, kissing her on both cheeks.

'It's going to be great fun. Thank you so much.'

As Charlie walked away her thoughts were a churning mess. This was a huge step forward in her quest to bring Michael Hawkins to justice, but was it a step too far? She was really glad Suzanne was no longer in Brazil; she would have a fit at the thought of Charlie getting into a plane with the man responsible for so many deaths in the past. And was she right in assuming that although Hawkins knew Suzanne very well, he'd no idea of Charlie's existence? *I guess we'll find that out on Saturday*, she thought.

But at the back of her mind there was another thought niggling her. Just what sort of a friendship was Mercy looking for? The way she'd reacted to Charlie's agreeing to visit Iguaçu could just have been a lonely woman in a strange land, happy at the thought she'd found at least one friend to spend time with. Or it could have been something quite different. Charlie wondered what the sleeping arrangements would be on Saturday evening.

Either way, it would be a great pity if Mercy was disappointed when she found out, as she would eventually, that Charlie was not the innocent writer she was pretending to be. And as this thought slipped across her mind, she remembered she'd promised to ring Annie over the weekend. That was going to be difficult. Charlie sighed inwardly and decided, on reflection, it was a good thing both her sister and her partner were half a world away and unable to see what she was getting up to at the moment.

CHAPTER 19

Cape Town, October 1960

As I went home from that first supper with Stefano, my mind was buzzing. There was a message for me, pinned to the board next to the public phone in the hallway of my lodging house: Amelia Marks called. She prays you will feel better soon and hopes to see you at tomorrow's class. *I stared at the words for a few minutes, before screwing the paper up and dropping it in the waste bin. I would be meeting my new friend again tomorrow evening and I had a feeling I was going to be too busy to play schoolteacher for a while—if at all.*

The next few days were the most exciting of my life so far. Each evening I hurried over to the hotel as the sun started to sink towards the horizon and, taking the path around the back, met Stefano in the garden. We chatted, he told me all about his travels, his hunts for fossils—and the fees people were willing to pay him for undertaking those hunts—and the other things he got involved with. He was only ten years older than me, but he seemed to have packed so much experience into those ten years. We always ate in the hotel. I suggested one night we might go elsewhere, so I could show him around the city I had adopted as my home, but he refused.

'I like the cuisine in this place, my boy,' he said, 'so why go looking elsewhere, where we might well be disappointed?' I nodded and decided I wouldn't make that sort of suggestion again.

Then one day, about two weeks after I'd first met him, Stefano turned up at the railway station. He had his little sample box with him, but no other luggage. It was just before noon and the train to Jo'burg was puffing on the platform, due to leave in five minutes time.

'Come, walk with me, Michael,' he said. I hadn't seen him go to the ticket office, but he had a piece of cardboard in his hand which he absentmindedly waved at the inspector as we strolled through the barrier, deep in conversation.

We stood on the platform together as the final few passengers scurried to find places. To be honest, I wasn't really listening to what he was saying. I was keeping an eye on my lads, making sure they were satisfying the passengers. After all, happy passengers are good tippers. But suddenly his words wrenched my attention back to him.

'I've got to leave town for a while, my boy,' he said, 'and I don't want you to go anywhere near Mount Nelson while I'm away.' I looked at him in surprise and he shrugged. 'A little dispute over the bill. I think it would be better if they didn't see my friend for a while.'

Before I could ask any more questions, the guard blew a whistle, and the train gave a lurch, its wheels slowly beginning to turn. Stefano darted forward, pulled open a door, and jumped through, slamming it behind him. He waved to me through the window and then in a cloud of steam, the train moved off and he was gone.

For the next few evenings, I stayed at home, lost for ideas and uncertain what had happened or why. Then one evening as I was walking out of the station, Frank called me over to his newsstand.

'Haven't seen you for a while, boy.'

'No, Frank, I've been busy,' I replied.

'Hmm, yes I heard. Too busy for Amelia and Joe, too busy for class.' I didn't say anything; just hung my head, kicking the dust at my feet. He cleared his throat and then continued. 'I'm having supper with them tonight. They said to bring you along. They said they'd love to see you.'

'Oh, I don't know, Frank...' I began, but he put his hand on my arm to stop me.

'Don't be silly,' he said, 'I know you let them down—and you probably feel a bit stupid, but these aren't people who hold grudges. These are your friends.' He stared at me as I struggled with my feelings, then let out a sigh of relief as I grinned and nodded at him.

'Okay, Frank, you're on. I'll see you over there just before seven.'

As Frank had promised, Amelia and Joe were nothing but perfect hosts that night. They welcomed me back into their home and never even mentioned that I'd been missing for a couple of weeks and had let them down. As we were leaving, Amelia gave me a quick hug.

'I'm going to class tomorrow evening,' she said, 'and the pupils would love to see you. Do come with me.'

Life went on as normal for the next ten months. I carried on with my own studies; tutored a few of the richer kids as they prepared for their exams; and continued to run the gang of porters at the station. And all the time, I was looking out for that one opportunity I needed to get myself into a better position within society, a job in an office somewhere.

I never went near Mount Nelson again. I met Sammie in a bar one evening a few months after Stefano had left and he filled me in on what happened.

'Your mate really stiffed everyone!' he said. 'Managed to talk his way into the best suite in the hotel, ran up huge bills in the restaurant,' I felt myself go hot at these words, 'and then ran out on us without paying a penny.'

'But how did he get out with all his luggage?'

'Oh, he left that behind!' I remembered Stefano had only been carrying his sample box when he got on the train. 'But, you know what? When we searched his room, all he'd left behind were suitcases! And they were empty. I reckon he only had them for show in the first place. No clothes or anything in them.'

Reluctantly I had to face the fact that my so-called friend wasn't the rich adventurer and traveller he'd made himself out to be, but was little more than a conman; and by the look of it, a conman who'd run out of luck—in Cape Town at least.

One morning, about a month after my twenty-first birthday, the station manager called me into his office as I was walking onto the concourse. We'd had very little to do with each other in the past. My regular payments to keep our gang in place were made each month to his deputy and although we nodded when we passed each other from time to time, we rarely spoke. Now, he sat at his desk and looked at me over the top of his glasses. In his hand, he held a thick white envelope.

'Not sure I approve of this place being used as a poste restante,*' he sneered as he threw the envelope across the desk at me, 'but it says* Private and Confidential, *so I thought I'd better hand it over straight away.' I didn't really know what* poste restante *meant, but I could guess. I picked up the envelope and glanced down at it. It was addressed to me in a sloping italic script, written in black ink:* Mr Michael Hawkins, c/o Cape Town Railway Station. *I didn't recognise the handwriting and had no idea who would be corresponding with me. I felt embossing on the envelope and, turning it over, was surprised to see the emblem of the Mena House Hotel in Cairo. The mystery deepened. I knew Cairo was the capital of Egypt, but had no idea where that was, and I certainly didn't know anyone who lived there.*

'Well,' asked the station manager, 'aren't you going to open it?' I looked at his weasely little face and something told me this was an envelope I shouldn't open in his presence. I left him at his desk, puffing and blowing and shouting after me about not giving the station as my address.

I shoved the envelope into my pocket and strolled around my little kingdom, checking everything was operating satisfactorily. One of my boys had been avoiding me for a few days and had failed to make his weekly payment. I knew he'd been working, but he'd managed not to be around at the same time as me. I asked some of his friends and they all denied any knowledge of his whereabouts. Something I would need to sort out before it got out of hand. Maybe I needed to make an example of someone before more of them thought they could get a free ride out of me.

But I could feel the envelope as though it was burning a hole in my pocket. Finally I nipped into the passengers' toilet. We weren't supposed to go in there, but the staff turned a blind eye so long as it was only me. It wouldn't do for any of the black kids to try and sneak in; but they all knew that anyway. Shutting myself in one of the stalls, I closed the lid and sat down, lit up a ciggie and opened the envelope. The letter was written on the same thick creamy paper in the same black ink. I pulled it out of the envelope and a small piece of card came with it and fell to the ground. As I bent to pick it up I caught sight of the signature on the letter: your friend, Stefano. *Gasping, I turned back to the beginning of the letter and began to read.*

My dear Michael

No doubt you will be surprised to hear from me after so long. Have you forgiven me for running out on you like that? I mentioned a bit of trouble at Mount Nelson, and you have probably heard all about that too, if you've seen your friend, Sammie. I do hope you didn't get caught in the fallout.

I've been moving around quite a bit since we were together in Cape Town and as you will see from the address, I have reached the very northern tip of this continent. I've had some interesting times, but to be honest, I'm not sure the Arabs like the Soviets as much as the black fellows down south seem to. I will be coming back down to South Africa, although not to Cape Town, within the next couple of weeks.

I have thought a lot about our discussions in the hotel gardens and I still feel there is a place for a smart lad like you in my projects. It's about time you broke out of the rut you've got into down there.

I am enclosing a ticket to Jo'burg. It's dated for the first of next month. That should give you time to settle your affairs down there and say your goodbyes. Although, a word of warning: don't be too open with people about your plans; you never know when you might want the benefit of complete anonymity. I hope to see you next month. You will find me at the Monarch!

Your friend Stefano.

I lay awake all that night tossing and turning as thoughts raced through my head. I knew Stefano was a conman at best; maybe a dangerous crook. He might not be the safest person to team up with. But on the other hand, the time I'd spent with him had been the most exciting fortnight of my life—and I wanted more.

I pushed all the lads at the station to make their regular payments a little early that week. A couple of them objected, but a quick cuff around the head was enough to quieten them down and no-one else seemed to want to object after that. They were going to be surprised when I didn't appear the following week, but I guessed it wouldn't be long before someone else would rise through the ranks to take my place; and at least they wouldn't have to fight their way in, as I'd had to with Enoch all those years ago.

I went to class with Amelia one more time, and had supper with her, Joe and Frank afterwards. She was full of news about a new company opening up in the neighbourhood.

'And, Michael, they're recruiting office staff! I've got you a form; I'll help you to fill it in.'

I smiled and took the form from her. It seemed only polite to do that.

'I'll have a look at it when I get home,' I said, 'and let you see it before I send it in.' She looked at me long and hard, and I almost blurted out my plans, then and there. But something stopped me; maybe the thought that they would try to dissuade me. As I left that evening, I hugged her extra hard.

'Goodbye,' I whispered as I walked away from their little house for the last time. When I got back to my digs, I realised I'd left the recruitment form on the table in their lounge.

CHAPTER 20

The phone rang as Suzanne was finalising the report on her investigations so far into Sunshine Supplements. It was Damien.

'Suzanne, hi.'

'Hi, Damien; good to hear your voice.'

'Yes, you too. How's the investigation going?'

'Not too bad. I've been doing some digging into the background of Sunshine Supplements and our Mr Nigel Atkinson. I'm just writing it up and you should have it by tomorrow morning.'

'Gee, that's great. And I've been busy at this end too. I've just sent you an email but I thought it would be easier to talk it through with you as well.'

'Hang on, then,' said Suzanne, 'let me open it up first.' She clicked into her Outlook folder and found an email with the subject *SS Report*. There was a brief covering note and a Word attachment. She clicked on the W icon. 'Okay, Damien, I've got it. Looks very comprehensive.' The document was seventeen pages long.

'Yes, there's a fair bit of detail in there—and I'll leave you to read through it at your leisure, but I wanted to emphasise a couple of things before you start. You'll see there's a list of names. Those are all the people I talked to in Brazil, plus some others I've met since I came back to the US. Not all of them have been showing the symptoms we're concerned about, but they've all been drinking Super Fit.'

'Well, that's okay. We need to talk to a cross section of users; so if some of them are finding they don't have problems, we need to record that too.'

'But when Lulana first got Super Fit, she swore by it. Said it was wonderful. And didn't show any adverse reactions. It was only after about three months they started to manifest themselves.'

'So it's important to have the timeline for people taking the supplement too.'

'And maybe interview some people more than once, over a period of time. Or ask some of the people with symptoms when they started experiencing them; how long they'd been using the supplement? It may be they were so used to it by then they failed to associate the symptoms with the product.'

'Or, and we have to face this fact, Damien, it may all be a coincidence and Super Fit might be completely harmless.'

'I don't believe that,' said Damien.

'No, neither do I, as a matter of fact,' she said, 'but we have to keep an open mind until we have some incontrovertible evidence that links Sunshine Supplements and Super Fit to the behavioural problems.'

The two discussed some of Damien's findings and Suzanne agreed to ring him later in the week, when she'd had a chance to go through all the interviews.

'And there's a separate list in there,' he said, 'of athletes from Europe; mostly UK, but also other countries. Can you cover those interviews?'

'Yes, of course I can. I'll do the ones closest to home first and then spread out if I need to.'

'Suzanne, you said you'd found out some interesting

background on the company and its boss?'

'Well, Sunshine Supplements isn't the first company our Mr Atkinson's been part of.'

'No?'

'No. He's been involved in five start-ups over the past twenty-odd years. Mostly in food supplements, although one was in health care—a homoeopathic company.'

'And what's he done with those companies? He's surely not running all of them, is he?'

'Oh, no. They've all been bought out by larger organisations from Eastern Europe. Made our Nigel a stack of money over the years, in fact.' She went on to tell her client that Atkinson seemed to work to a pattern. 'There will always be a start-up product that pushes up the value of the company just before the buyout takes place.'

'That's very interesting. And would I know of any of these start-up products?'

'It's unlikely. In all cases apart from the homoeopathic one, the star product has later been taken off the market. There's always been a valid reason; either a change in regulation or lack of demand, but it seems a bit odd that none of the stars has survived absorption into the larger company.'

'Haven't any of these companies heard of due diligence?'

'Apparently not. Either that or they know about the problems and don't care.'

'Money laundering?'

'Possibly. I need to talk to a few friends in the city before I can make a judgement on that. And that would explain why there's so much investment gone into the Super Fit production plant. It's far too high-tech for a food supplement under normal circumstances.'

'And do you think Sunshine Supplements is heading for a takeover as well?'

'Yes, I do, at some point. There's a rumour that some investors are sniffing around, looking at its potential. But let me do some more digging and get back to you. And in the meantime, I'll start interviewing the folks on this list.'

'Okay, Suzanne. We'll talk in a day or so—and let's move quickly on this. Too many of my friends are taking this thing for me to sit back and let it hurt even more of them.'

Over the next couple of hours, Suzanne tried to contact seven of the people on Damien's list. One was out of the country and not expected back for another two months. Two refused point blank to talk to her, or even to admit they were taking the Sunshine Supplements product. Three were happy to talk, even though only one of them seemed to be having any problems. The seventh was a sprinter called Annabelle Swift. She lived in Somerset and as Suzanne was planning to drive down to the West Country that week to visit her parents, she arranged to call in to the pretty little village just outside Bristol on her way past the following day.

'It's only a short distance from the motorway; I should be there around two pm, if that's okay,' she told Annabelle when she spoke to her on the phone.

When they met, Suzanne was surprised to see Annabelle was tiny and frail looking. She sounded breathy and looked like a schoolgirl in her early teens, although Damien's notes told Suzanne she was actually nineteen and in her second year at university. She had a coughing fit at one point and confirmed to Suzanne she was not actually training at the moment due to breathing problems.

'But I'll soon be fine again,' she confided. 'I'm taking Super Fit and it's helping me a lot. I'm hoping the doctor signs me off next week. I can't wait to get back to training again.'

Annabelle was adamant she'd suffered no ill effects from the Sunshine Supplements product. Quite the opposite in fact.

'All my friends have been commenting on how glossy and healthy my hair has got since I started using it. Why, some of them are even considering taking up a sport, just so they can be eligible for it!'

Suzanne wrapped up the interview quickly. There didn't seem to be anything untoward going on with Annabelle, apart from her coughing, which could hardly be blamed on Super Fit. She took a few more details of usage and then said her goodbyes.

But as she continued on her journey down the M5, she couldn't get the image of the frail young runner out of her head. She made a mental note to herself to give her a ring the next day to check how she was. But she was driving, she didn't have a notebook to hand—and the visit to her parents drove other things out of her mind.

It was another four days before she remembered she'd meant to phone Annabelle. She rang the cottage three times that day, but there was no answer. The following morning, she dialled the number just after nine o'clock. The phone was picked up but instead of Annabelle's voice, it was a male that answered.

'Hello, this is Suzanne Jones. Could I speak to Annabelle, please?'

'Are you a friend of hers?'

'Well, not a friend, actually. I came to see—'

'She's not here.' And the phone was slammed down. Suzanne stared at the handset, perplexed. What was that all about? Should she try again? Maybe later, when hopefully Annabelle would be at home.

But she never did make that call. Later that day, she got an email from Damien with a link to the *Somerset Weekly Gazette Online*, reporting the shock death of a young sprinter following an extreme allergic reaction. The report said the medical authorities were baffled as to exactly what the deceased athlete had been allergic to. But it was the name that jumped off the screen at Suzanne. The deceased woman's name was Annabelle Swift.

CHAPTER 21

Despite her apprehension, Charlie's first time in the company of Michael Hawkins was a lot less stressful than she expected. They met at Congonhas Airport and apart from a brief conversation when Mercy introduced 'Rose Fitzpatrick, her friend from England' to her father, he ignored both of them. As soon as they took off, he pulled a sheaf of papers out of his calfskin briefcase, took a slim gold pen from his breast pocket and settled down to read. He didn't raise his head until the pilot announced they were coming in to land at Aeropuerto Internacional de las Cataratas del Igauzu and they were to refasten their seat belts.

The plane taxied to the section of the airfield reserved for private transport, and stopped. Two limos with blacked out windows drove across the tarmac and stopped at the side of the plane, while ground staff wheeled the steps over and positioned them by the door.

Hawkins disembarked first. The back door of the first limo opened and a short, squat man in expensively casual clothing jumped out and hurried to shake Hawkins by the hand. Then, clapping him on the shoulder, he escorted him to the car. Mercy and Charlie stood uncertainly at the bottom of the steps. Out of the second car emerged a much younger version of the first man. Hawkins looked over his shoulder and called across to Mercy.

'This is Chico. He'll look after you girls this afternoon and we'll meet up for a drink before dinner tonight.' And with a wave he climbed into the car which drove away.

'Well,' said Charlie, 'it looks like we're on our own.' She looked across at Chico who was standing silently to one side, waiting for them to acknowledge him. 'Right, Chico, what do you have planned for us?' As she said this, Charlie hoped she wasn't coming over as too forward, but Mercy seemed to have suddenly become very withdrawn. What was wrong with her?

Unusually for a Brazilian of his age, Chico's English was poor. Charlie, who was no linguist, had picked up very little Portuguese since arriving in Brazil. She was going to have to rely on Mercy to act as interpreter. But in fact, Chico had very little to say for himself anyway and after a few attempts at conversation, they decided to treat him as a tour guide and enjoy the visit on their own.

When they'd dropped their bags at the hotel, the two women, with Chico trailing behind them, made their way down the stairway to the cliff-side path along the rim of the falls. Everything was shrouded in mist when they first arrived at the top of the cliffs. They could hear the water thundering over the rock face below them, and feel the spray as it splashed across their faces, but all they could see was an impenetrable grey blanket. They walked faster than Chico and he had very soon vanished from view.

'Chico reckons this will disappear soon,' Mercy said, linking her arm through Charlie's. She gave a shiver. 'But if it doesn't, I think we should head back to the hotel and have a swim. We can always come back tomorrow. The weather is forecast to be better in the morning—and apparently the best time to see the falls is at dawn anyway.'

'You could be right,' said Charlie, looking upwards, 'but I do believe there's a gleam of sunlight up there. Let's just hang on a while longer.'

The women stood huddled together leaning on the railing, and after a short while, Charlie knew she'd been right. The sun was definitely coming out and the mist began to clear. Then without warning, it was gone and the whole vista was laid bare. Charlie heard Mercy gasp and felt her squeeze her arm.

'Would you look at that!'

The falls stretched out before them, fold after fold of fractured cliffs over which millions of gallons of water tumbled to the river bed below. Light glinted on the water, myriad rainbows played through the spray and the roar of the falls seemed to intensify with the sight.

Charlie was surprised to see tears pouring down Mercy's cheeks.

'Mercy, what's the matter?'

'It's so beautiful; I've never seen anything like it.' She rubbed her hand across her face. 'Thank you so much for coming with me. It wouldn't have been the same without someone to share it with.'

'Hey, you're welcome. I'm really enjoying this,' said Charlie, realising, as she said it, how true her words were. She felt a tiny stab of guilt that she was here under false pretences. This guilt was a habit she'd tried, but never quite managed, to break herself of in the past. There was always someone innocent, someone she felt drawn to. But now she stifled that thought, reminding herself that no matter how innocent Mercy might be, her father deserved whatever he had coming to him. 'It's great you asked me rather than one of your other friends.'

But Mercy just shrugged.

'What other friends? You're the first person I've really talked to since I got here.' She stared out over the cliff top and then turned towards Charlie, her face crumpling again. 'I've been so lonely...'

'But surely your father must know lots of people. He's been here for a long time, hasn't he?'

'Not really, no. He's had business connections here for ages, and he had the villa built more than ten years ago, but he's only lived here for about eighteen months. He certainly doesn't seem to know many people—or not people my age, anyway. And he doesn't like me spending time with his friends.' She stood staring out over the water again. Then she grabbed Charlie's arm in a tight grip. 'He seems so nice and friendly at the moment, doesn't he? But you should see him when he gets angry.'

Charlie wasn't sure she believed this. Suzanne had told her she'd never seen Hawkins lose his temper once, the whole time she'd worked for him when he was masquerading as Sir Fredrick Michaels. That was one of the things her sister remembered particularly about her erstwhile boss. His calm under all conditions. But Mercy was nodding her head vigorously. 'Sometimes, when he gets in a real rage, I'm so frightened of him.'

'Well in that case, why don't you leave him and go live somewhere else?'

'How can I? I'm his daughter, but I don't have a Brazilian passport yet. I'm only in this country at his behest.'

'But that's not right,' said Charlie. 'If you're frightened of him, there must be something we can do.' At once, Mercy's smile broke through the tears, as the sun had broken through the mist just a while before.

'Will you help me, Rose? I need to get away from him. Help me come up with a plan. I'm sure we'll be able to do it together.' Then she tucked her arm through Charlie's again. 'Come on, let's not spoil this weekend, thinking about unpleasant things. We'll go back to the hotel and have that swim. We can come back here in the morning and look at the falls again.'

By the time the women finished their swim and got changed, Hawkins was waiting for them in the bar. He introduced them to his companion, whom he referred to as *'Senhor Diego*, a business associate of mine.' Then he apologised for not being able to join them for dinner.

'Our business discussions have overrun somewhat, so we're going to continue them while we eat, in the private dining room. You would only be bored listening to all that shop talk, so I've booked a table for you girls on the roof terrace. You can watch the falls as you eat. We'll have lunch together tomorrow, I promise.'

'Tell me, Mercy,' Charlie asked casually as they walked towards the elevator, 'what sort of business is your father in?' But the other woman just shrugged her shoulders.

'I don't know, really; he never talks about it.' Then she shuddered. 'But some of his so-called associates are a bit scary. They make Senhor Diego look like a pussycat.'

Charlie had been relieved to find she had a room to herself in the hotel and although there was an interconnecting door to the adjoining suite, where Mercy was sleeping, it was locked. As she got ready for bed after a long, very enjoyable evening, she reflected on the fact that Mercy Gove Hawkins was actually very good company. She felt guilty once more at the inevitable disappointment when she discovered her new friend was not what she claimed to be. *But then again*, she thought, *if she really is afraid of him and does want out, maybe we can fix the situation without too much disappointment after all.* Her final thought before she drifted off to sleep was of Annie. She really must remember to ring her in the morning.

CHAPTER 22

Johannesburg, October 1961

I left Cape Town on the first day of October 1961 and met Stefano more than a day later in Jo'burg's famous Monarch Hotel. It had been a long, tiring journey, sitting upright throughout the night, but after all those years of watching other people getting on and off trains, I was fascinated. Electrification had only partly been installed and at Beaufort West we jumped onto the platform to stretch our legs while the locomotive was replaced with the more familiar steam engine for the remainder of the journey via Kimberley and Klerksdorp. But I also had lots of time to dream and get excited about the future. I had no idea in what direction my life was going, but I didn't think I would ever be returning to my days of carrying bags for passengers and teaching spoilt little rich kids to do their sums.

Stefano greeted me like a long-lost brother, gathering me into his arms in a tight bear hug and then kissing me on both cheeks. He must have noticed my embarrassment at this; I certainly felt hot when he let me go. He burst out laughing and slapped me on the back.

'I'm sorry, my boy,' he gasped between laughs, 'I forgot how reserved you Brits are.' He took a deep breath and shook his finger at me, although his eyes still sparkled with laughter. 'In my country, men are not afraid to show their emotions.' He paused and looked at me with his head on one side. 'Mind you,' he went on, 'a lack of emotion, maybe even a good poker face, could be a real asset to us in

the future.' Then he took my bag from me. 'Come on, let's get this up to the room and sort you out some food. And tomorrow, we really must get you some better clothes.'

The next day was a whirlwind of activity and I just kept my mouth shut and went with the flow. We headed for one of the best malls in the city, where Stefano was greeted as a respected customer by all the shopkeepers. I acquired two new suits, several shirts, underclothes and the best pair of leather walking shoes I had ever seen. And in each shop, Stefano airily waved a hand and told them to 'put it on my bill, old boy.' And they did. At every single place we visited, we walked out with bags full of stuff, without paying a single penny.

This was a different Stefano from the casually dressed ageing hippie I'd met in Cape Town all those months ago. He was beautifully dressed, with neatly tied cravat, well-trimmed hair and moustache and brightly polished shoes.

'It's a question of image, my boy,' he told me when I asked him about the change. 'When we met in Cape Town, I was an archaeologist, a fossil hunter; I'd been living rough (or at least that was the story) so I needed to look the part. Life is very different here, and I'm showing the punters a different face.'

It took me a while to learn exactly what role Stefano was playing, but for the moment, I was happy just to spend time with him and learn about his life—or at least the parts he was willing to show me. But gradually, I realised he, or I guess I should say we, had fingers in many different pies.

Stefano introduced me to his other 'associates' as he called them. There were two men from his home town of Kharkov, which he told me was on the western edge of the Soviet Union. He referred to them as his cousins and although I was never sure whether this was a true family relationship or just a figure of speech, he certainly trusted this pair with his secrets and, on more than one occasion, his life. Then there were three South Africans, two black and one white. These he used as messengers and runners; they were on the margins and he didn't share much with them, but they were useful when a more local level of knowledge was needed.

And as for the schemes themselves, or his projects, as he called them, they ranged from extortion and protection rackets to the occasional professional hit. Stefano never got his hands dirty himself, but he controlled every move and called all the shots.

After we'd been in Jo'burg for nearly a year, he decided we should move.

'All this apartheid nonsense is bad for business,' he declared one day after one of his runners had narrowly avoided being detained by the local police, just for being in the wrong place at the wrong time. 'We need a country where whites and blacks can mix more freely. We'll give Mozambique a try.'

We packed up our stuff, sneaking it out of the hotel one bag at a time, and hiding it in the left luggage lockers in the station. When it was all clear, we slipped out ourselves one evening and never returned. I believe Stefano had paid some of the bills earlier on, to keep them happy, but we still left them with a huge outstanding account.

'A true gentleman never pays his bills; isn't that right, Michael?' he said as we left the hotel for the very last time.

We took a train to the border and from there transferred into a car arranged for us by one of the local associates. The Soviet cousins had gone on before us into Mozambique, but we were leaving the runners behind.

'There will always be people available, willing to do anything for a few pence,' said Stefano afterwards. But as we said goodbye to these three men who had helped us no end in our projects, I had a lump in my throat, and even Stefano seemed to be shedding a tear, although he swore it was dust in his eye.

We settled in Lourenço Marques and as Stefano had surmised, it was much easier to operate and fit in. Society was more integrated and the inconveniences of apartheid hadn't made it across the border.

Within a few months, we were well established and even found ourselves a place to live. The idea of squatting rent-free in one of the best hotels had been amusing for a while, but there always seemed to be staff around, changing the bedclothes, cleaning the rooms, delivering room service—and we had never been sure how many of them we could trust. At least one of the waiters at The Monarch had realised what we were up to and actually tried blackmailing Stefano. He disappeared the same evening, and no-one else tried the same trick, but it made us even more wary in Mozambique.

Of course, we weren't the only people in the country who were trying to make a living from their wits and other people's energy. There were several gangs already operating in the capital city and as we guessed, they were not too happy at the idea of new kids on the block taking some of their opportunities away.

One night we were meeting a new client to arrange a spot of business. At least that's what we thought. But it turned out to be a trap. We were cornered in a dark alleyway by two thugs, who told us they had a message from the boss.

'Who does he think he is? James Cagney?' growled Stefano. We stood back to back as the two huge men approached us. I saw a glint and realised the one closest to me had a knife.

'Watch out, Stefano, they have knives,' I whispered, before ducking down, tackling my opponent around the ankles and bringing him crashing to the ground. They say the bigger they are, the harder they fall, and it was certainly true in this case. He went down like a ninepin, catching his head on a railing as he did, and lay very still. I checked over my shoulder. Stefano was having no trouble dealing with his opponent, and as I watched, the thug dropped his knife and ran for the end of the alleyway, back into the busy street and apparent safety.

At that point, mine groaned and opened his eyes. I picked up his knife, which had slipped from his grasp, and plunged it into his throat.

'A message back to your boss,' I said softly. 'There are some new boys in town and they're not to be messed with.'

He gurgled once, as blood dribbled out of his mouth and spurted from the knife wound. I jumped out of the way and watched from a distance until he stopped moving and I was sure he was dead. As his hands slid from his throat to the floor, I spotted something shining in the moonlight. He wore an ornate pinky ring; green and red flashes and gold lettering around the edge. I reached over and slid it off. It fitted my little finger perfectly. I've worn that ring ever since to remind me no matter how high up the ladder you climb, there will always be someone behind you, waiting to pull you down.

Standing, I walked away from him, and from Stefano, and bent over, retching as my stomach emptied itself of its contents. I guess the first time is always a shock, something never forgotten.

Stefano waited until I'd cleaned myself up, then put an arm around my shoulder and we went home. There he broke out a bottle of his favourite vodka and toasted me as his saviour. I wasn't at all sure that was true, but it was good to hear he appreciated me. It made the flight from South Africa and everything I'd left behind worth it.

That night, Stefano sat me down and gave me full details about all the projects he was involved in. I'd known about some of them; he'd even given me responsibility for one of the smaller ones. But now, it was as though he believed I was truly worth trusting; worth bringing completely on board. I don't know what his cousins thought about it. I never asked—and they never offered any comments, but from that moment on, I was seen as the number two to Stefano Mladov. When he wanted something special sorted out, he sent me along—and people started treating me with respect, just as I'd seen them treating Stefano up to then.

CHAPTER 23

Next morning, Charlie was woken by an urgent tapping on her hotel room door.

'Rose, are you awake? Hey, Rose, wake up!' She recognised Mercy's voice and glanced at the clock as she rolled out of bed.

Shit! Five-thirty am! What on earth could be that important at such an ungodly hour? Grabbing a robe and throwing it over her naked body, she groped for the door handle and peeped out.

'Mercy, what's the matter? Are we on fire?'

The tall African woman gave a bark of laughter.

'Don't you remember? We agreed to go and watch the dawn at the falls. Come on, we'll miss the sunrise if you don't hurry.'

It was beginning to come back to Charlie. Their view of the famous falls shrouded in mist yesterday afternoon, then the sun breaking through, revealing the wonderful sight. And Chico's recommendation that they go back this morning and watch the sunrise. It had seemed such a good idea when they'd talked about it yesterday, but that was before a late dinner and a protracted drinking session in the bar afterwards. How did Mercy manage to look so fresh this morning? Charlie was sure they'd drunk the same number of cocktails.

'Come on, sleepyhead; get moving,' said Mercy now, jumping up and down like a child on Christmas morning.

Dousing her head under the cold tap helped clear some of Charlie's cobwebs before she threw on joggers and a fleece, and within twenty minutes, the two women were striding down the path from the back of the hotel, arriving at the platform above Garganta del Diablo just as the first finger of light pierced the air above the surrounding hills.

At first, it was like gazing at a smudged monochrome picture, all blues and whites with just the faintest tinge of pink. Slowly, as the sun struggled to break through the horizon of roiling clouds, the sky turned bruised, mauve, purple and orange, contrasting with the stark black of the foliage, and reminding Charlie of sunset in Africa. Then as the sun broke through the cloud, the palette turned to greys and greens and outlines became clearer, sharper. For a brief moment, the water took on the colour of the sun, thundering over the fourteen separate falls of the Devil's Throat like curtains of gold. But this quickly faded, leaving the white sweeps of foam like so many living glaciers.

They stood in silence for ten minutes, and Charlie wondered if Mercy's heart was beating as loudly as hers. To start with there was only a muted sound of falling water, but as the light increased, so did the intensity of the sound and finally, as day broke, the full force of the water impacted on her senses. She didn't think she'd ever seen anything so impressive.

Mercy gave a great sigh and turned towards Charlie, tears sparkling in her eyes.

'I am so glad you're here,' she said. 'If I'd been on my own, I wouldn't have even got out of bed; I would have missed this—and this may be the only chance I ever get to see it.'

Hey, that's a bit final, isn't it?' asked Charlie. 'So you're really set on doing a runner then?'

The other woman nodded.

'Yes, definitely. Meeting you, making friends for the first time, has made me realise how my father is stifling me. I need to get away.' She gripped Charlie's hands and squeezed them, painfully. 'You said you'd help me; did you mean it?'

Great, thought Charlie, *I've just started to get close to Hawkins and Mercy wants me to help her run away. That's going to really piss him off.* She knew this would limit the time she had left to sort out how to trap Hawkins into giving himself away.

'Rose,' Mercy looked nervous, 'you promised! Will you help me?'

'Of course I will,' Charlie said, although she could feel her heart sinking. 'What do you want me to do?'

'My father keeps close tabs on me. When I'm in the house, there are always people there and even if I'm out and about, one of his men is always around.'

'Not when you're at the sports club, surely?'

'Yes, even there. You probably wouldn't notice; they're trained to blend into the background. But I know I'm never really alone. I need some sort of diversion. We're going up to Rio next week, for Mardi Gras and I was hoping to get the opportunity to slip away during the parade.' She looked at Charlie with a serious expression on her face, then she smiled and nodded her head. 'That's it; come with us to Rio. If I'm with you, he's likely to be less vigilant.'

'Oh, I'm not sure that's a good idea...' but Mercy was now nodding her head vigorously.

'Yes, definitely, that's what we'll do. I'll tell him we're going down to watch the parade together, we can lose his minders in the crush and with a bit of luck we'll have time to get away before they realise we've gone.'

'Yes, but where will we be gone to?' Charlie asked. Mercy shrugged.

'Not sure about that; I need to do some more thinking.

Let's talk again later.' She dropped Charlie's hands, which she had been clutching throughout, and gave a laugh. 'Come on, race you back to the hotel. I'm starving. Let's see if the restaurant is serving breakfast yet.'

Charlie started to run after her, but the slope was steep and she slowed to a walk after a few metres. She had a lot of thinking to do herself. She'd had one problem: how to trap Michael Hawkins into giving himself away and thus push him towards arrest and punishment. Now it seemed she had two problems. Not only did she have to deal with the father, but the daughter was going to do something rash and expected her to help. How on earth had she got herself into this situation? She desperately wanted to talk things through with Suzanne, but something told her that wouldn't be a good idea. Her sister would want her to get away and leave them be; or worse still, she would insist on coming back out to Brazil to help her. And that wouldn't be a good idea at all.

Suddenly a thought struck her and the simplicity of the solution made her laugh out loud with delight. There was one other person who hated Michael Hawkins as much as the Jones sisters, one person who would sympathise with her current plight—and might very well have the answer to her problems. Francine Matheson! In her early days as an MP, long before she became Parliamentary Under-secretary in the Department of International Affairs, Francine had made a mistake. A mistake which Hawkins, in his persona of Sir Fredrick Michaels, had exploited two years ago when making his escape from Britain. She would be able to help; probably with both sides of the problem. That was it! As soon as she was back in São Paulo, she would phone Francine and ask for her help.

CHAPTER 24

By the time she'd finished her phone conversation with Francine on the Sunday evening, Charlie had put together a clear plan of action, although she wasn't going to tell Mercy just where she'd got her information from. Nor did she plan to tell her the place of refuge she'd arranged for them was actually a safe house connected to the British Embassy.

The two women met as usual at lunchtime on the Tuesday morning after their trip to Iguaçu. Hawkins' daughter was jumpy, more anxious than usual, and eager to talk about their plans for Rio. She seemed grateful and relieved to hear Charlie had some thoughts about how she could run away from Hawkins.

'I've found us a safe place to hide for a few hours,' she said, 'and then friends of minc will smuggle you to the airport, where I've secured you a place on a flight out of Brazil.'

'Where will I be going?' Mercy asked, 'And won't you be coming with me?'

'No, I don't think so, Mercy. It will look more suspicious if both of us disappear together. I'm going to go back to your father and say we got separated in the crowd.

It's easily done and if we lose your bodyguards at the same time, he can't say anything, now can he?'

She dodged the question of where Mercy would be going. Taking her into protective custody might seem like an extreme measure, but if Hawkins was brought to trial, as Charlie hoped he would be, then Mercy could well be an important witness, with her knowledge of his early life in Africa before he became a senior public servant in Her Majesty's Government. And Charlie didn't want her disappearing before they had a chance to question her. So a quick trip across the Caribbean to the nearest British territory seemed a good move in the first instance.

The two women moved on to discussing the practicalities of Mercy's escape. She told Charlie that since she'd come to Brazil, her father had given her a generous allowance and she'd taken the opportunity to build up quite a good wardrobe. But she knew she wouldn't be able to take much of it with her.

'We're only supposed to be going to Rio for a few days, so I won't get away with too much luggage,' she said.

'And besides, you're running away during an evening out. Difficult to take suitcases with you, I would have thought,' replied Charlie.

Mercy shrugged.

'It's a pity, but let's face it, I arrived in this country with nothing but the clothes I stood up in. I can always leave the same way.'

'Oh, I'm not sure it's quite that bad,' said Charlie. 'If you pack a small bag, I'll take it to my friends earlier in the week and they can hold it for you. I take it you've got some money?'

'Well, I've got credit cards.'

'No, that's no good!' Charlie was overly emphatic and realised one or two of the diners at the surrounding tables were looking curiously at her. Luckily she was speaking in English, so not everyone would understand their conversation. Nevertheless, she lowered her voice and smiled apologetically at her companion. 'Sorry, but even if your father doesn't cancel them, it's not a good idea to use them. They'll pinpoint your location—and since you presumably don't want to be found again...'

'Okay, so I need cash,' said Mercy. 'I'll draw some out over the next couple of days.'

'And if you wear some of that swanky jewellery you were flashing around last weekend,' said Charlie with a grin, 'you can always hock that if you need some more cash.'

The women agreed they would put their plan into action on Tuesday, the last night of their visit, and the last day before Ash Wednesday and the start of Lent. Which left Charlie with just a week to get closer to Michael Hawkins and try to find his weak spot. She needed to step up her activities.

Over the next three days, Charlie managed to manoeuvre herself into dinner invitations twice at the Hawkins residence. The first time, Hawkins was going out and although he was pleasant enough when they met, telling Charlie he was pleased to hear she was accompanying them to Rio, he didn't stay long. Waving a hand and reminding Mercy not to wait up for him, he disappeared through the front door, followed by his chauffeur. Mercy pulled a face.

'He's going to one of his meetings at *Il Paradiso*.'

'Isn't that the strip joint everyone's talking about?'

'That's the one! He tells me he's only going because that's where his client likes to meet, but he always comes home stinking of cheap perfume. I think he enjoys it alright!'

Charlie was amused at the look of prudish distaste on her friend's face but thought it better to keep this to herself. She took the opportunity of having a snoop around the house, even finding her way into Hawkins' study. She was just trying all the desk drawers, which were frustratingly locked, when she heard Mercy outside in the hall calling for her. She poked her head out of the door, using the lame excuse that she'd got lost looking for the bathroom. Luckily Mercy hadn't seen as many B movies as she had, and took her explanation at face value. She clicked the door closed behind Charlie and pointed her in the right direction.

'It's a good job my father's not here,' she said when Charlie re-joined her in the dining room. 'No-one goes into his study uninvited—and certainly not when he's not here.'

The second time she was invited to dinner was the evening before they left for Rio. Hawkins wanted to get away early the following day—'more business meetings, I guess,' said Mercy—and as Charlie had told them she was staying in student accommodation on the other side of the city, they suggested she spend the night with them, ready for the early start. And this time, Hawkins stayed in and joined them for drinks on the terrace before dinner. It was the first time Charlie had the chance to study her quarry up close and she could see why he'd managed to get away with so much for so long.

Put simply, Michael Hawkins could be very good company when he wanted to be. Casually dressed, clean-shaven and with his hair trimmed very short and dyed a natural-looking pepper and salt, he appeared at least ten years younger than the sixty-seven Charlie knew him to be. He looked directly at her when he asked a question, and maintained eye contact, nodding encouragingly, as she answered him. She could feel herself starting to like this man, against her will, and reminded herself, that just like Kipling's Shere Khan, Michael Hawkins was a deadly enemy, even if he didn't always appear that way.

It was after dinner, as Mercy was out of the room, that Hawkins dropped a bombshell.

'Rose, have we met before? I'm sure I know your face

from somewhere, but I can't place it.' Charlie felt like a bucket of ice had been tipped over her. She struggled to keep her face straight.

'I don't think so, Michael. I'd have remembered if we had.'

'I saw you at the sports ground, you know. On the weekend of the race meeting. The day Mercy won her medal. I thought I recognised you then, too.'

'Maybe you saw me in the newspaper,' Charlie was thinking rapidly and the words came out before she had time to fully polish the story, but it would have to do. 'I won a couple of competitions a few years back; was quite the darling of the press for a few months.' She pulled a wry face. 'It didn't last, of course. You're only as good as your last book.'

Hawkins stared at her, slowly rubbing his temples. Then he shrugged.

'Maybe that's it. But I'll keep thinking. It'll come to me.' He pointed at her and winked. 'I never forget a face, you know.' At that moment, Mercy came back into the room and his attention turned to his daughter. But it was a long time before Charlie could still her racing thoughts.

CHAPTER 25

Lourenço Marques, August 1967

I met Grace Gove in the most prosaic of ways, at the grocery store in her home town about two hours' drive from the Mozambique capital. We had been approached about getting involved in a new project, a casino being built in the countryside, and Stefano sent me up there to see what was going on. I'd come to the conclusion there was nothing in it for us. The guys organising the project were losers, all of them, and the chances of the place having many customers, short of running tourist buses out there each night, were slim to say the least. And although the activities of FRELIMO hadn't reached this far yet, rumours of guerrilla movements were being whispered in every bar I visited. I was about to ring Stefano and tell him I was on my way home when I heard someone singing.

She had the sweetest voice I'd ever heard. She was singing softly to herself as she stacked cans on the shelves at the back of the store. The tune sounded familiar, and I realised later it was one of the ones we used to sing during the services Joe Marks held in his Cape Town church. If I'd realised that, I might have taken it as a sign to leave well alone, made that phone call to Stefano, returned to Lourenço Marques and forgotten all about Grace. But that wasn't what happened.

I stayed in that little town for the next ten days. On the first day I just smiled at her as I walked past. On the second day I tipped my hat to her and said, 'Good morning, Ma'am.' She smiled up shyly at me from beneath her long dark lashes, but said nothing. By the fourth day she'd got over her shyness and plucked up the courage to talk to me. By day seven she'd agreed to come out with me for a walk in the evening. And on day ten, when I got to the bus stop to pick up my ride back to the capital, she was waiting for me, a small bag clutched in her hand and a look between trepidation and expectation on her face. I had begged her the previous night to come with me, but until that last moment, I didn't think she would agree. We said very little on that two-hour journey back to the city, just held hands tightly. I'm not sure which of us was the most nervous.

We'd have been even more nervous if we'd known what Stefano's reaction was going to be. It was one of the few times he yelled at me; and certainly the only time I ever yelled at him.

When we got back to Lourenço Marques, it was early evening and Stefano was in the local restaurant he had bought and turned into his HQ. He was just beginning his usual evening meal of something typically Russian he'd taught the local cooks to make— borsch *or maybe* pilmeni*—when we arrived. I walked in first and his face lit up when he saw me.*

'Michael, my dear boy! Welcome back.' He jumped up and shook my hand then gave me a bear hug. 'You've been away so long. You must have so much to tell me. Is the business going to be good..?' but he stopped himself from going any further and slapped me on the shoulder. 'Come, have some food first and then you can tell me all about it.' He turned back to his table, but I caught his arm and stopped him.

'No, wait, Stefano,' I said, 'first there's someone I want you to meet.' He turned back to me with a confused expression on his face. I opened the door and beckoned Grace in. She had been waiting outside until I called her and as she walked in, she was biting her lip and staring at the ground in front of her. 'Stefano, I'd like you to meet Grace Gove. She's come down from the town with me.'

He stared at me for a few seconds, then it was like a shutter coming down on his face. He turned towards her, with a smile that warmed his lips but didn't quite reach his eyes.

'Miss Gove, how do you do?' He indicated a spare chair at the

table and clicked his fingers to the waiter to set another place. 'Do sit down and join us; you must be hungry after your journey.'

That was the longest meal I can ever remember eating and we sat in silence for much of the time. Stefano asked me a couple of questions about the trip, but seemed distracted and didn't appear to be listening to my answers. Grace said nothing apart from a whispered 'please' or 'thank you' when someone spoke directly to her.

At last we finished and as Stefano stirred strawberry jam into the thick black tea he insisted on drinking at the end of each meal, he finally looked at me.

'Where will Miss Gove be staying tonight?'

'I'm going to book her into one of the rooms in the hotel across the street from us,' I said, feeling rather than seeing the look of disappointment on her face. I wanted to say she would be staying with me, but chickened out at the last minute.

'Well, why don't you take her over there now,' my boss replied, 'and come back here afterwards. You can brief me on your trip then. I'm sure Miss Gove would be very bored if we started talking business at this point.'

We picked up her case and I took her hand. As we walked along the street to the little hotel, she looked up at me.

'I don't think your friend likes me.'

'Who, Stefano?' I tried to laugh off her concerns. 'No, he's fine. He wasn't expecting you, that's all. I'll talk to him and explain the situation. So you'll only have to stay here a night or two. Then we'll sort something out.'

I booked her into the hotel and saw her safely to her room. She begged me to stay with her, but I knew Stefano was waiting for me, so I kissed her goodnight and promised to call in for her first thing in the morning. Then I walked back down the road to the restaurant.

'You idiot! What are you thinking?' Stefano yelled at me the minute I walked in. It was late and we had the place to ourselves, which was just as well. 'Or are you thinking at all?' he went on. 'You're certainly not thinking with your brain, that's for sure.'

'Stefano—' I began, but he wouldn't let me finish. He jumped up from the table and began pacing backwards and forwards, waving his hands around.

'How could you be so stupid? Bringing your money-grabbing little tart here; introducing her to me. You'll be telling her all about our projects next.' I stared at him in disbelief. He'd never spoken to me like this before. Finally, he sighed and sat down at the table again. 'Look, Michael, I understand that you get lonely sometimes, need a bit of female company. We all do. But you go to visit them at their place, on their territory. You don't bring them here. You don't introduce them to your partners. And you don't ever, EVER, risk them finding out about our business.'

As he lapsed into a brooding silence, I started to reason with him, talking quietly at first. But my anger grew as I spoke and by the end of it, I was shouting as loudly as he had.

'Number one, I've not told her anything about our business. She thinks I'm a salesman for farm machinery. Number two, I don't see that I have to get your permission to have friends—you're my business partner, not my father. And number three: she's not money-grabbing, and she's not my tart—she's a respectable young lady.'

At that he looked up and sneered at me.

'Respectable? Really? Tell me, Michael, just how difficult was it to persuade her to come away with you? How long have you known her, anyway? Three days? A week?'

'Ten days,' I replied sullenly.

'Oh, pardon me,' he said with exaggerated politeness, 'ten whole days.' He looked at me, his eyes cold. 'And you think that's long enough to forge a meaningful relationship, do you?'

'Sometimes it doesn't take that long,' I said, but quieter now, worrying about his reaction.

'How do you know you can trust her? She might find out all about us and then go to the police. Hell, she might even be a police informer.'

'Oh, come on, Stefano. She's a girl I met in a grocery store miles away from where we operate. How could she possibly be a police informer?'

'Well, she might not be now, but she could become one in the future. She's a weak link; I don't like weak links.'

'Of course she's not a weak link,' I shouted at him, still unable to accept what he was saying. 'She's a perfectly nice young lady and I

think I'm falling in love with her.' At this he turned towards me once more and the sneer on his face was unbearable.

'Love? What do you know about love? You've only just met this little tart.'

'I know enough to recognise it when it comes along,' I yelled, jumping up and marching to the door. I turned as I yanked it open, letting the cool air from outside waft over me. 'And for the last time, she's not a little tart. She's the woman I love—and I'm going to marry her—so get used to it.' And I marched out of the door, slamming it behind me.

I stomped across the road to our lodgings and threw myself onto my bed fully clothed. But despite being tired from the journey and the emotional trauma of the past few hours, it was a long time before I got to sleep. I lay, staring up into the darkness and listening to the ceiling fan creaking above me, until the light started creeping through the blinds, telling me dawn was approaching.

We were married a month later in the tiny church at the end of the street. I was just twenty-seven and she was two years younger.

Stefano came to the service, even gave Grace away in the absence of anyone else to do it. Afterwards, we repaired to the usual restaurant for a slap up meal and Stefano made a speech, wishing us luck.

We never spoke again of our argument on the night I brought Grace to Lourenço Marques. Stefano was polite, but never more, to her. And it seemed as though my relationship with him was unchanged; but sometimes, I wondered whether he still told me everything. There were times when I thought maybe he was keeping secrets from me.

Grace found herself a job working for the pastor who married us. Each day, she would go off to work after breakfast, and return home in time to cook my tea for me. She never asked about the business I was in, and I never talked to her about it. If I had to go out again in the evenings, or was late coming home, she accepted my explanation without question. And for the moment, I thought I was the happiest man alive.

CHAPTER 26

'Look, Damien, we can't blame ourselves.' He had flown over to London the day after they'd heard about Annabelle's death and now Suzanne watched him pacing up and down the office banging the back of one hand into the curved palm of the other. 'Even if I *had* rung her; what could I have said that would have made her change her mind?'

'Logically, I know that's true, Suzanne,' he said, stopping his pacing and facing her. 'She refused to accept there was anything wrong with the Sunshine Supplement product. But you could have told her about the other athletes who've had medical problems.'

'No I couldn't! That would have been most unethical.' Suzanne took him gently by the arm, steered him to the window seat looking out over the Thames, and pushed him down onto it. 'Now, you just sit there and calm down. I'm going to put the kettle on.'

'Right,' she said a few minutes later, pushing her way through the door with her hip, 'let's have a drink and talk about the next steps.' But the window seat was empty. She looked around and found Damien sitting at her desk rapidly banging on the keyboard. 'What are you doing with my laptop?'

'I'm doing a search on the internet.' Suzanne watched as Damien tapped a few more keys and then sat back in frustration.

'It's no good! I just can't work my way through this like you do, Suzanne. It keeps bringing up all sorts of irrelevant sites. How on earth do you do it?'

'Practice, dear Damien, practice!' Suzanne said, grinning at his obvious confusion. 'Now come and have your coffee and explain to me what it is you're looking for. After all, that's what you pay me for, isn't it? I'm nowhere as good as Charlie at this, but she's taught me quite a lot in the last couple of years.'

Damien left Suzanne's desk and returned to the window seat. Taking a mug of coffee, but declining the proffered biscuits, he stared out of the window for a while. Then he turned back and smiled.

'You're right, of course. I'll define what I want and you can work your magic for me.'

The pair worked on their search for over an hour, defining and refining their search criteria, looking for anything relating to aggressive behaviour, running, and herbal products. But they got nowhere. Finally Suzanne flexed her shoulders and stretched her arms wide to ease the strain in her muscles. She turned to Damien and rubbed her hand across her forehead.

'You know, I can't help feeling we're looking at this from the wrong angle. We started by talking to users of the Sunshine Supplements product and asking them if they've been having any adverse symptoms.'

'Correct.'

'Well, unless there's something wrong with every dose—'

'Like contamination?'

'Yes, like contamination—unless that's happened, then statistically the majority are probably going to be okay, aren't they?'

'Because Atkinson's not going to try and sell a product that's contaminated, or affects all the users, now is he?'

'Of course not. There are just too many tests, even on a food supplement, that would spot that straight away. And that facility looked to be quite well run, hygienically speaking.'

'So what do you think is the problem?'

'We know that many of the users are unaffected by Super Fit. I think there's something in the formulation that only affects a small percentage of users.'

'What do you call a small percentage?'

'It could be as low as nought point one per cent,' she said with a shrug.

'So it's a low risk to most people—'

'And for anyone that is affected, the reaction seems to vary from the aggression we saw in Brazil to, possibly, a fatal allergic reaction. So the effect is almost random, unless you happen to be allergic to the problem ingredient—in which case the risk for you is a hundred percent!'

'So we're looking for a needle in a haystack?' said Damien. 'How many users do we have to talk to in order to find the tiny percentage affected?'

'That's what I meant when I said we were approaching this from the wrong angle. What I want us to do is search for any unexplained deaths associated with allergic reactions, especially in the young, and especially if they are athletes, either amateur or professional.'

'Wow, that's a specific search, Suzanne. How far do you think we're going to get with that?'

'Without Charlie, perhaps not very far, but we could at least make a start, to see if there's anything there. And in the meantime, I'll get on to my contacts around the various agencies to see if they've got anything in their adverse reaction databases.'

'So we're going to ignore the aggression for the moment—'

'—and concentrate on the deaths instead. Correct.' She put down her mug of tea, cracked her knuckles dramatically and started hammering her keyboard.

The results, when they looked at them, were staggering. Suzanne identified five teenagers in the United Kingdom, all promising athletes, who had died of unexplained allergic reactions in the previous twenty months. The Sunshine Supplements trials had been running for just under two years. In three cases, she was able to trace their coaches and confirm they'd been using Super Fit at the time of their death.

Suzanne next made an appointment to see her former boss at the European Medicines Agency. On her arrival, the receptionist greeted her like the old friend she was. But once she was shown into Marcus Findlater's office, the temperature dropped several notches.

'I was surprised to get your call, Suzanne,' was his opening comment once she was seated opposite him, across his wide uncluttered desk. 'I thought you consultants,' almost spitting the word, 'knew everything and didn't need the help of us lowly regulators.'

'Oh, come on, Marcus! That's hardly fair. I have nothing but the utmost respect for all regulators, especially you guys I've worked with.'

'That didn't stop you disappearing over the wall though, did it?'

Suzanne bit her lip and decided silence was her only option at this point. In the aftermath of Sir Fredrick Michael's supposed suicide, when everyone was falling over themselves to elevate him to the misguided status of sainthood, it hadn't been possible to tell people the true facts of the case. When the International Health Forum was subsequently disbanded, Suzanne returned briefly to work in the EMA. But her experiences in IHF had made her sceptical of intergovernmental organisations. She'd left soon afterwards and set up the consultancy with Charlie. And despite their obvious disappointment, and even disapproval, at her decision, she had never thought her former EMA colleagues were anything but consummate professionals.

'Anyway, you're here now,' continued Marcus. 'What can I do to help you?'

'I have a project I'm working on that's thrown up some disturbing information,' Suzanne said. 'I've only been able to look at the situation in the United Kingdom so far; but I suspect it might range far wider than that. I was wondering if someone could interrogate the European databases for me.'

She went on to tell Marcus about Sunshine Supplements, about Damien's growing concerns, about their trip to Brazil and the investigations she had continued since her return.

'The trouble is, Marcus, as it's classified as a foodstuff rather than a medicine, it's not regulated as tightly outside of America. Damien is trying to get someone within the Food and Drug Administration to take a look at it, but they're so pushed for resources, it's not been given any priority so far.'

'But if it's a foodstuff, how do you think we can help?'

'I found my latest information by looking at unexplained adverse reactions. I thought you might take the same approach across the rest of Europe.'

'And just how did you find that information, might I ask?'

Suzanne thought about the answer she always got from Charlie when she asked the same question.

'Believe me, Marcus, you don't want to know!'

Her former boss stared at her for a moment, then started laughing.

'Okay, Suzanne, I'll get someone to take a look. But the systems aren't fully integrated, so it's going to take a while to get responses back from the other twenty-six member states. I'll get back to you if we find anything.' He stood and held out his hand, indicating the meeting was over. 'Good to see you again, Suzanne. Sorry I gave you a hard time when you arrived; and remember, if you feel like doing a bit of a poacher turned gamekeeper act, there's always a position for you here.'

Suzanne expected to wait a long time for the response from the EMA, but two days later Marcus rang and asked her to come back to see him again. This time, there was no icy atmosphere and she was offered coffee on arrival.

'Suzanne,' he said as she sipped her drink, 'we've only had results back so far from a few of the agencies, but there's enough data already to raise our suspicions, even without hearing from the rest.' He picked up a sheet of paper from the pile on his desk and scanned it quickly before looking up at her. 'We've identified three unexplained deaths of young athletes in France, one each in Spain and Malta, and four in Germany. We've contacted our friends in the Food and Drug Administration in the United States, and they uncovered a shocking eleven cases in the past eighteen months. Over half the deceased were taking Super Fit at the time of their death. But because it was a food supplement, it hadn't featured in their medical histories and wasn't picked up as a possible cause of the anaphylactic shock.'

'That's dreadful,' said Suzanne. 'But at least we now have something we can use against Sunshine Supplements, don't we?'

But Marcus didn't look at all convinced.

'I'm afraid not. All we've got is a lot of suspicions and some circumstantial evidence that could well be argued away as coincidental. And with resources being what they are...' He shrugged and pulled a face at her. It was his 'I'd love to help, but I'm not sure there's anything I can do' face. She was starting to remember why she'd not always enjoyed working for Marcus Findlater.

'And the information you've given me?'

'Is unofficial, I'm afraid. We can't be associated with an off-the-record investigation initiated by a member of the public with a bee in his bonnet.'

'Then why did you bother calling me in?' she asked, unsure whether she felt more angry or depressed.

Marcus rolled his eyes at her.

'Because although I can't be associated with this case at the moment, there's no reason why I shouldn't offer some help to an independent consultant who is in a position to help said member of the public. Especially when that consultant is so well-known to us.'

Suzanne grinned and, standing, shook his hand.

'Okay, Marcus, message understood. I'll be back when I've got something more concrete. And thanks for your help.'

That afternoon, Suzanne had a phone call. It was the last person she would have expected to hear from.

'Ms Jones, Suzanne,' said the familiar male voice, 'it's Atkinson, Nigel Atkinson here.'

'Mr Atkinson.' Suzanne didn't even attempt to keep the icicles out of her voice, 'I am surprised to hear from you. What can I do for you?'

'Suzanne, I wanted to appeal to your better nature. Your investigation is killing our company. People are going to lose their jobs, their livelihoods.'

'But people are losing their lives. That's even worse, isn't it?'

'Not true; not proven! I was devastated to hear of those tragic deaths—such promising young athletes—but it's all a terrible coincidence. There's nothing in my supplement that could cause death.'

'I don't believe in coincidences! And although we may not have any proof yet, I know it's out there—and we *will* find it.'

Atkinson sighed and then started again, his tone sorrowful.

'Suzanne, I'm begging you. Please stop this cruel witch hunt now. If it will help persuade you, I'll stop all production of Super Fit. Just stop stirring things up, please.' He paused then continued: 'I'm going to level with you, Suzanne. There's a major multinational interested in our portfolio, and we're approaching a very delicate time in the negotiations. I'm not doing this for myself; it's for the workers; I want to protect their jobs, make sure they can look after their families. And it's all about to come together; they're ready to join the party. Do you really want to have the collapse of this merger on your hands?'

'I can live with it,' said Suzanne. 'I've seen your history of start-ups and mergers. In most cases, the wonder products are pulled from the market within twelve months, and several of the factories have been shut down. So people's livelihoods are destroyed anyway. The only one who really profits is you, isn't it, Nigel?' There was a long pause. Then Atkinson responded.

'You seem to have a very poor opinion—', but Suzanne had had enough.

'Goodbye, Mr Atkinson,' she said, 'don't call again. My investigations will be continuing.' And she put the phone down with a gentle but firm click.

She sat, staring at the phone, her head buzzing. She knew there was something she was missing. What was it Atkinson had said? Something about coming together; joining the party. What party? Why did those words sound so familiar? She reached for her laptop, opened the search engine, typed in the two phrases and hit enter. And just like that, it was all there before her. And she finally remembered who the old guy in the Sunshine Supplements factory was. She grabbed the phone and dialled Damien's number.

CHAPTER 27

Charlie slept very little; her mind raced with thoughts of the upcoming trip to Rio. How could she get the much-needed evidence about Hawkins before Mercy ran away and her links to the family were severed? Or worse still, before Hawkins remembered why Charlie's face was familiar. She had been so sure she'd never met him. But it looked like she might be wrong. She'd used the Rose Fitzpatrick identity before. If Hawkins searched for her online, he would find articles about the one-hit-wonder author who was the darling of the literary world for a few brief months some years ago; but it was a pretty thin veneer and anyone who knew their way around the internet would see through it. She just had to hope Hawkins wasn't that anyone.

At four-thirty am, she gave up trying to sleep, rose and showered. By the time Mercy tapped on her door ninety minutes later, she was packed, had tidied her room and was striding up and down, still worrying.

'Now, there's a surprise,' the other woman said as Charlie opened the door. 'I was sure I'd have to come and pull you out of bed again!'

'Are you kidding?' said Charlie, pinning a grin on her

face. 'I've always wanted to see the Rio Carnival.' But as Mercy frowned at her, she rested her hand lightly on the woman's shoulder. 'Don't worry; I know this is an important trip and I won't let you down. But it won't hurt to have a little fun to start with, now will it?'

Hawkins was waiting downstairs for them and after a quick bite to eat, he shepherded them out to the waiting limo for the short drive to the private airfield they'd used previously for the visit to Iguaçu. The same Cessna 525 was waiting for them. Hawkins told Charlie he hired the plane when he needed it.

'It's easier to have someone else look after all the paperwork and maintenance,' he said. 'Although we use it so often these days, I'm thinking of buying one.' He turned to his daughter. 'How do you fancy flying lessons for your next birthday, Mercy?'

As she watched her friend clap her hands in glee and give her father a hug and a kiss, Charlie marvelled at her acting abilities. She certainly didn't look like someone who was afraid of her newly-discovered father and was planning to run away at the earliest opportunity. *Still, I guess we're all acting a part here, today*, she mused, as they walked up the steps and settled themselves in the luxurious cabin.

Once again, Hawkins immersed himself in a pile of papers and didn't look up or speak to them until they started flying over the outskirts of the city. Mercy gasped and grabbed Charlie's arm, pointing out of the window.

'Look, Rose, it's Christ the Redeemer!' They watched in silence as the little plane flew past the most famous symbol of Brazil and headed down towards Santos Dumont Airport.

They landed and parked at a remote spot away from the commercial shuttle terminal and watched from the tarmac as an eight-seater minibus drove towards them. Judging by the gleaming paintwork and gold lettering emblazoned along the side, Charlie guessed this was no ordinary minibus company. Hawkins seemed to read her mind.

'I hire a concierge company to manage all aspects of my visits to Rio,' he said. 'They handle transport, find appropriate accommodation and make bookings.'

The 'appropriate accommodation' was not, as Charlie had expected, one of Rio's many five-star hotels. When they left the airport, the minibus turned not towards the city, but northwards, along the broad highway skirting the coast.

'So where's the famous Copacabana Beach?' said Mercy.

'Infamous, more like,' said Hawkins. 'You need to keep your wits about you and your hand on your valuables when you go there.' He turned from the front seat and smiled at the two women. 'It's in the other direction, south of the bay. And Ipanema is the other side of it. But I think you'll find your options for sunbathing are going to be a little less crowded and a little more exclusive than that.'

They left the highway behind and turned into a small marina, where tiny dinghies jostled for space with much larger yachts. The minibus pulled up at the jetty of one of the biggest vessels. Charlie and Mercy gasped. Hawkins turned to them, grinning like a schoolboy whose party trick has just gone very well indeed.

'Yes, I thought you'd be impressed.'

'Wow,' said Mercy, 'when you told me we were staying on a yacht, I was thinking much smaller than this.'

'This isn't yours, is it?' asked Charlie.

Hawkins nodded his head.

'Well, we don't own it, if that's what you mean; but for the next few days, this is the humble abode we can call home.'

The boat looked to Charlie to be brand new, or at the very least, recently refurbished. It was at least seventy metres long, painted cream and blue, with highly polished wooden railings and trim. The name on the prow was *Pride of Kharkov.* A row of crewmen, together with the gold-braided captain, stood to attention on the jetty waiting to welcome the guests aboard. *Wait until Suzanne hears about this*, thought Charlie. Mercy grabbed her arm and pulled her towards the gangplank.

'Come on, Rose, let's go and explore,' she said, back in excited child mode.

The two women quickly found their way around the boat, and within a short time, they had settled in and were lying beside the swimming pool on the sun deck. Hawkins strolled along the deck to join them, wearing a straw panama, tailored shorts and deck shoes. He threw himself into a lounger next to Charlie, who felt herself suppressing a shudder.

This was surreal. This man had masterminded an operation making and selling counterfeit drugs in Africa—and probably beyond; was responsible for the deaths of numerous people, especially children; and on a more personal level was connected to a plot to kidnap and imprison her sister in the African jungle. Yet here she was, lounging around next to him on a luxury yacht. And still with no plan for how to unmask him and bring him to justice.

'I'm going to spend the rest of the morning getting some work done,' Hawkins said, 'and I have a quick meeting this afternoon.' Mercy looked up at him and pouted. 'Yes, I know, sweetheart, we're supposed to be on holiday, but this is the end of it, I promise. From tomorrow, I'm all yours.' He thought for a little while then went on. 'You girls can go and explore the city a little; I'll arrange for a car and driver to take you around and keep you out of trouble. Then this evening we'll have dinner and watch the fireworks from here. You'll get a great view.'

'But what about the carnival?' asked Charlie, 'Isn't that what we've come to see? Won't we miss all the fun from here?' If she and Mercy were going to put their plan into action, they needed to be mixing with the crowds in the streets, not watching from afar on an isolated boat. Hawkins raised an eyebrow at her and she wondered if she had gone too far. But to her surprise, it was Mercy who responded, looking quite put out.

'If my father wants to eat dinner here, than that's what we'll do,' she said. She turned to Hawkins. 'What time do you want us back here, Tata?

'Well, we won't be eating until after nine pm, so there's no hurry,' he said, then turning to Charlie 'and don't worry, Rose. Carnival goes on for another three days and we'll have plenty of time to mix in with the hoi polloi. I've got tickets for the Sambadrome for tomorrow night and we'll drop in one of the balls after the parade. Trust me, my dear, by Tuesday you will welcome a quiet evening out here on the boat.'

Somehow, Charlie doubted if it would come to that, but she kept her mouth shut and just smiled at Hawkins and his daughter, who for some reason, suddenly appeared a much tighter unit than she'd realised. What on earth was going on in Mercy's mind?

'Okay, what was that all about?' she asked her companion an hour later as they sat in the back of an air-conditioned Mercedes that collected them from the jetty and headed for the city.

There was no reply. Mercy was staring out of the window, picking at the handle of her shoulder bag with nervous fingers. She jumped as Charlie touched her arm and the eyes that turned towards her were unfocussed. Charlie didn't think she'd heard the question.

'Mercy, are you okay?' She shook her arm gently and the girl blinked once before flashing her old smile.

'Of course I am. Why do you ask?'

'Well you seemed miles away—and I was asking why you jumped to your father's defence like that? I would think you would prefer to be out in the crowds, rather than on the boat. How are we going to manage to break away from him out there?' But Mercy just smiled and patted her hand.

'Relax, my friend,' she said. 'It'll be fine. I'm beginning to think everything is going to work out just perfectly.'

After that, the driver rolled down the screen separating him from the passengers and started an explanation of where they were going and what they were going to see. His rapid Portuguese was beyond Charlie's level of competence and she gave up trying to follow him. She would let Mercy bring her up to speed if there was anything she needed to know.

It seemed to Charlie they'd walked for hours! And shopped for hours too. She had never considered shopping for clothes as a pastime. Her regular approach, if anything so rare could be considered regular, was to decide what she wanted, pick a single venue and if, as was often the case, she couldn't find what she wanted, give up in disgust and wear something she'd had in her wardrobe for years. But Mercy was the complete opposite.

They'd visited every clothes shop in the Rio Sul shopping centre—and some of them more than once. Mercy had tried on dresses, skirts, tops, and shoes. So many shoes. And she'd given her credit card a good bashing.

Charlie questioned Mercy's logic in buying a load of new clothes she was never going to wear, but her companion only laughed at her.

'This is what my father would expect me to do,' she said, as they piled the bags into the boot of the limo and threw themselves back into the soft leather-clad seats. 'We're in one of the best shopping centres in South America. Why wouldn't I take advantage of it?' She stared at Charlie for a few moments in silence then went on. 'And you know, it might help confuse the issue when I do go.'

Charlie didn't understand this point and her face must have shown that, as Mercy continued. 'We've been talking about my running away and about how we do it before my father has a chance to find me?' Charlie nodded. 'But how about if he thinks I've been kidnapped—or worse—won't that muddy the waters and give me more time to get away?'

No, Charlie thought, *that won't help things at all. It will simply make Hawkins all the more determined to get his daughter back*. But she was unable to convince Mercy it didn't make sense. In fact her companion seemed to have stopped listening to her. Charlie was starting to get a really bad feeling about all of this. And she still hadn't come up with a plan for trapping Hawkins. She knew she was running out of time.

They'd chosen a shopping centre in Botafogo, as it was close to Ipanema, where they planned to watch the afternoon's street band parade. Charlie looked longingly at the iconic statue of Christ as they passed it in the distance, and Mercy smiled and patted her arm.

'The afternoon's really not the time to go up there,' she said. 'It's way too hot and it'll be much too crowded.' She'd been chatting to the driver and seemed to have everything worked out. 'We can come back early in the morning and take the funicular up to Corcovado to watch the sunrise. It will be like Iguaçu all over again.'

CHAPTER 28

Lourenço Marques, September 1969

For two years, Grace and I were blissfully happy. I know that sounds like a cliché, but it's true. It was like I was two different personalities. During the day, and often in the evenings as well, I was Stefano's right hand man. I ran important projects on my own, although not the biggest ones; he held them back for himself. I sorted problems. In fact I made problems go away. And there were quite a few at that time. But when my working day was over, I would go home to our little apartment—we had long since moved out of the digs near Stefano's HQ—and be the perfect husband. It was idyllic, it was safe, it was different—but in the end, it became boring.

I met Honey one evening when Stefano was holding a meeting in the casino he owned. She waltzed in with a couple of young men in tow. She was coloured—the result she told me later of a long-term liaison between a Portuguese trader and his housekeeper. She was high octane, sparkling, laughing at everything. I wanted her from the minute I saw her. But there was one big problem; well, two if you count the fact I was married to Grace—but somehow that didn't seem to matter. No, the big problem was that Honey was the mistress of a local army leader. He was a man who ran our part of the city with a rod of iron. He used a private gang of thugs to deal with anything he couldn't do legitimately with his official troops. It was only by his grace and favour we were able to operate as we did. It cost us a lot of money each month to keep him happy, and it was worth it. But suddenly none of that mattered either.

Stefano introduced us and she offered me her hand. I bowed, kissed the back of it and would have let it go, but she held on to my fingers just that bit longer than was necessary and looked me straight in the eye, with a challenging look on her face. The message couldn't have been clearer if she'd written it down. Then she removed her hand, blew me a kiss, and turned back to her companions. She didn't speak to, or even look at, me again, all evening, no matter how much I stared at her. Stefano noticed the direction of my eyes.

'Oh no you don't, my boy!' he said, clapping me on the shoulder and steering me towards the bar. 'You've been a fool over a woman once already, and you've got away with it. This is completely different. You can't afford to go there.' I nodded at him and laughed.

'Yes, I know, Stefano,' I replied, 'but there's no harm in window shopping, now is there?'

As Honey left the casino that night, she walked over to our table and bade Stefano goodnight. Then she held out her hand to me and as I returned the gesture, I felt a small card sliding into my palm. I pushed it into my pocket and as soon as I could, excused myself and headed for the men's room.

The card was printed with her name and an address in the best part of the city. On the back was printed in large, childish writing: He's away. Tomorrow, 3pm.

My head told me I should throw the card away, destroy it even, and forget all about the bewitching woman who'd given it to me. But I was listening to my heart, not my head at that moment.

I kept that appointment the next day, and again the day after, and the day after that. Then she told me her patron was returning to the city that night—and it was all over. I bowed over her hand one last time and returned to the casino and Stefano, somewhat relieved. It had been heady, wonderful, too much to take in—and I didn't think I could have carried it on much longer. Each evening I'd returned to Grace, feeling sadder than the day before. That night I took her in my arms as we went to bed and swore to myself I would never do anything again to harm this woman who loved me so much and deserved to be treated with respect.

Honey's body was found floating in the harbour two days later. She had been brutally beaten, raped and then strangled. Stefano called me to his office that same afternoon.

'You know I have to kill you, don't you, Michael?' were his first words. I looked around wildly, but there were only the two of us there. I was ten years younger than him, much stronger and in better shape. I thought I could take my chances against my old friend physically, but mentally, would I be able to harm him? Maybe I was about to find out. But then he laughed and clapped me on the shoulder.

'I always knew it would come to this at some point, my boy. I think it's time you went home, don't you?' I must have looked as puzzled as I felt because he laughed again. 'England! I think it's time you went home to England.'

The next morning, Stefano picked me up from home and took me to a warehouse he owned down on the docks. He left me hiding there while he sorted everything else out. He arranged for a homeless drifter, who sometimes came to the restaurant kitchen door for scraps, to meet with an untimely accident. Then he dressed the body in my clothes, slipping my cigarette case into the jacket pocket, and had it dropped over the side of a boat outside the harbour, leaving the tides and the fishes to do their work.

He found me new clothes, arranged for papers in a new name, and reminded me of everything he'd ever taught me about archaeology and fossils during our early days together in Cape Town. Then one week after Honey's murder, he handed me papers for the Queen Katherine, a cruise ship due to sail from Cape Town for Southampton. Under cover of darkness, he sent a car to collect me and take me to the South African border.

Three days later I walked up the gangplank of the newly commissioned liner and went to find the purser in his office.

'Good afternoon, sir,' he said, 'how can I help you?'

'Michaels,' I said, shaking his hand, 'Fredrick Michaels. I'm your archaeology lecturer for the upcoming voyage.'

CHAPTER 29

The driver dropped them at Ipanema beach and agreed to return for them in a couple of hours. It was approaching five o'clock and the crowds were jostling for space along the boardwalk.

'Come on,' Mercy said, grabbing Charlie's arm, 'let's go and get a drink; you must try the coconut water. We can watch the parade from there.' They dived into a kerbside bar and Mercy called for drinks. Then she wriggled her way through the crowd until she was leaning on the railings overlooking the street. Charlie followed in her wake. The crush was so great, the women were pushed against one another. Mercy linked her arm through Charlie's and gave a contented sigh.

As the parade drew near, the excited chatter of the crowd swelled to a cacophony of sounds. People spilled out of the bars and cafés onto the street to join in with the dancing and singing. There was every skin tone from palest white to deepest black. A brass band, shirts emblazoned with their name, played trumpets and trombones. A solitary figure, like a modern day Tin Man from Oz, blew a whistle repeatedly while striking his metal chest, turning himself into a living instrument. Costumes in bright colours, some made entirely of feathers, flitted like exotic birds among the crowd. To Charlie's eyes, it began to merge into a seething rainbow-coloured living tapestry. Her head buzzed as the smells of coconut, beer, pancakes and fried pastries mingled with the sweat of the crowd. And above it all was the throb, throb, throb of the samba drums.

As her senses reached overload, Charlie realised her companion was no longer watching what was going on in the street, but was staring at her. Mercy lifted her hand to brush a strand of dark hair away from Charlie's damp brow, then leaned forward and kissed her. Her lips were cool, dry and very soft. Charlie remained quite still. She didn't return the kiss, but she didn't pull away either. The sounds from the street faded and all Charlie could hear was a rhythmic drumming sound. She wasn't sure if it was the samba drums or her own heartbeat she was listening to.

Mercy pulled away and smiled at her. With one hand she continued to stroke her face, while the fingers of her other hand feathered softly over Charlie's leg, slowly moving upwards towards her thigh. Then she leaned forward once more, only this time her lips brushed Charlie's ear.

'I'm so glad you agreed to come with me,' she whispered. Then she turned her attention back to the parade.

This can't be happening. This mustn't happen, thought Charlie. But almost of its own volition, her hand moved across to Mercy's and gripped tightly. The wandering fingers wandered no more, but the two hands, one white, one coffee coloured, remained melded together as the parade continued on its way.

When it was time to return to the boat, Mercy linked her fingers with Charlie's as they strolled along the edge of the beach. The sun had disappeared behind the mountains and the water glowed dully like liquid gold. In the bars and cafés, lights were beginning to appear. In the distance, they could see their car waiting for them.

'You don't have to go back,' Mercy said. Charlie glanced across at her companion and saw she was staring intensely at her.

'Back to São Paulo? Of course I do. I've got research to do, I've only got a short while left here in Brazil...'

Mercy was grinning widely.

'No, silly, I mean you don't have to go back to Britain. You have no ties there. You could stay here.' She swung round in front of Charlie, blocking her path and grabbing her hands. 'Stay, Rose. Stay here with me. We could have such wonderful times.'

She put her arms around Charlie, pulled her to her and kissed her. But this wasn't the cool kiss of before. This was full of passion, demanding a response. And Charlie felt that response beginning to blossom. Her arms were around Mercy's shoulders and she could feel the other woman's taut body pressed against her. She returned the kiss, mouth open, tongue exploring.

But at the back of her mind she could hear a voice urging 'no'. A quiet Scottish voice; the voice of someone who desperately wanted to trust her. She grabbed Mercy by the shoulders and pushed her gently but firmly away.

'No, Mercy. I can't. We can't.'

'Why not?'

'Because—'

'We're both adults. I want you. And I know you want me too.'

'Yes, but—'

'Once we're free of my father, we can do what we want; be what we want.'

Charlie took a deep breath and shook her head slowly, hating herself for what she was about to say.

'It won't work, Mercy. I lied when I said I had no ties. I have a partner back home. She—'

The blow came so fast, there was no time to duck. Mercy lashed out and back-handed Charlie across her cheek. Then she turned on her heel and marched towards the car.

Stunned, but unwilling to be left alone on a Rio street at night, Charlie shook her head to clear the ringing in her ears and then ran after Mercy, catching up with her at the car.

As the two climbed into the back seat, the African woman pushed herself into the corner and stared out of the window. They sat in silence as the driver started the engine and began the drive back to the marina.

Charlie's thoughts were in turmoil. She needed to placate Mercy before they reached the boat and then just had to hope she wouldn't say anything to Hawkins, although given her comments about being free of her father, that that was probably a safe bet.

It wasn't the first time she'd been in this situation. On several occasions, her undercover roles had called for her to fake emotions. Once she'd even been engaged briefly to an Eastern European smuggler. So why was this so different? Partly it was that Scottish voice in the back of her head. Annie was special. Annie was for keeps and Charlie didn't want to screw that up.

But if she was honest, she was frightened. Frightened that the emotions wouldn't be fake. And she wasn't sure she would be able to deal with that when the time came to part.

As the car drove into the marina, Charlie was still no closer to an answer, but Mercy turned to her and put her hand out to touch Charlie's bruised cheek.

'Rose, I'm so sorry. I was wrong to assume you would feel the same as me. And I was wrong to hit you.'

'That's okay, Mercy. I shouldn't have led you on. And in other circumstances—' but the African woman rested her finger gently on Charlie's lips.

'Hush,' she said, 'we'll say no more.'

While they were getting changed for dinner, Charlie heard noises and bustle coming from the engine room and the bridge. Then a whistle blew and she felt, rather than heard, the engines starting up. By the time she joined her host and his daughter on deck, they were moving out of the marina and heading to the edge of the bay.

'Mercy suggested we take a bit of a tour,' Hawkins explained, 'and we'll have an even better view of the fireworks from further along the coast.'

They anchored in a small, deserted bay just north of Copacabana beach and Hawkins told the captain they would stay there until morning. The crew seemed happy at the opportunity for a night off duty and, leaving one young sailor behind 'in case the boss needs anything', they climbed into the motor boat and headed for the shore. In the distance, the lights of Rio shone brightly, but once the noise of the outboard motor had faded, all was silent and dark around the *Pride of Kharkov.*

The crew had laid a table out on deck and a gentle evening breeze blew, relief from the burning heat of the day, as the three helped themselves to lobster, pasta with truffles, and a delicate lemon mousse. Afterwards, Mercy poured brandy into three cut crystal glasses and handed one each to her father and Charlie. The three settled in companionable silence, just as a rocket arched across the sky, signalling the start of the evening's firework display. When it finished fifteen explosive minutes later, Hawkins reached across and patted Mercy's arm.

'All a bit different from Mozambique, isn't it?' he asked. His daughter turned her face towards his. Charlie could see the boat's lamps reflected in her eyes and wondered if it was tears that made them shine so brightly.

CHAPTER 30

'What was it like, Mercy?' asked Charlie. 'Tell me about your childhood.'

The other woman stared out into the darkness and said nothing for a long time. Charlie wondered if she'd not heard the question. But then, she shook herself and turned towards her, giving Charlie a gentle smile as she began to speak.

We didn't have much when I was first growing up. My mother worked in a bar to earn enough to feed us. From as long ago as I can remember, she would take me with her each evening and leave me in the back room while she worked. To start with, I was in a Moses basket, sleeping most of the time. There was an old nurse, the mother of one of the waiters I think, who used to keep an eye on me. If I woke, she would tell me to shush, or give me a piece of biltong to suck on to keep me quiet.

As I learnt to walk, they put a rein on me so I could wander around the room but not get out. Sometimes she brought an old toy for me to play with: a stuffed lion with only one ear; or a rattle carved from cedar wood and bound with leather straps, with peas inside to make the noise. Once I remember there was a puppy. I think it had lost its mother; we fed it with warmed milk and they let me hold the bottle. Afterwards, I would play with it; the two of us tumbling together in the dirt. I pulled at my mother's hand as we walked towards the bar each night, eager to get there and see my little friend. But then one night, it was gone. The old woman told me it ran away. I never saw it again!

Then when I was seven, everything changed. My mother found herself a new job, working as a hostess in a fancy club down on the main street. And she introduced me to her boss, Rene Lopez. He had a young brother, Guido. He was about fifteen, I think. As part of her wages, Guido agreed to teach me to read. My mother always regretted she hadn't learned her letters when she was a child and she was determined I would have a better chance in life than her.

'I don't want you working in no bar or club, child,' she said to me when she told me about the deal with Guido.

I don't think either of us was particularly happy about the arrangement, but Guido was scared of his brother, and I always did what my mother told me to. So we started meeting two or three times a week in the evenings—and within a short while, I was able to read.

For my birthday, Rene gave me a Bible. It had an embossed cover and really nice paper for the pages and he suggested I keep it at the club. He thought it might get damaged if I took it home to our shack. But I could read it whenever I wanted to; and of course, I did—at every opportunity. From then on, I could be found each evening, curled up in the storeroom, or in the dancers' dressing room, reading, reading, reading.

I was fourteen when my mother first got ill. She was unable to work and spent most of her days in bed from then on until she died. I got a job in an office, leaving her on her own during the day and then hurrying home to her as soon as my day's work was done. I didn't have many friends anyway, and those I'd made—mostly from the district where we lived—got fed up with me turning down all their invitations and stopped asking me out.

But I didn't mind. Mama and I were perfectly happy. If she was having a good day, she would go to the market to buy food and might even start preparing the evening meal. I would finish it when I got home and then we would sit together outside our front door, watching the sun go down and chatting about my job, the neighbours, the government; about anything at all. Or I would read to her. She loved stories and could remember all sorts of details. We would sit there together happily until the light faded and then I would help her get ready for bed before going to sleep myself.

When I finally lost her, I cried myself to sleep every night for months. Some of the neighbours tried to comfort me, but I was lost without her. For a while, I had to leave the city altogether; there were just too many memories in that little shack.

I found work in other offices, other places; one boring job after another. There was nothing to get home for, nothing to work for. There were times when I thought I should just throw myself under a train. That way, I reasoned, I would be able to see my beloved mother again.

With time, the memories began to fade a little. Not completely, of course. I wouldn't want that. But there was a little less pain each night. Sometimes I found myself laughing at something on the television, or something someone had said. And I'd realise that for a whole hour, or afternoon, or even a day, I was able to forget all about my mother and that I'd lost her. I went back to the city, found myself another boring job, making a little money, with somewhere suitable to live—and I even started making a few friends.

Mercy stood, walked over to the rail and stared out into the darkness once more. Then she turned and directed her sparkling eyes once more towards Hawkins.

'So, Tata, how right you are,' she said. 'I think you can certainly say life was never like this. No, indeed.'

CHAPTER 31

***Queen Katherine*, out of Cape Town, October 1969**

On long cruises, the lecture programme is always an important part of the entertainment. After all, there's only so much time a passenger can spend staring out to sea. And if I say it myself, the lectures by Fredrick Michaels on fossil hunting were one of the highlights of the trip. Of course, I'd never actually been on a fossil hunt, but I'd spent so much time over the past nine years listening to Stefano Mladov's stories and handling the samples in his collection, I had a fair few anecdotes I could use. And of course I also had a vivid imagination. Throw in the occasional Latin term—real or otherwise—and, providing there were no Classics scholars in the room, I was home and dry. For my first lecture, the audience was a little sparse. But by the second one, word had started to spread, and by the third one, every seat was filled. There were even a few disgruntled people who didn't manage to get into the hall—and I had to run some of my lectures twice in the same day, just to accommodate everyone.

I was timetabled to speak every three days—and the rest of the time I was free; free to roam the ship, to leave behind my little bunk in the crew's quarters and find myself some company. Strictly speaking, I was only supposed to use the second class areas, but as a guest of a bona fide passenger, I could go anywhere. And there were plenty of takers for the role of companion. Especially the ladies. Most of them were the blue rinse brigade, old enough to be my mother, if not my grandmother; and although I wasn't above a bit of cross-generational fraternising if I could see an advantage in it, there were also a sprinkling of younger women who were only too happy to relieve the boredom of the long voyage. And for the first few days, that was enough to keep me occupied.

Pauline Wilson was more of a challenge. She came to my lectures and sat at the back, never asked a question and slipped out on her own as soon as we finished. She didn't seem to have any friends. One of the other women, always happy to gossip, told me Pauline was recently widowed and was returning home to the UK. I wasn't really listening to the stream of chatter, until she uttered the words:

'I understand she's loaded. Her husband was a prospector; left her pots of money.'

From that moment on, I was determined to get to know Mrs Pauline Wilson. I started 'bumping into her' several times a day; we progressed from a nod, to a smile, to a greeting; and within a week, she invited me to dine with her at her table in the first class lounge. It was a very quiet meal; quiet on my side, that is. I asked the occasional question to keep the story going and then sat back and listened as she poured out her heart.

Samuel Wilson had been a South African prospector, living and working in the diamond region somewhere in the Transvaal. She was a secretary in a diamond firm in London, unmarried and with both her parents dead. They met when he went to England to sell some of his stock; he courted her, captured her heart and carried her back with him to Cape Town three weeks later. They'd not been particularly happy. She'd found him to be a bully once they settled down to married life, but he at least provided her with security and she'd stayed with him for ten years. Then he caught malaria and died very suddenly. She was horrified and was going back to England, because, 'I can't stay in Africa; it's too dangerous. Look how quickly it stole my husband.'

That first night, I walked her back to her cabin after dinner, kissed her hand and bid her a goodnight. I could feel her watching me as I walked away, but resisted the temptation to look back.

For the next few days, I made sure I was around her quite a lot of the time, but only in the distance. I didn't push it. I didn't need to.

The line was baited; all I had to do was wait for the fish to bite. Five days later, she waited for me when my lecture was finished and invited me to dine with her again. She told me she found my company relaxing and appreciated the fact I was happy to listen to 'an old woman talking about her lost husband.' I told her she couldn't be more than three years older than me. And although there was actually a ten-year age gap, she didn't correct me. And from there on, it was easy.

The captain married us on the last day before we arrived in Southampton. He seemed a little uncertain about the rush, and was a bit sniffy with me when I raised the subject, but Pauline Wilson was a rich, influential woman and once she pointed out she was a shareholder in the cruise ship company and a personal friend of the owner, there was no more argument. We joined the cruise in Cape Town as strangers; we arrived in England as man and wife. Fourteen years after I'd been tricked into a journey to South Africa, I was back. I had a new name, a new wife and a considerable fortune behind me. Life was beginning to look up.

Arriving back in England as Michael Hawkins the runaway would have been dismal; and even as Fredrick Michaels, archaeology lecturer and fossil hunter, I would have had difficulty getting established in 1960's Britain. But as Fredrick Michaels, second husband to Pauline—deeply in love heiress—doors opened as if by magic.

The following October I enrolled at King's College, Cambridge as a mature student to study Politics, Philosophy and Economics. We bought a bijoux cottage on the outskirts of the city where we spent the weeks. During the day, Pauline played at keeping house—or at least harried the cleaner and the gardener as they attempted to keep house for her—while I attended lectures and tutorials. In the evenings, I worked on my assignments while she read or sewed in the background. And at the weekends, we returned to the apartment in London where we wined and dined with her first husband's old friends and I schmoozed my way into the best circles in town. When I graduated in 1973 with a First Class Honours degree, it was but a small step into the Civil Service and from there I was on my way.

Pauline was in many ways a very silly woman and I quickly grew bored with her company, if not with her money. But she loved me, and our daughter, born just ten months after we docked in Southampton. She never complained if I was late home or stayed away for a night or two occasionally. We were, to my mind, the perfect couple.

I didn't expect to hear from Stefano Mladov again and was just grateful our friendship was strong enough for him to defy his powerful patron and smuggle me out of Mozambique. But one day, three years after I'd joined the Civil Service, I received a letter, postmarked Kharkov. We kept in touch over the next ten years, as he divided his time between two continents. In 1985, life finally got too hot for Stefano in Africa, especially as Mozambique had recovered from the War of Independence only to slip into civil war instead, so he put one of his cousins in charge of the African 'projects', and returned to Ukraine, and his long-suffering wife; by this time, they had three children, two boys and a girl. The youngest, Nico, was born in 1978.

The Mladov family became quite prominent in Kharkov. They were involved in all sorts of industries, including the pharmaceutical business, which was quite big in USSR, and at the time Stefano made contact with me, they were making a fair living with semi-legal activities in Russia and Ukraine. In 1991, the Soviet Union burst apart and Ukraine became an independent state. Changes in regulations and the aftermath of independence pushed the Mladovs to look elsewhere for income and they started setting up counterfeiting operations in Africa.

They used small factories in rural parts of Zambia and Tanzania to make drugs which were distributed to neighbouring countries. In time, Nico was given the job of managing the schemes 'on the ground' in Africa. He spent most of his time over there. But a couple of weeks a year, he would come to visit me in England. It wasn't that easy for a Ukrainian to travel to Britain, but there were always trade delegations or other official trips being arranged. By this time, I was working in the health ministry and we began to work together on projects and schemes that made me a tidy sum. I began to see there might be a time when I would be independent of Pauline, maybe be able to walk away and live life as I wanted for a change.

It was all going so well. And then I made a mistake and misjudged someone. Someone I thought would be useful, pliable and easy to manipulate. But she turned out to be anything but.

The International Health Forum was first mooted in 2002, just after 9/11. There was a spirit of co-operation around that seemed to be born partly out of guilt. How could we have let those things happen, in America, in this day and age? The effect on counter-terrorism was obvious, but it also spilled over into other global issues, and counterfeit medicines was one that came in for a lot of publicity.

I'd been in the health ministry for years; I'd recently been knighted for services to international welfare, and I was just a couple of years off retirement. I was seen as a safe pair of hands. The job was advertised in all the usual channels, but I'd indicated my willingness to serve and the position was mine even before the advertisement went out. Banda was already up and running in Zambia and talking it through with Stefano and Nico, we could see great advantages in my being at the helm of the anti-counterfeiting project.

But I wasn't going to do the day-to-day work. There was far too much dashing around involved. So I advertised for a project leader, to act as my deputy. And that's when I met Suzanne Jones. On paper, she was perfect for the role. Her background was in industry before she'd transferred to the Medicines Control Agency and then been fast-tracked into the European Medicines Agency. She was a smart cookie; I knew that. But I assumed that with her lack of experience, she would be conscientious but ineffectual. After all, she would be dealing with some of the most bureaucratic and male chauvinist countries in the world.

I'm still not really sure how it happened, but the whole thing began to unravel. She had inside help; from people in Swaziland and Uganda. People who let their emotions get the better of them. And then our production manager went rogue and made a full confession before killing himself.

It was all such a waste! Years of planning down the toilet. Our network in Southern Africa was completely destroyed. We were going to have to start again from scratch.

And, not content with causing havoc in Africa, Ms Jones then brought the whole thing back to England, right to my doorstep. It was time for me to disappear.

All the plans were in place anyway. I'd had the Brazilian operation set up for years; the villa was built and ready for occupation. It just meant bringing everything forward by a few months. But it was irritating to be working to someone else's timetable rather than my own.

In fact, I probably wouldn't have known anything about it until it was too late if it hadn't been for a tip-off from Francine Matheson. *She thought she was being so clever, calling me out in front of the PM that night. But I've eaten bigger fish than her for breakfast many times!*

And luckily I knew things about Francine. *Things from her past, before she rose to her current giddy heights. She was a very junior MP when we first met at the conference in Africa. I didn't know how her indiscretion would be of use to me, but I knew it would at some point. And with Nico's help, I set her up, made it look like she was involved in the counterfeiting. The whole thing was very tenuous. It would have been embarrassing for her if it had come out, but it wouldn't have stood up under close examination. But it didn't have to. It was enough to make the pair of them—Suzanne and Francine—slow down in their investigations; just long enough for me to get away and move to Brazil.*

And then, finally I was free, with my new, or should I say my old, name. Free of those wretched investigations; free of my silly wife Pauline. Free to carry on with my business unhindered. And for a while, I was content. But I started to think about the old days, back in Mozambique. I wondered about Grace. I decided to see if I could find her. And I asked Stefano if he could help.

For a while there was no word. Then one day, I got a call. Poor Nico had met with a tragic accident in Kiev and was found in the river. But Stefano's other son, Mikhail, was coming to São Paulo to meet me. I never allow any of my business associates anywhere near the villa, so arranged to meet him at a favourite haunt of mine near the cathedral in the city centre. And the news he brought me turned my life upside down once again.

CHAPTER 32

'It was ancient history by the time I went to college,' Suzanne said. Damien had jumped in a cab and come straight over to the office when she told him she'd worked out a huge piece of the puzzle. 'But they still taught the psilocybin story when I studied pharmacy in the 1980s.'

'Psilocybin? What's that?'

'It's an hallucinogenic alkaloid found in some toadstools. They're sometimes called magic mushrooms or shrooms.'

'What are they used for?'

'These days, very little. They're regulated or prohibited in many countries around the world, but for a brief time in the early 1960s they were legal and were being hailed as some kind of wonder drug. Have you ever heard of Timothy Leary?'

'Yes, I think I have,' Damien said, nodding. 'Isn't he the guy Richard Nixon described as 'the most dangerous man in America'?'

'That's the one. He was a great advocate of mind-enhancing substances and, at the time, he had been encouraging the use of LSD; hence Nixon's comment.'

'And what does he have to do with psilocybin?'

'Well, before he became public enemy number one, Leary was a respected psychology lecturer and researcher at Harvard. It didn't last very long and Leary was fired after some of his students were discovered taking LSD in the laboratory. But before that, he was instrumental, with a couple of colleagues, in establishing the Harvard Psilocybin Project and carrying out behavioural studies on students and seminarians. And that's where the phrase 'joining the party' comes from.'

Damien held up his hand.

'I'm not sure I'm following all this, Suzanne. What does a disgraced teacher from more than forty years ago have to do with Sunshine Supplements? You don't think he's behind all this, do you?'

Suzanne laughed and shook her head.

'No, of course not; Leary died back in 1996. And coming to the party wasn't one of his phrases anyway. The one he was best known for is 'turn on, tune in and drop out'.'

'So where does the phrase come from?'

'One of the seminarians involved in the study was the second son of a British earl. He went under the wonderful name of Rufus Armstrong Jenkins. And as the spare in the family, he was naturally going into the church.'

'What?' Damien pulled a face and Suzanne realised she'd lost him again.

'Sorry, Damien. I know the English nobility is a new subject to you. We have a joke in this country about the importance of breeding an heir and a spare. The first son takes on the title and the property on the death of his father. And the second son is the spare, in case anything goes wrong with the succession. Under normal circumstances, the route for that second son is either into the military or the church.'

'And this Armstrong Thingy was a second son?'

'Armstrong Jenkins. Correct. But after getting involved with the Harvard Psilocybin Project, he left the seminary and carried on the research started by Leary and his mates.'

'And this was all in the States?'

'Only to start with. Psilocybin is registered as a Schedule 1 drug with a high potential for abuse; and it's illegal under US Federal Law. But, for example, it's only been banned in this country since 2005. So there are still places around the world where its use is legal.'

'And Armstrong Jenkins has been taking advantage of that?'

'Yes, he's been an advocate of its use ever since. He even put up a strong case for declassifying it at some point. And that's when he started using the phrase: come together; join the party.'

'But it's a fairly innocuous phrase. Are you sure it's not just a coincidence that Nigel Atkinson used it?'

'On its own, yes, it could be. But I've checked very carefully; gone back through all the pictures I can find on the internet and I am positive that the old guy I saw at the Sunshine Supplements factory—the same old guy that Atkinson ejected from his party at the sports ground—was Rufus Armstrong Jenkins.' Suzanne sat back in her chair and nodded at Damien. 'I'm still not sure what's going on, but if Rufus is involved, I'm willing to bet there's a link to either psilocybin or a similar entheogen—that's the general term for psychoactive substances.'

Damien made Suzanne go back to the beginning and go through the whole story again, just to make sure he understood what she was saying. Then he came up with all the sceptical questions he could think of, to try to disprove, or even just weaken her conclusions. But in the end, he had to agree with her. It looked as though Nigel Atkinson was involved in some way with the old researcher. And when they further investigated the nature and history of psilocybin, they found papers talking about the anxiety and paranoia suffered by some users. They also discovered a study from the 1970s which concluded that the dosage of the drug was very hard to control due to its source as plant material.

'So, to summarise,' said Damien, as Suzanne closed down the laptop at the end of a long research session, 'we have a link between Nigel Atkinson's Sunshine Supplements and an elderly researcher who has spent his life trying to win acceptance for a mind-enhancing drug. A drug that comes from a natural source and is therefore difficult to manufacture under controlled conditions.'

'But which is known to cause paranoia in some users,' concluded Suzanne. 'And I've been having another think about that analysis you had done on the material Lulana left behind.'

'But if I remember rightly, it didn't show anything dodgy, did it?' said Damien. 'All my friend found was *yerba maté* tea and a few vitamins. Certainly nothing of an unusual chemical nature.'

'What methodology did he use, do you know?'

'No idea, I'm afraid,' Damien said with a shrug. 'It's all alien to me. But I can ask him. Why?'

'Well, I'm wondering just how sensitive his instrumentation would be. This is a university lab, right? He probably used gas chromatography for separation, but if he used IR or NMR for identification, they are less sensitive methods and would only tend to find the functional groups.' Suzanne realised Damien's eyes had glazed over; she laughed and patted his hand. 'Look, all I'm saying is that his method might not have been sensitive enough to pick up traces of another organic material among all the herbal matter. We may need to get a sample to a specialised government laboratory.'

'But we don't have any more samples, do we?' said Damien.

'No, I'm afraid not. Looks like we need to add that to the task list too.'

The pair called it a night and headed across the road for one of Sanjay's curries. And it wasn't until later the following morning that the final piece fell into place for

Suzanne. She found reference to an article Rufus Armstrong Jenkins had co-written, singing the praises of homoeopathic medicines. Like many pharmacists and classical medical professionals in the western world, Suzanne was very sceptical about homoeopathy. Invented in the eighteenth century, it was an alternative system of therapy which used highly diluted substances, claimed to enable the body to heal itself.

'And, to be honest, it doesn't matter in this case whether it works or not,' she told Damien when she phoned him to give him the news. 'The point is the quantities of the material we're looking for could be so dilute, they're incapable of analytical detection.'

'But in that case, it wouldn't have any effect on people, would it,' asked Damien.

'That's not necessarily so. We're talking about extreme allergies, here. And we know from our experience with penicillin that people who are allergic can be affected at sub-analytical dosages.'

'So if Sunshine Supplements is using psilocybin or a similar material in very dilute quantities, it's not going to be provable in the laboratory,' he said. Suzanne sat in silence for so long that Damien finally asked, 'Are you still there, Suzanne?'

'Yes, I'm still here,' she said. Then she sighed. 'It's no good, Damien. This is all supposition and conjecture. The only way we're going to catch these guys is to get back into that factory; into that locked room, in fact.' She paused and then went on. 'I'm going back, Damien; back to São Paulo.'

'Then I'm coming with you,' he replied.

'That's sweet of you,' she said with a smile, 'but don't you have exams coming up? I think you should go back to college and wait until you hear from us.'

Suzanne didn't mention her other reason for wanting to go back to Brazil. She'd not heard from Charlie for the past three days. If she was honest, that wasn't unusual; she was used to her sister doing a disappearing act. But given what she was investigating, it would be good to get over there and see what she was up to.

PART III

CHAPTER 33

Charlie didn't remember falling asleep. She had no idea how long she'd been out for but she had the mother and father of all hangovers. She didn't think she'd had that much to drink, but something had to explain the seven dwarves and their mates who were tunnelling through her head, trying to beat their way out. And the foul taste in her mouth. And the absence of any memory after hearing Mercy's quiet voice in the darkness, reliving her youth.

Then she realised something that pushed all these other thoughts into the background. She was lying on her side, on the hard, metal floor in the pitch dark—and she was unable to move. Her arms appeared to be tied behind her back and her ankles were fastened together too.

'What the fuck...?' She tried to sit up and then stopped suddenly as waves of nausea threatened to overcome her.

'Lie still, take it gently. The nausea will pass in a minute.' The voice in the darkness was the first indication she wasn't alone. Michael Hawkins was in here—wherever here was—with her.

'What's going on? Why am I tied up?'

'I'm afraid I can't answer that, my dear. I seem to be in the same predicament as you.'

Charlie struggled to loosen the ties around her hands, but they refused to budge and it only made her head pound even more, so she gave up. Then she had a thought.

'Mercy? Mercy, are you in here, too?' There was no response. 'Michael, where's Mercy? Do you know? And what the hell's happening here? Is it pirates? Are we under attack?'

'I'm afraid she's not here,' responded Hawkins. 'It's a very small room. I can touch one wall with my toes and the other with my head. If there was a third person in here, we'd be able to feel her.'

'Have you tried shouting?'

'No, I only came to a little while before you did, Rose. I was waiting for you to wake up. What do you remember?'

'Nothing! Not a thing.'

'So let's go back to what we *do* remember.'

'Well,' said Charlie, 'I remember leaving the limo in the street. Coming back here, moving out into the bay. Then we waved the crew off in the motor boat for their night out and sat on deck, eating dinner and chatting, watching the fireworks. Mercy talked about her childhood. But after that, *nada*! How about you?'

'Pretty much the same as you. I certainly don't remember strangers boarding the boat or being tied up.'

At that moment, the door flew open, blinding them as the darkness was wrenched away to be replaced by bright sunshine. A tall figure stood in the doorway, silhouetted by the light. Hawkins realised who it was while Charlie was still blinking against the light.

'Mercy! Thank God! Are you alright? What the hell's happening?'

The tall African woman said nothing for a few seconds and then when she spoke, Charlie was shocked to hear laughter in her voice.

'Oh yes, Tata dear, I'm perfectly alright. In fact I've never felt better.'

'Can you untie us?'

'Of course I can—but I don't think I'm going to. At least, not just yet.'

There was a stunned silence. Charlie was starting to suspect she might have misjudged her new friend. She tried to keep her voice calm and reasonable.

'Mercy, please help us. Your father's not well...' but Mercy only laughed again.

'Oh, I think you'll find my father is perfectly well, Rose. You've no idea how good he is at playing a part.'

'Mercy,' Hawkins said, 'what's going on?'

'Oh, you'll find out soon enough,' she said. She waved her fingers at them. 'Don't go away. I'll be back in a little while,' and she pushed the door closed. There was the sound of high heels clipping along the deck—and then silence.

'Right,' said Charlie slowly, 'so now we know. Not pirates; not strangers on board. I rather suspect your daughter might have drugged the brandy last night.'

'You think?' growled Hawkins, a note of sarcasm in his voice. But then he sighed. 'Sorry, Rose, I shouldn't take it out on you. And we seem to be allies in this, whatever this is, so let's just see if we can work together, shall we?'

They talked through a number of possibilities for a while, but neither of them could come up with any reason why Mercy should be behaving as she was. After a while, they lapsed into silence. Charlie's head had cleared but she was starting to get cramp from the awkward position in which she was lying. It was difficult to think straight in such circumstances. But it wasn't the first time Charlie had been in a situation like this and she knew the next encounter with Mercy was crucial.

True to her word, Mercy returned within less than an hour.

'Right, let's get you two somewhere more comfortable,' she said. 'It's going to be a long night.' She helped Michael Hawkins to his feet, cut the ties around his ankles and pushed him out of the door. 'I'll be back for you in a while, Rose,' she said. Charlie fancied Mercy's voice was a little softer when talking to her, than her father. Maybe the issue was with him, rather than her. In which case, maybe, just maybe, there was a chance to talk her round to letting them, or at least her, go.

When Mercy finally returned, she hauled Charlie to her feet, freed her legs, and guided her out of the room, which turned out to be a storage locker on the lower deck, towards the stairs, and up to the living quarters. The sun was starting to dip in the west and Charlie guessed it was late afternoon. They went into one of the cabins and Mercy clipped the tie holding Charlie's hands together. At the same time, she pushed her hard so she stumbled across the room and half-fell onto the bunk. By the time she righted herself and whipped around to face the other woman, she was looking straight down the barrel of a classic shooting pistol.

'Stop right there,' said Mercy. 'Running's not the only sport I've been training in. I can shoot straight—and I will use this if I need to. Although it would be a little wasteful and I'd have to reorganise my plans.' She gestured towards the *en suite*. 'Go and make yourself comfortable. But leave the door open. And don't try anything silly!'

Afterwards, Mercy made Charlie walk in front of her down the corridor to the main lounge. Hawkins was lying on the floor, hog-tied once more. He looked up at the two women and glared silently at his daughter. For a moment, Charlie felt sorry for him; until she remembered just who this man was and what he'd done to her friends and family in the past.

Mercy ignored him and pushed Charlie towards the sofa.

'I won't tie you up again—unless you give me cause to mistrust you. And you're not going to do that, are you, Rose?' Then she hauled Hawkins to his feet, untied his ankles, and pushed him down on the sofa next to Charlie. Finally, she kicked off her shoes, curled up on a banquette at the other side of the room and pointed the gun at both of them.

'Right, we're going to do some storytelling. I always loved storytelling when I was a child. How about you, Rose?'

'Yes, I did, Mercy,' she replied. 'But I'm not sure this is the time for storytelling. How about you explain what's going on.' Mercy laughed. It wasn't a pleasant sound.

'I'm surprised you haven't worked it out already. You're *so* smart.' Charlie didn't have to fake the confusion she was feeling.

'Mercy, I thought we were friends—'

'Friends! That's really funny. Why on earth would I want to be friends with someone like you? We have nothing in common!' She stared at Charlie who thought she might just possibly detect a hint of regret in the other woman's eyes. But then it was gone. 'I gave you your chance, Rose. Asked you to stay with me. You could have shared it all with me. But you made it quite clear you weren't interested in me. And I don't take rejection well.' Her voice wobbled a little at these words, and Charlie dared to hope Mercy would have second thought. But then she took a deep breath and laughed harshly. 'So, my little British 'friend', at this point you're nothing more than a useful device. But don't be hurt; you're still an important part in my plan.'

'And just what is your plan?' asked Hawkins wearily.

'Oh, no, Tata dear, let's not rush things and spoil the fun. We've got all the storytelling to go through first.' She sat up straighter and pointed the gun at Hawkins' head. He flinched but kept silent. 'Right, now last night I told you the story of my early life in Mozambique. Let's just say I didn't tell you the whole truth. Oh no, there's quite a bit more to tell. But first,' she pointed at Hawkins, 'I want to hear *your* story. I want to hear how you came to be in Mozambique; and why you left; and what you've been doing since then.'

Hawkins was shaking his head almost before she'd finished speaking.

'Mercy, you know all this. I told you my story when we first met.'

'Oh, I know you told me the sanitised version,' she sneered, 'but now I want the truth. I've been doing some research and I know some of it already. But I want to hear it all—from your own mouth. And believe me when I say I've been doing my homework. So if you try lying or missing parts out, then I will know about it.'

This should be interesting, thought Charlie. *I wonder how much will tally with what we've already found out.* She wondered where her phone was; it would be perfect if she could get a recording of Hawkins' story. Of course, he might deny everything afterwards, or say he was forced to speak under coercion, but it would certainly help their case.

Then she realised she was kidding herself. She was stuck on a boat moored off a remote coast and Mercy was holding a gun to her head. Bringing Michael Hawkins, or even Sir Fredrick Michaels, to justice was the least of her problems right now.

CHAPTER 34

Night had fallen by the time Michael Hawkins stop talking. There was a short silence before Mercy stood suddenly and snapped on the overhead lights.

'Such a pretty story, Tata dear, but I think you've left out a couple of major elements.'

Charlie had been so absorbed in listening to him tell his story she'd almost forgotten about the predicament they were in. But now the sneering voice of her tall African friend—or she supposed that should be former friend—pulled her straight back into the here and now. Hawkins was looking confused.

'No, I don't think so; I've told you everything,' he said.

'Well, I suppose that's true, in a way,' said Mercy. 'After all, once you left Africa, you no longer knew or cared what happened to my mother, did you?' Hawkins said nothing, but just stared at his daughter. 'You had your new life and your new wife. So what did it matter what happened to poor little Grace?' She stood up and walked over to Hawkins, who flinched and pulled his head away as she waved the gun in his face. 'Well, we've heard your story; now I'm going to tell you the bits you missed.'

The day you disappeared, Grace had a surprise for you. She'd suspected for a while she was pregnant, but that morning she'd been to the doctor and had it confirmed. She shopped for all your favourite foods: prawns, peri peri chicken and fresh mango. She dressed in her smoky nut brown silky dress—you remember, Tata, the one you bought her because you said the colour reflected in her eyes—and dressed the table up real special. Then she sat and waited for you to come home. But you never did, did you?

She waited for seven days, wondering where you were, whether you'd had an accident, scared to go out and ask your friends, frightened of what she might hear.

Then the week after you left, a rumour started circulating: you'd fallen out with the army chief, and Stefano had been forced to kill you. She didn't believe it for one minute. She always said she would have known if you were dead. And even when that body washed up in the harbour, a body so battered by the waves and eaten by the fishes that it was unrecognisable, but wearing your clothes and with your cigarette case in his pocket, even then, she didn't believe it. And she was right, wasn't she? Because you weren't dead. You were living it up on a luxury liner with your new woman.

Two days after you were declared dead, Stefano went to visit Grace. He wanted her out of the apartment. She broke down, telling him there was a baby on the way—that's me, remember?—and she had nowhere to go, no friends or family in Lourenço Marques. He suggested she go back to her home town, but she didn't believe her family would have her back.

Stefano finally relented. He told her she could stay in the apartment for free until the baby was born, but after that she either had to find somewhere else to live or work for him. And at the time, that sounded like a great deal.

Well, in time, I was born and Grace told Stefano she would stay and work for him. She thought he was offering her a job in one of his bars—and so he was to start with. The story I told you last night—you know, the one where I spent evenings in the little back room while my mother served the customers—that was true. But what I didn't say was that as my mother recovered from the birth and started looking happier and healthier, she attracted the attention of the wrong sort of customer. The sort of customer who took a woman upstairs to one of the special rooms, used her, abused her and then left, laughing.

Grace tried to object, told Stefano she was a good girl, a good mother. But to no avail. He insisted she do what he told her to. And gradually, she spent more time in the rooms upstairs and less time behind the bar.

I was about five when I realised there was something wrong with my mother. When she came to collect me in the mornings, she would be confused, slurring her words. Sometimes she would cry, shout at me for the slightest thing; other times she would ignore me for hours on end and I would have to beg some food from the woman who ran the cake shop at the end of the street. It was a couple of years before I realised Stefano had turned my mother into a junkie in order to keep her under control.

We rubbed along like this until just before my eleventh birthday. Then one evening, Stefano called me over to his table. I was big for my age, but I was still a child. A child, Tata!

There was another white man sitting at the table with him. I'd seen him in there before; very tall, running to fat and with a heavy moustache and beard.

'Ah, Mercy, my dear,' Stefano said, pulling me towards him and putting his arm around me, 'I want you to meet someone who's especially keen to get to know you. This is Marco Gomez, Lourenço Marques' great army chief. He's a very important man.' The other man leaned forward and took my hand in his huge paw. He smiled at me, a smile that sent shivers down my spine, and when he spoke, his breath was like the river water when the tide is low and full of stinking garbage.

'My dear, I've seen you several times in here and wanted to meet you. Sit down, join us.'

I was trembling, not sure what was happening, certain it was not good. But Stefano steered me to a spare seat and pressed my shoulder really hard—I can still remember his fingers digging into me—and poured me a drink.

I was so frightened, I drank the whole thing without asking what it was, and although it was thick and creamy, like milk, there was something else in the background; something fierce and strong.

For a while, the two men ignored me and talked to each other about things I didn't understand, couldn't follow. I wondered if they had forgotten me and even tried to slip away, but as soon as I stirred, Stefano put his hand on my arm again.

'Now, young lady,' he said. 'I want you to be nice to Marco; he's a really good friend of mine.' Gomez stood and held out his hand to me. Stefano smiled and nodded. 'Go on, child; go with him.'

So I did. I walked across the room, hand in hand with that odious man, climbed the stairs with him and entered my own private hell. I was ten!

Afterwards, he walked away without a backward look. But at the door, he paused and said one thing I have never forgotten.

'Your father took my love from me. Now the debt is paid!'

I lay on that stinking bed for hours, sobbing. At some point, my mother found me. She seemed quite lucid that day, gathered me up, took me home, bathed my wounds and swore she would never let anyone hurt me again. But of course, that was a promise she was unable to fulfil. The next night, she was back on the drugs, back whoring again and there was no-one to protect me.

By the time I was fifteen, my mother was unable to work. She was old before her time, losing her looks and riddled with disease. There was this new sickness going around. Some said it came from monkeys, others thought it was a curse from God. But wherever it came from, it spread rapidly and killed people way before their time.

Stefano tried to make me take my mother's place in his brothel. And there were a few times when I did what he asked. After all, nothing could be worse than being raped by a vicious thug at the age of ten. And some of the punters were even kind to me, giving me extra money which they told me to hide when I left the room.

One mistake I was determined not to make was to follow my mother down the drug route. I refused all offers from Stefano and never again ate or drank anything in any of his restaurants.

By the time my mother died, it was a blessed relief. Her body was destroyed; so was her mind. Once she stopped working for Stefano, he stopped feeding her drug habit. I locked myself with her in the apartment and held her hand as she sweated, shouted and screamed her way through cold turkey. It was dreadful, painful and dangerous, but I didn't want her to remain dependent on a drug we couldn't afford. It took weeks, and in the end, she was free of it, but by that time her mind was gone. For the rest of her life, just a few short months, she sat in the apartment staring at the wall, often with tears rolling down her cheeks, sometimes calling your name. She only ate when I fed her, took no interest in her appearance, and in fact, if I didn't insist, she sometimes didn't even get out of bed all day.

Meanwhile, I was trying to keep us fed and the rent paid. Stefano tried to evict us, and we would have been out on the streets if it wasn't for, of all people, Marco Gomez. He visited me once or twice more in the brothel but I was older, better able to deal with his cruelty. When Stefano suggested we must leave, I went to see Gomez and begged for his protection. I promised him once my mother was at rest, I would go to him and live as his mistress. And the stupid man believed me! He actually believed a child he'd raped and brutalised would agree to live openly with him when she was older. But it worked. Stefano never threatened me with eviction again.

My mother was just forty-three when she died. No age at all for a normal young woman, but her life was anything but ordinary. And we have you to thank for that, don't we, Tata? As I stood by her grave on that arid hillside one sweltering morning in June, I swore I would find a way to be revenged on you for my mother's life and death. Of course, at the time, I had no idea how I would do that, since you were apparently long dead. But my mother swore to her dying day you were still alive. And when Stefano's son told me all about your new life in Brazil and your wish to be reunited with Grace, I knew my chance had come.

CHAPTER 35

Charlie choked back tears as she listened to Mercy's story. She couldn't imagine what it had been like for the young girl, but she was beginning to understand the rage she was feeling against her father. Hawkins himself seemed shaken by the revelations. He said nothing, but Charlie could see he was struggling to remain composed. He stared at his feet, apparently unable to meet his daughter's eye.

'So, now you know, Tata dear,' said Mercy, 'all about the lives you wrecked after you'd thoughtlessly fled back to England.'

'But I never forgot your mother,' Hawkins said, his voice little more than a whisper. 'That's why I asked Stefano to send Mikhail to Africa.' He finally raised his head. 'Mercy, I know there's nothing I can do to make up for the terrible suffering you and your mother endured, but I hope I can make the future better for you.' Mercy laughed. The sound sent chills down Charlie's back.

'Oh, you're going to make my future very good indeed, Tata,' she said, 'but unfortunately, you're not going to be around to see it.' She stared at him for a few moments, as though debating with herself, and then nodded. 'But I guess there's one final part of the story you might as well hear.'

Mikhail didn't have to go to Africa to find me. I wasn't there. In fact I hadn't been there for twenty years.

One day, not long before my mother died, she gave me a message to take to Stefano. She wanted to see him. Well, to start with, he refused, but I told him she was dying, and he finally agreed. When he arrived, Mother sent me away. But I didn't trust him, so crept back and listened at the window. My mother was lying in bed; Stefano stood by the door, looking like he couldn't wait to get away.

'Stefano, I don't have much time,' my mother said, 'so I need you to tell me the truth. What happened to Michael? What happened to my husband?'

'Grace, we've been through this many times,' he replied harshly, 'Michael did something very stupid and he had to pay the price.'

I could see my mother was getting frustrated with him.

'I don't believe you! I've never believed you! I would know if Michael was dead.'

'But you saw the body!'

'Pah! That thing you pulled out of the harbour? That wasn't my Michael. I know it and you know it!' She stopped, taken by a violent coughing fit and pointing to the glass of water on the table. Stefano handed it to her and then sat on the chair next to the bed. When she'd finished coughing, he took her hand.

'Grace, I'd like to help you, but I can't. I'm sorry.'

My mother was silent for so long, I wondered if she'd fallen asleep, but finally I heard her sigh.

'Alright, Stefano, I won't ask you again. Not for me, anyway. But I'm worried about Mercy. She's going to be all on her own. For her sake, I'm begging you. Please find Michael, wherever he is, and tell him he has a daughter. She's his responsibility now. He needs to look after her.'

Stefano was shaking his head.

'Grace, I don't think that's a promise I can keep. But, I promise you I will do what I can for your little girl.'

My mother didn't tell me about the conversation with Stefano, and I didn't tell her I'd been eavesdropping. And two weeks later, as I stood at her graveside, Stefano took me to one side.

'Mercy, what are you going to do now?' he asked.

'Oh, I'll be alright,' I said. I might only have been fifteen, but I was used to looking after myself.

'Marco Gomez tells me he has an arrangement with you?' My heart plummeted at those words and I looked around wildly, to make sure my tormentor and would-be patron wasn't nearby. I'd been trying to forget the promise I'd made out of desperation. Stefano went on. 'If you're happy to go through with that, then that's fine. But,' he looked shrewdly at me, 'you're not happy with it, are you?' I pressed my lips together to stop them trembling, and shook my head. 'Well, I have a suggestion to make. This civil war looks like it's not going to be settled any time soon and I'm getting too old for all this. I'm going home; to my wife, my children. Come back to Ukraine with me.'

At first, I thought he was joking, making fun of me. I hadn't even known he had a family. But eventually, I realised he was serious. For more than ten years, Stefano had been spending part of each year back in Kharkov. His wife, Katya, had given him three children, a daughter and two sons. And now he was offering me a home with them. I don't know why he did that. Maybe he felt guilty about my mother, or about how I'd been treated. I never asked him. I was just happy to have an escape from Marco Gomez.

The next twenty years were tough, but nothing compared to the previous fifteen. I was older than all Stefano's children and although Katya was kind enough, the rest of the family treated me as the intruder I was. The sight of a black face in the Soviet Union was unusual and many times I was harassed on the street. But I ignored the problems and concentrated on learning everything I could. I went to school, then college. When Stefano found I was quick at figures, he involved me in the business, at least the local ones. By the time I was twenty-five, I was running several of his factories for him and was known as a tough character who wouldn't be taken for a fool. You mentioned 'poor Nico' earlier on, Tata. Well poor Nico thought he could get the better of me. He found out the hard way I don't like to be crossed.

Then one day, Mikhail, Nico's older brother, came to see me at the factory. We had grown to tolerate each other over the years and sometimes, it almost felt like we were friends.

'Papa wants me to go to Brazil,' he told me. 'He's had a strange request from your father. But I need to know what you want me to do.'

It was as though I had been punched in the stomach. I stared at him in silence as I fought to get my breath back. In fact, I said very little that day, just listened to everything Mikhail had to say. But by the time he was ready to leave for the airport, I had my plans in place, my story straight.

'Do not tell him I am in Ukraine,' I said. 'I want him to think I'm still in Africa.'

'But what if he decides to go there to meet you?'

'He mustn't. Tell him you found me and I am happy to hear about him. Tell him I want to go to Brazil to meet him.' I'd thought this all through. 'And, Mikhail, do not tell him how my mother ended up, or what my life was like before your father brought me here.'

'So what will I tell him?'

'Tell him we survived. Tell him my mother found a friend, let's call him Rene Lopez. We'll give him a son called Guido.'

'And so, Tata, we made up this story and we told Stefano what Mikhail was going to say, so there would be no confusion.'

Mercy stared out of the window for a few moments. Then she looked back at Hawkins with a cold little smile on her face.

'But it seems Stefano didn't trust me as completely as I thought, did he? I never knew, until this evening, that he was in touch with you all that time. He never told me about you—and he obviously didn't tell you about me. I don't know why; but I will find out. Believe me, Tata, I will get answers from Stefano Mladov when I've finished with you.'

CHAPTER 36

Charlie sat tall and straight, staring at Mercy, determined not to distract her by moving in any way. But her mind was seething. Mercy was speaking slowly and distinctly, pausing to take a deep breath occasionally, and with only a slight break in her voice as she relived her life so far. She looked as though she had forgotten her audience, except the gun was still pointed straight at Michael Hawkins, and the hand that held that gun was rock solid, with never a tremor in it.

Finally, Mercy stopped talking and sat silent for a minute or two. Then as though waking from a deep sleep she shook her head and refocused on her father.

'Right, Tata dearest, now you've heard the full story. Anything to say before I end your miserable life?'

Hawkins looked back at his daughter and tears welled in his eyes.

'But Stefano's son told me your mother was safe, cared for. You told us the same last night. Why invent the story about Rene Lopez?'

'I couldn't take the risk, Tata, that you would be ashamed of me. I didn't want anything in my past to make you change your mind. Now I knew you were alive. Now I had the chance for revenge. I needed you to want me. But now that need's gone. The truth can't hurt anymore.'

'I'm sorry, Mercy, so very sorry. I had no idea. If I'd only known—'

'Known what?' she spat. 'Known my mother was expecting me, or known she would end up as a whore and junkie whore at that! Or known your daughter would have to fight to stop herself from going down the same road. Which do you wish you'd known?'

'All of it,' Hawkins whispered.

'Yes, well, that's easy to say,' she sneered, 'but what exactly would you have done about it? Would you have stayed and looked after us? I doubt it! I think you would still have run away to save your own miserable skin!' Hawkins made no reply. Mercy rose to her feet and gestured to Hawkins with her gun. 'Right, I've had enough of this; let's go!'

She paid no attention to Charlie, almost as though she'd forgotten she was there. And that was the chance Charlie was waiting for. She sprang to her feet and launched herself at Mercy, hoping to rugby tackle her to the ground. But at the last minute, the other woman side-stepped her and, twisting as though on a knife edge, brought the gun down sharply against the side of Charlie's skull. She went down with a thud and everything went black.

Once again, Charlie had no idea how long she'd been unconscious. She was lying on the ground, with her cheek pressed against the thick Persian carpet. As she started to sit up, her head smacked at her and she stopped, trying to swallow down the wave of nausea that threatened to wash over her. She wriggled her fingers and was relieved to find that Mercy had not got around to retying her wrists. She was free to move—if she could.

Someone was shouting from the deck outside the

salon. The large window on the port side had been opened earlier to let in the night breezes and the voice was coming from that side of the boat. Charlie wondered where the crew was. Why hadn't they come up from their quarters to see what the commotion was about? She raised herself gently to her knees and looked out of the window. Hawkins was lying on the deck, curled into the foetal position and Mercy was standing over him, taunting him and pointing the gun at his head.

'Sod that for a game of soldiers,' muttered Charlie. She wanted Hawkins to stand trial for what he had done, and be fittingly punished. She was damned if he was going to get an easy way out, here in the middle of the sea.

The door to the salon, which was opposite the window and led out to the starboard deck, was pulled to, but there was a chink of light shining through below it. With a bit of luck, Mercy might have left it ajar, or forgotten to close it. Charlie lowered herself back onto the carpet and inched her way across the room. The lamps were still lit and if Mercy looked across at the window at the wrong time, she was likely to spot Charlie moving, but that was a risk she would have to take. She just had to hope Mercy was too involved in taunting her father to think of anything else at the moment.

Charlie hooked her fingers under the bottom of the door and pulled it gently towards her. When it was about half open, she slid through and reaching up to the handle, pulled it shut behind her. Then she stood up.

The blood rushed to her head and she was reminded once more of the stinging blow she'd received from Mercy's gun. But there was no time to think about that now. The deck ran all around the central salon. If Mercy was still in the same position as before, she would have her back to the stern. Charlie crept in that direction. She could hear Mercy quite clearly now. Again, she wondered where the crew had got to. But she couldn't rely on them anyway. After all, they were hired by the Hawkins family; they should be loyal to Michael Hawkins, but they could well be allied with Mercy.

As she reached the back of the salon, she ducked down into a crouch. Turning the corner, she came face to face with the young crewman left on board the previous night by the captain to look after them. He was sitting slumped against the wall, his legs stretched out in front of him, his eyes open and staring sightlessly at her. The blood that had gushed from the wound at his throat made a dark stain down the front of his once pristine uniform. It looked like he'd been dead for hours.

She poked her head around the corner and then drew back rapidly. Mercy was standing over Hawkins, just a few feet away. She was still holding the gun.

Charlie looked around for a weapon and spotted a rack of sports equipment, including a baseball bat. It was perfect. It reminded her of the rounders bats they played with at school. She had always been very good at rounders.

She took a deep breath and ran around the corner, heading straight for Mercy and Hawkins. The African woman spun on her heel at the noise, but before she had time to pull the trigger, or react in any way, Charlie brought the bat around in a double-handed swipe, worthy of any first team batsman. She felt, as much as heard, the impact as the bat hit Mercy's wrist. There was a scream, whether of anger or pain was unclear, as the gun flew out of her hand and slid along the deck.

With another scream, this time definitely of rage, Mercy flung herself at Charlie, clawing at her face. Her momentum threw the two women down in a heap and Charlie groaned as her head hit the deck. Even her headache was starting to get a headache.

Mercy twisted herself sideways, sat astride Charlie's chest and wrapped her hands around her throat. As she struggled to remove the fingers of steel, Charlie saw a figure rise from the deck behind Mercy. Was Hawkins going to come to her aid? But with his hands still tied behind his back, there was nothing he could do. He turned and scurried towards the bow, hiding himself behind the lifeboat station.

Charlie interlocked her fingers and forced her clenched fist between Mercy's arms and then threw her hands apart, bringing her fists down hard on the other woman's wrists. The pressure on her neck slackened. Only slightly, but it was enough. She bucked her whole body upwards and sideways, and Mercy fell off and rolled against the wall of the salon.

Charlie jumped up and stood panting, watching as Mercy tried to recover. The place where they were standing was narrow and there was no room to manoeuvre. She needed to lure the other woman to a wider space. Glancing over her shoulder, she spied the stairway leading up to the sun deck on top of the salon. As Mercy began to stir, Charlie turned and ran towards it.

'Yes, you can run,' screamed Mercy, 'but you're not going to get away from me that easily.' Charlie heard the thud of bare feet on the deck as Mercy chased after her.

She reached the stairs seconds before her pursuer and raced to the top. The sun deck was wide, flat and empty at the stern, with steps thirty metres away, leading down to the swimming pool and a row of loungers at the bow end.

Charlie ran to the other side of the deck and turned to face Mercy, who was holding her right wrist in her left hand and grimacing. Blood trickled down the side of her face from a gash along her cheekbone. She was breathing heavily. Charlie stood still, waiting for the other woman to make the first move.

Mercy prowled around the deck, keeping her eyes on Charlie throughout. Neither woman was armed; Charlie had lost her weapon in the struggle on the lower deck, but at least Mercy's gun was also gone. Charlie was just beginning to wonder if she would be able to talk her way out of this situation, when Mercy began to speak.

'You know there's no-one else to help you, don't you?'

she said. Charlie looked down towards the entrance to the crew's quarters and Mercy laughed. 'Oh, come on! You don't really think there's anyone else on board, do you? Don't you think they would have appeared by now?'

'Well, I've seen your handiwork downstairs, but I was wondering where the rest of the crew had got to.'

'I paid them off, sweetie. When they headed off for their night out, I told them we would manage on our own today; that they were to take the day off and come back to pick us up tomorrow. Mind you, it didn't come cheap. It took a fair wedge of my money to convince them, well, Tata dearest's money really—ironic isn't it? The man who's going to get killed is paying to send his possible rescuers away.'

'So your plan is to kill Michael, or maybe both of us?'

'Oh, definitely both of you! My father assaulted you; you fought him off; killed him in self-defence. And were so guilt-ridden you killed yourself too.'

'And what about you?'

'Me? Oh, I'd taken a sleeping pill and slept through it all. I think I will play the grieving daughter and friend rather well.'

'But what about our plans? You running away, me helping you?'

'Run away?' Mercy gave a contemptuous laugh. 'Why on earth would I want to run away? I've got everything here I would ever want. All I need to do is dispose of my father,' she spat on the deck as she said the words, 'and make him pay for what he did to my mother. Then I will take over his businesses as his rightful heir.'

'So you've been planning this for a long time?'

'Ever since I arrived, Rose dear; ever since I arrived. I couldn't do anything too soon; that would look just too suspicious. But now I'm settled in, accepted as a dutiful daughter, grateful even. All I'm going to be accused of is an unfortunate choice of friends! Tragic really.'

As they talked, Mercy edged ever closer. Charlie moved

slowly backwards, aware there wasn't much space left between her and the edge of the deck.

And then it came. With a snarl, Mercy launched herself towards Charlie—who made no effort to defend herself.

At the last minute, she stepped sideways and stuck out her foot. Mercy tried to check her flight, but the momentum was too great. She tripped over Charlie's leg and fell headlong over the edge of the deck. Immediately below them was the covered shape of the starboard lifeboat. Charlie watched as Mercy flew through the air, and landed awkwardly, striking her head on the edge of the boat as she did so. She struggled to her feet and stood, swaying slightly, her eyelids fluttering.

At that moment, a skyrocket arched up into the night sky behind her, signalling the start of that night's firework display. The explosion of sound came an instant later. Mercy jumped at the noise and spun around, just as a wave hit the boat, rocking it and tugging at the anchor. She lurched sideways, tried to regain her footing and teetered on the edge before slipping over the side and down into the inky darkness of the water below.

'Noooooooo!' The screech split the night and Michael Hawkins rushed out from his hiding place on the other side of the boat and raced to the starboard hand rail. Charlie ran down to the deck below and joined him at the side. But there was no sight nor sound of Mercy. She had simply vanished.

CHAPTER 37

Charlie undid the ties binding Hawkins' hands and for more than an hour they searched for Mercy; shouting her name, stabbing the darkness with flashlights, staring into the dark waves below. But there was nothing. She was gone. Whether she was unconscious when she fell into the water, or whether she got caught in rocks and weeds under the surface, wasn't clear. But even her father had to admit she wasn't coming back.

Charlie left him standing on the deck and clawed her way in the dark to her cabin where she fell on her bunk, fully clothed. The shock and pain of the previous twenty-four hours finally caught up with her. The last thing she heard was a dragging sound, followed by a splash. Then all was quiet.

When she awoke, the sun was high in the sky. Michael Hawkins was still standing where she'd left him, clinging to the rail and staring at the deep waters beneath him. He looked like he'd been there all night. And yet, he must have moved at some point. When Charlie checked the stern deck, the body of the young crewman had gone.

'I loved her. I truly loved her.' Hawkins' voice was low, hoarse and full of despair. 'I've done a lot of things in my life I'm not proud of. She was the one shining light in the whole sorry mess.'

Charlie put her hand on Hawkins' arm. Briefly, she saw not a man who had lied and cheated his way through life; not a man who had caused the deaths of countless children, and probably adults, in his greed; not even a man who had kidnapped and tortured her sister. For that brief moment, she saw just a man who'd lost his daughter and was grieving.

'Come down to the galley,' she said, 'and let me make you a drink. Have you been here all night?'

But Hawkins carried on talking as though he'd not heard anything she said.

'She didn't love me. I realise that now. All these months, we've been living a lie. But it was worth it.'

Charlie realised she wasn't going to get through to Hawkins at the moment, so she went down to the galley in search of food and something to drink.

As the sun gradually climbed into its noonday position, with no sign of the crew returning, Charlie got on the radio and called for help.

Within a short while, a large motorboat appeared on the horizon, bearing the logo of the Brazilian Coast Guards. They dropped a couple of sailors aboard the stranded vessel, who quickly had the engines started and the boat heading back towards the marina.

As she stood at the rail, watching the skyline of Rio get ever closer, Charlie heard a step behind her. It was Michael Hawkins. But such a different man from the broken, grieving father she'd seen just a while before. He had shaved, changed and was back to his normal dapper self. As he reached her side, she began to speak.

'Michael, I am so sorry—,' but he waved away her words.

'It's over, Rose. I thought she was my daughter, but I was obviously mistaken. No true daughter would treat her father like she did.'

'But what are you going to tell the police?'

'Police? In this place? During carnival? What's the point?' He shook his head. 'I've ordered the plane to be ready for this afternoon. I'll take you back to São Paulo and then I will say goodbye to you.'

'And will you go back to England for a while? You need a breathing space and staying in Brazil will only remind you of Mercy.' But the words were barely out of her mouth before he rounded fiercely on her.

'Never! Why would I want to go back there? I have everything I could need here—everything! And I don't wish to hear that woman's name again—ever!' He turned and walked off towards the lounge.

Charlie watched him ruefully. She'd thought for one moment she would be able to persuade Hawkins to come back to England voluntarily. It would be much easier to get him arrested once he was back on British soil. But it had been a long shot and it obviously wasn't going to work.

Oh well, thought Charlie, *it was worth a try. I guess I'm going to have to revert to Plan B. I just wish I knew what Plan B was.*

Back on dry land, Charlie and Hawkins went in search of the missing crew in the various dockside pubs and drinking dens—and in the third one they tried, they were lucky. The captain and first mate were enjoying a drink and a laugh together in front of the fire. Their jaws dropped when Hawkins strode across the bar and slammed his fist down on the table.

At first they seemed reluctant to say why they'd failed to return from their evening ashore. The guilty pair looked around furtively.

'Miss Mercy, she is not with you?' asked the first mate.

'No,' replied Hawkins coldly, 'Miss Mercy is not with us. You won't be seeing her again.' The pair looked at him curiously, but he didn't elaborate. 'I'm waiting,' he said.

The captain finally spoke.

'Two nights ago, Miss Mercy, she told me she was organising a little surprise for the two of you. She said she wanted to do it all herself—and she gave us a holiday. Told us we could have two days off. We were to return tomorrow morning.'

'But you're *my* crew,' said Hawkins through gritted teeth. 'I hired the boat; I give the orders, Not my—, not Miss Mercy.' The captain grinned at Hawkins, nervously.

'True boss, but Miss Mercy, she even scarier than you!'

'And she paid us well, boss,' chipped in the first mate. But their smiles faded as Hawkins slammed his palm flat on the table.

'Well I hope she paid you very well indeed,' he said quietly. 'I've been speaking to the boat's owner. And you are both fired!' And as he stood up, he leaned heavily over them. 'And you can tell the rest of your worthless crew they're out of a job too.' Then, turning on his heel, he strode out of the bar, leaving Charlie to follow in his wake.

But as she began to walk away, the captain pulled at her sleeve.

'What about the fire?'

'Fire,' she said, confused, 'what fire?'

'Miss Mercy she said there might be a small fire on board, and we were not to worry. If the boat was damaged, she would pay.' Charlie shrugged her shoulders.

'Well, she must have changed her mind; there's been no fire on board. In fact that's one of the few things that hasn't happened!'

She hurried outside and found Hawkins waiting impatiently for her. He had hailed a cab and was chatting to the driver.

'We'll go back to the boat to collect our things, then go straight to the airfield. We're due to take off in an hour.'

'Michael, those sailors weren't really expecting to go back to the boat,' she said, as they drove along the waterfront to where their boat was moored.

'I know. They were lying,' he said. 'That captain wouldn't drink, or allow his crew to drink, on the day he was expecting to go to sea.'

'He told me Mercy mentioned the possibility of a fire. What do you suppose she meant by that?'

'Rose, I told you I don't want to hear her name again,' Hawkins said, then turned to stare out of the window. Charlie was left alone with her thoughts. It looked as though Mercy had planned to set fire to the boat, but had she planned to kill them first? And had Mercy planned to die with them? They would never know, but somehow, Charlie doubted it.

The flight back to São Paulo was a silent one. Hawkins seemed withdrawn and although he swore he would never speak of, or think about, his daughter again, Charlie suspected he would grieve for a long time.

When the plane landed, Hawkins preceded her down the steps to the tarmac. Then, turning, he held out his hand.

'Rose, I'm sorry you were involved in all this. I don't think we will meet again, do you?' She took his outstretched hand, but it was the merest of touches, as though he was brushing her out of his life. 'Goodbye, Rose,' he said, and turning towards his waiting car, he left her standing alone.

'Oh, don't worry about me,' she said out loud. 'I can take a taxi.' But he was gone.

During the drive back to her hotel, Charlie finally gave in to the chilling thought she'd been trying to avoid all day. Hawkins had said they were unlikely to meet again. He was tired and probably still in shock following the events of the past forty-eight hours. But at some point he would remember Rose Fitzpatrick sitting quietly by his side throughout the hours he had recounted his story. She would constitute a risk to his security. And she knew Michael Hawkins would not be willing to allow that risk to remain. Luckily, he didn't know her real name or where she was staying, but even so, the whole affair had suddenly got even more dangerous than before.

CHAPTER 38

Sitting in her hotel room a couple of hours later, Charlie scribbled down everything she could remember from Hawkins' history, and that of Grace and Mercy. She still had no proof, and Hawkins was still holed up in Brazil, but there was enough detail of his past life, she suspected, to cause the police to investigate. Most importantly, there was news of Hawkins' change of name and second marriage during his voyage back from South Africa all those years ago. Hopefully that, together with the pictures of Hawkins Charlie had taken during their trip, would be sufficient to raise interest in a case which to all intents and purposes was dead the day Sir Fredrick Michaels' clothes and car were found abandoned in the coastal car park in Kent.

Charlie packed her bags and phoned the airport; there was a seat free on the flight leaving the following day. She booked it. There was nothing else she could think to do here in Brazil, and she couldn't spin out her investigation of Nigel Atkinson any longer; it wasn't fair on Damien. She just hoped the whole experience hadn't been a dangerous waste of time. She tried, for the fifth time since arriving back at the hotel, to ring Suzanne. She knew her sister would be worrying about her. But there was no answer on the office landline or at the flat, and her mobile was switched off. Where could she have got to?

Reluctant to pass the evening on her own and unwilling to spend more money on an expensive meal in the hotel restaurant, Charlie headed down town to a little bar and café she'd frequented with Mercy over the weeks before they left for Rio. She took a table in a dark corner and ordered a beer.

'Drinking alone?' The male voice was deep and only slightly accented. She looked up warily but was pleased to recognise Felix, the guy from Mercy's running club. She'd met him a couple of times since that first morning and had found him good company. As far as she could tell, he still hadn't recognised her or remembered how they'd originally met.

'Felix, what a nice surprise,' she said. 'Will you join me? I was just going to order some food.'

He grinned and pulled out the chair she pointed to.

'Sure, why not. Great to see you again, Rose.' He took a long pull from his beer and then putting the glass down, turned towards Charlie, with a serious look on his face, 'I wanted to say how sorry I was to hear about the accident in Rio.'

'How did you know...' Charlie began, but then realised, 'of course, through the club.'

'Yes, we heard from her father earlier this afternoon. He told us there'd been an accident and she wouldn't be returning.' He shook his head. 'How very sad. She was such a talented athlete—and a nice lady too.' Charlie kept quiet, deciding not to disabuse him of his view of her late friend. It wouldn't help anyone to know just what had happened on the boat. Felix went on: 'In fact I sometimes wonder how such a nice woman could come from such a terrible father. I guess it's the fact she was out of his influence for all her formative years.'

'Maybe,' said Charlie, noncommittally. Then she realised what he had said about Michael Hawkins. 'Tell me;

what do you have against Michael Hawkins?'

'Not a lot at the moment, and most of it is circumstantial. We know he's involved in deals with some of the drug cartels in Colombia and Peru. And he's been quietly buying up properties in São Paulo and Rio for the past decade. Let's just say he's not one of the most enlightened landlords in the country.' Felix paused and gave a deep sigh. 'In fact that's how I first got involved in all this. My grandmother was one of his tenants. She got behind with her rent and he evicted her. She died not long afterwards.'

'Felix, I'm so sorry.'

'And although the doctor's certificate says pneumonia, I will always blame Michael Hawkins. If she'd stayed in her own home, it wouldn't have happened.'

'But that's very difficult to prove.'

'Of course it is; and evicting someone who's behind with the rent may be immoral, but it's not actually illegal. Believe me, I looked for some sort of proof that Hawkins broke the law, but he's very clever. He does everything by the book.'

'Not always he doesn't,' said Charlie. Then she put her hand over her mouth as she realised what she'd done. Her companion turned to her and gripped her arm tightly.

'What? Tell me! What do you know about Hawkins? Is it anything I can use against him?'

'No, I don't think so; not here in Brazil, anyway.' She took a deep breath and stared at the young man, as her mind churned. Could she trust him? Was it safe to be open with him? She'd always considered herself a good judge of character—although her recent experience with Mercy had dented her confidence somewhat. But his next words were as shocking as they were unexpected.

'Rose,' he said, taking her hand, 'or should I say, Charlotte, you saved my life once. I know I can trust you. How about you taking a chance and trusting me as well? Maybe together we can do something?'

'Saved your life,' she stuttered, 'what do you mean?' But even to her own ears, the words sounded unconvincing and she wasn't surprised when he laughed at her.

'Did you really think I would forget you? The woman whose team finally ended my ordeal and got me back home?' He shook his finger at her. 'You can grow your hair, you can change the colour, you can even change your name. But your eyes will always give you away.'

'How long have you known?'

'I recognised you as soon as we met. I would have said something before we parted that day, but I wanted to see if you would recognise me. I was going to tease you on your lack of observation.' He grinned. 'But then you started asking questions about Mercy and I couldn't be sure what you were doing here in Brazil, so I kept quiet.'

'Well, in my defence,' she said, 'I recognised you too. But I was under cover and you were an added complication I didn't need.'

Charlie stared at him, her thoughts undecided. Then she thought: *What the hell? I'll be out of here tomorrow*. She told Felix everything she knew about Michael Hawkins, his early life in South Africa and Mozambique, his transformation into Sir Fredrick Michaels when he returned to England, his involvement in the counterfeit drug trade and the brush with death that caused for her sister, Suzanne. Then she brought him up to date on the latest chapter, with Hawkins faking his own death and fleeing from Britain to South America when his schemes looked likely to come unravelled. And, reluctantly, she told him about the nightmare on the *Pride of Kharkov,* destroying his original picture of Mercy.

'And now, I'm going back home with a bit more information, and a verbal confession, which I'm hoping will enable us to get some interest from the police.' She rubbed her hands across her face. 'But to be honest, I'm wondering if we're ever going to get anywhere with it. He was a respected civil servant who's believed to have taken his own life while the balance of his mind was disturbed. No-one's going to want to reopen that case.' She paused and sighed, 'And even if they did, he's safely here in Brazil. Look how long it took to get Ronnie Biggs back to England. And in fact, despite the 1997 treaty, we were denied permission to extradite Biggs. He came home on his own in the end. I suspect that wouldn't happen with Hawkins.'

Her companion looked at her thoughtfully. Then he nodded his head.

'But it would help your case, would it not, if he was back on British soil and could be identified?' he asked.

'Absolutely, it would. But I can't see that happening, can you?'

He shrugged his shoulders and smiled at her, tapping the side of his nose.

'Oh I don't know. You never know what can be arranged, do you? I have an idea, but I need to think it through before I talk about it.' Then he picked up the menu lying on the table. 'Now, Rose, or should I say, Charlotte, let's forget all about Michael Hawkins for the moment and enjoy the rest of our evening. I'm starving; let's eat.' Charlie grinned at him and nodded. Then she held out her hand to shake his.

'Charlie,' she said. 'My friends call me Charlie.'

Felix didn't say anything more about his idea during the rest of the evening, and Charlie was left wondering exactly what he was planning. In the cab back to the hotel, she decided to cancel her flight of the following day, and extend her room reservation for a little longer.

As she crossed the foyer on her way to the elevator, she heard the one voice she'd really been missing: Suzanne's.

'Charlie, there you are! Where on earth have you been? I was beginning to get really worried.' She turned and threw herself into her sister's arms. After the two women had hugged, she pulled away.

'I've been into the city for supper. And I might ask you the same question. I've been trying to ring you all afternoon.' She wondered if Suzanne would miss the fact she'd deliberately misunderstood the question. She guessed not; and she was right. Her sister gave her one of her 'I may be the younger sister, but I'm the adult' looks; then smiled and took Charlie's arm.

'Well, I guess we have a lot of talking to do, don't we? But let's not do it here. Your room or mine?'

'Oh, definitely yours,' said Charlie with a grin. 'Mine's been occupied for a good while and yours is still going to be neat and tidy.'

CHAPTER 39

By the time Suzanne had brought Charlie up to date on her investigations and the conclusions she and Damien had reached on Sunshine Supplements and Super Fit, Charlie was finally ready to tell Suzanne the full story of her encounters with Mercy Gove Hawkins and her father. Neither sister was completely happy about the actions of the other, but in the end, they were just glad to be reunited and safe, if only for the moment. By the time they finished talking it was almost dawn. Charlie left Suzanne getting ready for bed and stumbled back to her room. They agreed to meet at lunchtime to start planning their next actions on the two projects.

Around two in the afternoon, Felix rang.

'Charlie, can you meet me downtown—same place as before—early this evening. There are a couple of guys I'd like you to meet.'

When the Jones sisters arrived at the bar just before six thirty, Felix was sitting at the same table. He was deep in conversation with a tall, well-built man, who looked to be in his late thirties. The two men stood then Felix looked over towards the door.

'Here's Benji; right on time! Ladies, sit down and I'll introduce you to the team.' The four were joined by a huge, baby-faced youth wearing a Grateful Dead tee-shirt. Felix caught the eye of a passing waiter and ordered beers all round. Then he turned to Charlie and Suzanne. 'Ladies, let me introduce you to the Trio de Paulo: this is Demetrio,' indicating the older man, 'or should I say Dr Demetrio. And this young man,' pointing to the large youth, 'is Benji. He's the best logistics brain I've ever worked with. Guys, this is Charlie from England and I'm guessing this is her sister, Suzanne. They've also had a run-in with our Mr Michael Hawkins and I think between us, we might just be able to come up with a solution to all our problems.'

Felix went on to explain that the three of them had served together in the Brazilian army; he and Benji had been doing military service while Demetrio was a regular soldier, serving in the medical corps.

'We were the only three in our troop from São Paulo, so we naturally oriented to one another and spent a lot of our free time together as well as sharing duties. When we were stationed here in the city, we often spent Saturday afternoons with my gran, enjoying her *feijoada*.'

'No-one ever cooked the pork and beans quite like Grandma,' Benji broke in, rubbing his not inconsiderable belly.

'We all loved Grandma,' said Demetrio, 'and that's why we were so upset when we heard what happened.'

'Well I can understand that,' said Charlie. 'When I heard what his gang had done to Suzanne, I just wanted to kill him.' She paused and shook her head. 'Actually, that's not true; we didn't know who was in charge at that point, but I wanted to kill someone—anyone.'

'And that's why I called the guys here tonight, Charlie. I think we can bring this whole messy situation to a satisfactory conclusion. But you're going to need to help us.'

'Me?'

'Yes, you. Hawkins has a small, unobtrusive but very effective security team. And after what happened on the yacht, he's going to be even more wary than ever. You need to lure him into the open. Then you can leave the rest to us.'

And as the three men explained their plan, for the first time, Charlie and Suzanne began to hope they might be able to solve the Michael Hawkins problem after all.

'Hawkins.'

When Charlie rang the phone number she'd been given by Mercy two weeks before, she expected it to be answered by the maid and she wondered if Hawkins would actually refuse to take her call. After all, he'd been quite clear on the tarmac when they returned from Rio: 'I don't expect we'll meet again,' he'd said.

'Michael, it's Rose, Rose Fitzpatrick.'

'Rose.' There was a long pause, then, 'what can I do for you?' Charlie took a deep breath and crossed her fingers.

'Michael, I think we need to meet.'

'I don't think we have anything to talk about, do you? That part of my life is over.'

'Oh I think when you hear what I have to say, you'll want to meet me. It's about something Mercy told me; and something she gave me for safekeeping. A diary...'

'Why would I be interested in the scribblings of that woman?'

'Because they concern you, Michael. Mercy told me not to read it, but after the accident, I didn't know what to do with it. I didn't want to just throw it away, but you didn't want to even hear her name.'

'Go on.'

'Well, I read it, Michael, and it makes very interesting reading. Let's just say Mercy already knew a fair bit of your story before you told us all about your time in Africa. And somehow, I don't think you'd want this book to get into the wrong hands; the police for example. Or the British Foreign Office maybe.'

'Are you trying to blackmail me?'

'Blackmail's such an ugly word, isn't it? Let's just say I think we could have a mutually beneficial conversation.'

The silence was so palpable this time Charlie could almost hear Hawkins thinking. Finally she heard him inhale sharply and slowly.

'Well you'd better come and see me, hadn't you? Tonight? Eight o'clock.' The thought was so ludicrous, Charlie actually laughed out loud.

'Yeah, sure. I come and see you and there's another unfortunate accident. I'd never be seen again.'

'Rose, Rose, don't be silly.'

'Listen, Michael, we're going to play this my way. Do you know the café in the park opposite the São Paulo Runners Club? I'm going for a run this afternoon, so I'll meet you afterwards in the café; at about four. There'll be plenty of people around and if I suspect any funny business, I'll be screaming so loud, they'll hear me in Downing Street.'

The running track was empty as Charlie warmed up. She rolled her shoulders to loosen the tension, touched her toes, circled her arms forwards and backwards, then gripped her ear to aid balance while standing on one leg to stretch her hamstrings. Jogging on the spot, she set the timer and started running. The circuit was a kilometre long, circular and hilly in places, providing a varied challenge. At the point furthest from the clubhouse, it passed through a glade of trees. An old disused track marked the boundary of the field.

On her first three laps, the track was empty. But the fourth time, there was a car parked under the trees. Charlie slowed her pace as she recognised the vehicle. She'd last seen it driving Michael Hawkins away from her the afternoon they flew back from Rio.

Charlie felt, rather than saw, the figure stepping out from the trees into her path. She dodged to avoid his outstretched arm, but he was too quick for her. One hand reached out and grabbed her, twisting her shoulder viciously, while the other pushed the barrel of a gun into her ribs.

'Shit, that hurts, Max. Let go!' But the driver just grunted and shoved her towards the car. As they reached it, the back door swung open. Michael Hawkins was sitting in the opposite corner, with a cold smile on his face.

'Get in, Rose. There's no point in struggling. You wanted to talk, so here I am.'

'I wanted to talk later, in the café. What are you doing here?'

But Hawkins laughed.

'I think you underestimated me, my dear. Why should I risk meeting you in a public place when we can talk much more comfortably here in private?' Then the smile disappeared, to be replaced with a snarl. 'Get in, now. I'm losing patience.'

Max pushed Charlie forwards and she fell into the car. She grabbed hold of the bucket seat and pulled herself into it, as far away from Hawkins as she could be. He looked across her to the waiting driver.

'Max, you stay out there. This won't take long, and then we will be taking Ms Fitzpatrick for a little drive.' Charlie shivered as the meaning of his words sank in. Max closed the door and walked a few feet away from the car. Charlie watched as he pulled a cigarette case from his pocket and lit up. Hawkins cleared his throat.

'Right, now, Rose. Let's not waste any time. Let me have the diary.'

'Oh come on; do you really think I'd have it with me?' she asked, trying to instil a note of bravado into her voice.

'Yes, I do, my dear. Otherwise, how were you going to

prove to me you have anything of real value?'

'Well, yes, I've brought a copy certainly, but the original's in a very safe place.'

'And we can talk about that in a little while. But show me the copy, then.' Charlie stared at him in disbelief. *Could this man really be that stupid?* She held out her hands, showing she was carrying nothing.

'I'm in the middle of my run at the moment. On my own. I'm meant to be meeting you afterwards. Why would I bring anything with me?' Hawkins stared at her silently, and then his eyes dropped from her face to the small key fastened with a safety pin to the waistband of her joggers. A locker key with a tiny number tag attached to it. Charlie moved her arm to cover the key, but it was too late. Hawkins smiled slowly and held out his hand. Charlie unpinned the key and passed it to him. She briefly considered jabbing the open pin into his outstretched palm, but figured that would only enrage him and bring the encounter with Max even closer.

'Thank you,' he said. 'We'll visit your locker in a little while. Now, about the original; you have two choices. You either tell me where it is and we go and get it now. Or I hand you over to Max who, believe me, will very much enjoy extracting the information from you.'

'Either way, you're planning to kill me, aren't you?'

'Oh, most certainly, Rose dear, but one way will be much quicker and less painful than the other.'

Charlie bit her lip, screwed her eyes up like a child waiting for a surprise and then exhaled noisily.

'Okay, Michael,' she said. 'You win. I'll give you the diary—but you can't blame a girl for trying. When I heard your story out on the boat, especially the part about you being that Civil Service bigwig who disappeared, I saw my chance to make a bit of money.' She shook her head. 'But I guess I was wrong.' She grinned and held out her hand: 'Well played, Michael—or should I call you Sir Fredrick? Tell me, do you miss your days in the International Health

Forum. You certainly had a great team working for you, didn't you?'

Hawkins was slipping her locker key into his wallet and taking no notice of her outstretched hand. But at her words, his head shot up and he stared at her, the colour draining from his face.

'Jones! Suzanne Jones! She had a picture of you on her desk! That's why your face was so familiar.' Charlie bowed to him; there was no point in hiding any longer.

'Charlie Jones, elder sister, protector and partner in crime, Sir Fredrick. Pleased to meet you.'

'I stopped being Sir Fredrick when I left England, Ms Jones! And I really can't say I'm pleased to meet you!'

Hawkins rolled down the window.

'Max, come here. Now!'

Then, several things happened at once.

The door on Charlie's side opened, someone grabbed her arm and pulled her out of the car. She stumbled and almost fell over the prone body of Max, which was lying on the edge of the running track. A figure, tall and well-built, jumped into the car in her place. A large figure, moving much faster than his size suggested, jumped into the front seat. Doors slammed, the engine started and as the car raced away, Charlie heard Hawkins give an enraged scream, rapidly silenced.

She took several deep breaths and then turned to the man standing over Max's body.

'You cut that a bit fine, Felix. I was beginning to think I really was on my own.'

'Never fear, Charlie, you were completely safe. But I wanted to make sure we had enough on tape to prove his identity.' Felix put his arm around her shoulder. 'Come on, time for you to get changed. We need to find out how Suzanne's been getting on.'

CHAPTER 40

Suzanne was waiting in the shadows outside the huge office building when the young woman with the flame-coloured curls came through the revolving door at precisely one-thirty pm.

'Still a creature of habit then, Megan?' she said, falling into step beside Nigel Atkinson's Irish PA. 'Lunch in the sunshine and a stroll around the shops before heading back?'

Megan jumped at the sound of her voice and stopped walking; then her face broke into a grin as she reached over to give Suzanne a hug.

'Hey, Suzanne, good to see you. But what are you doing here? Nigel said he'd had you run out of Brazil. I thought you were back in the UK?'

'Well, I was, but let's just say some more information came up and I needed to be back here.' Then she took the other woman by the arm and started walking her down the street. 'Look, can we go somewhere a little less public? I need to talk to you.'

Ten minutes later, the two women were installed in a booth at the back of a coffee bar off the main drag. Megan told Suzanne it was packed in the evenings, but tended to be quieter at lunchtime. They ordered drinks and snacks, then Megan turned to Suzanne.

'Okay, shoot. What did you want to tell me?' She paused and pulled a rueful face. 'Although why I should even be talking to you after the stunt you pulled, I'm not sure.'

'Yes, I'm really sorry about that,' said Suzanne, 'and especially about having to deceive you, but when you hear what I've got to say, I hope you'll agree it was worth it.'

Suzanne told Megan about Damien's original approach, his suspicions about Super Fit, and their plan to trick Nigel Atkinson into letting her see around the factory.

'And I have to admit, apart from that locked room and the old guy's suspicious behaviour, I didn't find anything of concern.' Suzanne shook her head. 'Quite the opposite, in fact. The place was just too clean, too high-tech for a supposed health drink.' Then she brought Megan up to date with the investigations she and Damien had carried out since they left Brazil. 'But there's no proof as yet. So you see, I really need to get inside that factory again. And that's where I thought you could help me.'

But Megan held up her hands and pushed her chair back from the table.

'No way, José! I nearly lost my job last time. Nigel already blames me for introducing you to him. There's no way I'm going to be able to get you back in there.'

'Not during the day, certainly. Charlie and I are hoping to get in at night. What can you tell me about the security systems?'

'Oh, come on; who do you think you are? James Bond?' Megan was shaking her head again. Suzanne put a hand on her arm and smiled gently.

'Yes, I know it sounds far-fetched, but we honestly can't think of any other way of getting the proof we need. Megan, people are dying, we're sure of that. And we're pretty sure your company is to blame. We really need your help.'

Megan stirred her coffee in silence for a long time, then looking up at Suzanne she gave a crooked smile.

'You really believe Super Fit is dangerous, don't you? This isn't another con?'

'Yes, Megan, I do; and yes, it's a con; but it's Nigel who's doing the conning.'

Suzanne held her breath as Megan remained silent again, then finally, the Irish woman nodded her head.

'Okay, Suzanne, I'll tell you what you need to know. But it's not going to be easy.'

'So the security guard's not going to be a problem,' Suzanne told Charlie later that evening after she'd reassured herself that her sister was unharmed by her encounter with Michael Hawkins. 'If we wait until tomorrow evening, there's only one on duty for the whole building and most of the time, he's sitting watching television in his little office.'

'And what about cameras?'

'Megan's going to switch the factory ones off before she leaves. She'll tell the guard they've malfunctioned and can't be repaired until the following day. So he won't be expecting to see anything on those screens.'

'And we can get into the factory without having to go through the offices?'

'Yes, there's an entrance around the back, where the lorries go in and out. It's on a quiet side road with nothing but warehouses on the other side, so we should be able to park there and slip in without being seen. Good of Felix to offer to drive, isn't it?'

Felix had wanted to come with the sisters, but Charlie persuaded him she knew what she was doing and that two people would be in and out faster than three. She had finally agreed to let him drive them there, and knew that would make their getaway quicker and easier than if they had to try and navigate the back streets of São Paulo themselves.

'And Megan's given you the codes for the gate and the factory doors. So that just leaves the locked room itself.'

'Yes, that's a pain, but apparently Rufus has a thing about modern technology; thinks 'they' can tell where we are all the time and insists on an old-fashioned lock and key for that one room.'

'And he keeps the key in his lab coat pocket, in his locker? How bizarre.'

'Isn't it?' Suzanne shrugged. 'Hardly the most secure of locations. But it just means we need to visit the changing room first. Shouldn't add much time.'

'Right then,' said Charlie, staring at the map Megan had drawn on a napkin and ticking a list off on her fingers: 'Three minutes from the gate to cross the factory yard and get in via the warehouse. Two minutes to the changing room; another couple to find the locker, break in and get the key. Then three minutes to the locked room. Allow five minutes to search and find the samples. And another four to get out again. We should be able to do the whole thing in less than twenty minutes.'

'So tell Felix to collect us at eleven-thirty pm. We should be back at the hotel and in bed before one am if nothing goes wrong on the way.'

'Wrong? What could possibly go wrong, sis?' said Charlie with a grin. 'I have done this before, you know.'

'Yes,' replied her sister, 'that's what I'm afraid of!'

CHAPTER 41

A dog barked as two figures in black crept along the street at the back of the Sunshine Supplements factory. Suzanne froze.

'Megan didn't say anything about dogs,' she whispered.

'That's not here; they're across the road,' hissed Charlie. 'Come on, let's get on with it.' Megan had told Suzanne the heavy main gates were operated from within the warehouse and couldn't be opened from the outside, except by Nigel Atkinson who had a remote control in his car. But to the left, a small pedestrian gate was fitted into the wall. This could be opened from either side by anyone with the correct code. Charlie reached up and keyed in the number Megan had given them. The sisters both heaved sighs of relief when there was a click and the gate swung open. 'Step one complete.'

'I was so worried they might have changed the number,' said Suzanne.

The factory was laid out around a large goods yard. Stacks of empty chemical drums provided long shadows across the moonlit expanse. The sisters slipped from one pool of dark to another and soon reached the pedestrian door next to the huge roller shutters on the warehouse.

Charlie keyed the number in. Nothing happened. She tried again. Again nothing.

'Are you sure Megan said to use the same number on both keypads?' she asked Suzanne.

'Positive. She said there's only one code across the whole factory, because people kept getting mixed up and locking themselves out of the system when they had multiple codes.'

'Well, it's not working!'

'It must be!'

'Well, it's not!' Charlie was hitting keys again. 'I've tried it three times.'

'Maybe it's a bit sticky. When Nigel took me around, he had trouble with one of the doors, had to key it in three times. And he...,' she paused and thought hard, 'I think he had to hit clear before it worked.'

'Clear? Where's that?' The women hadn't switched a torch on, scared that the security guard might be looking out of a window at just the wrong moment. 'Oh, for goodness sake, where's the torch?' She pulled a pencil light out of her pocket and clicked it on briefly, shielding the beam with her arm. 'Right, there it is. Let's try that.'

The light went out, and Suzanne heard yet another series of clicks as Charlie keyed the number in once more and this time, there was a final, louder click as the door swung open. They were inside.

'It's this way,' said Suzanne, visualising the layout from her visit with Nigel. Within less than a minute, they were in the changing room, a closed area with no windows. 'Okay you can switch the light on now.'

They quickly located locker number 37, which Megan had told them belonged to Rufus Armstrong Jenkins. It was locked with a cheap padlock which lasted no time at all against Charlie's lock pick. It snapped with a crack and clattered onto the tiled floor. In the silent building, the noise seemed deafening and the two women froze. Charlie clicked off the torch and they stood in silence, straining to hear. But there was no-one and nothing to be heard. As Charlie switched the light back on, Suzanne pulled open the locked door and then shrank back in disgust.

'Yuck! Smells like something's died in here,' she said. The locker was stuffed full of clothes, old jumpers, jackets and a grubby white lab coat. The shelf was overflowing with books, used pizza boxes and paper bags. 'Good thing I'm wearing gloves.' She reached in and grabbed the lab coat. 'Here it is,' she said, pulling a large, ornate key from the pocket.' She shoved the lab coat back in the locker and pushed the door shut. But the contents were overflowing and it swung back open again.

'Leave it, sis,' said Charlie, 'there's no time for being tidy.'

The women crept out of the changing room and along the corridor, past the windows into the packing hall. Last time Suzanne had been here, it was a hive of activity, with machines and operators working together to fill the sachets of Super Fit. Now it was dark and empty. Moonlight flooded through the windows on the outside walls, giving enough light for them to see where they were going.

'This is it,' said Suzanne, stopping in front of the small green door labelled *Private.* She turned the key, and the door opened inwards. Charlie flashed the torch around the room. It was about four metres square and one of the side walls was packed from floor to ceiling with cupboards, while the other was covered by dark curtaining material. In the centre was a standard laboratory bench with sink, gas taps and shelving full of bottles. There was a strong fusty smell in the air. On the back wall, there was a row of windows just below ceiling level. Charlie pointed to them.

'Well, no-one can see in; but we can't switch the light on. You're going to have to manage with just the torch.'

Suzanne was pulling on the cupboard doors, all of which were locked. Charlie walked across to join her.

Suddenly the lights were switched on. The sisters spun round and stopped dead at the sight confronting them.

The rightful occupant of the laboratory was standing in the doorway, grinning at them. But it wasn't the sight of the man himself that caused their consternation, so much as the gun he was pointing at them. Rufus Armstrong Jenkins was unkempt, with long greasy hair and heavily wrinkled skin, looking even older than he actually was; but the hand holding the gun was completely motionless.

'Good evening, ladies,' he said, giving them a mocking bow. 'How nice of you to drop in. I don't usually encourage visitors, but it does get lonely here sometimes, especially when I'm working late on my experiments.' He leaned across and twitched away the curtain, revealing row upon row of small cages. As the light flooded in, the occupants stirred and several threw themselves at the bars. Suzanne realised what the fusty smell was. Rodents! 'Hello, my pretties,' he went on, 'we seem to have guests. So you need to perform nicely tonight.' Then he stopped, looked down at the gun, then at the sisters, then at the cages. 'No, I'm not going to be able to do this on my own, am I? I'm an old man; you're two strapping young women.' He looked confused and seemed uncertain of his next move.

'It's Rufus, isn't it?' said Suzanne quietly. 'Rufus Armstrong Jenkins. I'm a great admirer of your work. I've read all your papers on the benefits of entheogens.' The old man smiled and seemed to swell in front of their eyes. Having seen how he was treated by Nigel Atkinson at the party, Suzanne suspected Armstrong Jenkins wasn't getting much respect or praise these days. 'Can we have a chat about your work? And then we'll get out of here and leave you in peace.'

There was silence for a few moments, and then the old man began to chuckle.

'Nice try, Ms Jones. But, you forget; I saw you that day with Nigel. The day before he found out who you were and threw you out.' He shook his head, still chuckling. 'He was so pissed at you that day. Everyone kept out of his way until he'd calmed down.' Then the smile was gone, replaced by a twisted snarl. 'So, no, Ms Jones, I don't think we will 'have a chat about my work' before you leave. In fact I don't think we'll chat about anything. I need to give Nigel a call. He will want to talk to you himself.' And with a speed that belied his age, he jumped backwards, pulled the door shut and turned the key in the lock. Suzanne gazed at Charlie in consternation.

'Now what do we do?'

But Charlie just shrugged and patted her on the shoulder.

'Well, I don't know about you, sis, but I'm going to finish what we came here for. Let's get that sample we want.' And to Suzanne's amazement, she turned back to the cupboards and started examining the locks once more. 'At least now we don't have to worry about working in the dark.' She pulled her lock pick out of her back pocket, inserted it into one of the keyholes, twiddled it around a few times and gave a satisfied grunt as the door swung open with a click. 'Bingo. Is that what you're looking for, Suzanne?' she said, pointing to a pile of plastic boxes. Suzanne pulled one out of the cupboards, snapped off the lid and nodded.

'Yes, I think this is it. I need to get it analysed of course, to be absolutely certain. But I'm willing to bet these are a type of psilocybin mushroom.' And glancing across to the cages, she went on. 'He must be using the rats to test out different strengths and combinations.' She pulled open a couple of other boxes and selected samples from each of them, stuffing them into a plastic bag before pushing them into the small rucksack she'd carried with her throughout. Then she turned to Charlie who was standing idly by the door. 'Okay, so now we have our samples. How do we get out?'

Charlie started laughing.

'Call yourself an auditor? Where's your powers of observation gone, Suzanne?' And she pointed to a large hook just by the door. A hook on which an ornate key was hanging. 'I reckon our host forgot about the spare key when he locked us in.' She reached up, grabbed the key and turned to the door. 'Right, let's get out of here.'

But the key slid part way into the keyhole then stopped. And it refused to turn. It looked like Armstrong Jenkins had left the other key in the outside of the door.

The sisters slumped down on the floor, as far away from the door as they could get. After a while, Charlie jumped up and pushed the cupboard door shut and relocked it.

'No point in letting Nigel and Rufus know we've seen the stuff,' she said when Suzanne raised her eyebrows at her. 'Keep your rucksack out of sight as much as possible. And we may yet be able to get away with it.' Suzanne couldn't see how that was going to happen, but she just nodded.

Then, after about ten minutes, they heard footsteps approaching along the corridor. The key grated in the lock and the door swung open. But instead of Nigel Atkinson or Rufus Armstrong Jenkins, the figure standing in the doorway was slight, female, and red-headed.

'Megan! What are you doing here?' cried Suzanne.

'I remembered Rufus was working late on his experiments and tried to phone you at the hotel, but it was too late. And your mobiles are both switched off. So I thought I'd better come and see if you were alright.'

'Great that you did, Megan,' said Charlie, 'but can we chat about this when we're out of here?'

The three women ran down the corridor, out of the back door and into the yard. But as they started to cross, the main gate swung open and full-beam headlights raked the space between them and safety. A four by four swept into the yard, with Nigel Atkinson at the wheel. Rufus Armstrong Jenkins was standing just inside the gate, looking towards the vehicle. The women threw themselves behind a stack of pallets and held their breath. They could hear the two men talking.

'I'm sure there's someone there.' The drawl was Nigel's. They heard his steps coming closer. Megan gave a sigh, then grinned.

'Oh well,' she said, 'I was beginning to miss home. If this doesn't work, I could be out of work again.' And squeezing Suzanne's arm, she stepped out into the light. 'Thank goodness you've arrived, Nigel. I was just coming for help!'

'What the devil are you doing here, Megan?' he growled.

'Well, it was like this,' she said. 'I realised I'd left my house keys on my desk, so I popped back in on the way home; I've been at a friend's house all evening. And while I was in the office, I saw that dreadful woman, Suzanne Jones, running through the factory towards the warehouse. She had someone else with her. I think they're hiding in there!' And grabbing his arm, she pulled him towards the door. 'Come on, you'll be able to catch them if you're quick.'

As their voices faded, Suzanne and Charlie slipped around the pallets and ran quietly towards the gate. Once outside, they peeped back in. Rufus Armstrong Jenkins was standing open-mouthed in the centre of the yard.

'Probably trying to work out how we got out of the lab,' whispered Charlie with a grin.

Suzanne flashed the torch up the road and from a car parked in the shadow of a building, there came a flash in reply. An engine started up and seconds later, Felix drew up alongside them. Suzanne jumped in but Charlie was still standing at the gate,

'Come on, Charlie!' hissed Suzanne. But her sister held up her hand in the universal signal for two minutes. As Suzanne watched, she pulled a tiny camera out of her pocket.

'Hi, Rufus, over here!' Suzanne heard her yell. There was a series of flashes in rapid succession, then Charlie threw herself across the pavement and into the car.

'Drive, Felix!' the sisters yelled in unison. Then Charlie handed the camera to Suzanne and pointed to the screen. A startled but clearly recognisable Rufus Armstrong Jenkins could be seen, standing right next to Nigel's vehicle, complete with the Super Fit banner along the side, just below the factory sign for Sunshine Supplements.

'Game, set and match, I think,' said Suzanne, hugging her sister. 'Damien's going to be delighted.' Then the sisters started laughing and it was some time before they could stop.

'Right, ladies,' said Felix when they'd finally quietened down. 'I take it you want to go back to the hotel?'

'Yes please, Felix,' said Suzanne, 'but only to pick up our bags. I think we need to get to the airport as soon as possible. There's a flight to New York leaving first thing in the morning. And it's got a couple of seats with our names on them.'

EPILOGUE

Suzanne phoned Damien from their hotel in New York and he flew up from Duke for the weekend. The three celebrated the success of the night raid on Sunshine Supplements and worked on their ongoing strategy.

'What do you reckon, Suzanne?' Damien asked 'Should we take this to the FDA here in the States or is it better going through your contacts in Europe?'

'Well, we've got enough samples to do both,' she replied. 'And I've got a contact in the Field Office here in New York. I'm sure he'll be able to set up a meeting for us at the HQ in Maryland.'

'So we can hopefully persuade them to take some of the samples, and then give the rest to your pal Marcus in London?' said Charlie.

'Precisely.'

Damien stood up and raised his glass.

'Ladies, a toast: to the Jones Partnership. Long make it prosper.' He paused and then grinned shyly at them. 'And I have some other news. I wasn't going to say anything; it's early days yet. But I've found her. I've found Lulana!'

'Damien, that's wonderful news,' said Suzanne. 'Where's she been?'

'Well, when she went home in disgrace, her parents shipped her off to her grandmother's house just outside Salvador. They knew their daughter wasn't naturally violent and suspected there was something strange going on. She's been virtually under house arrest for the past six months.'

'But she's okay?' asked Charlie.

'Yes, and what's more, she wants to see me again. I'm going down to see her over the Easter holidays.'

Three days after the sisters return to England, they presented themselves at the Houses of Parliament and after the customary security checks, were shown to the office of the Parliamentary Under-secretary in the Department for International Development. Francine Matheson jumped up when she saw her visitors and rushed around the desk to hug both of them.

'It's so good to see you guys,' she said, 'You seem to have been having fun in Latin America.'

'Well, I'm not sure you could call all of it fun,' replied Suzanne, 'especially Charlie's experience in Rio.'

'But we've certainly got some interesting stories to tell you,' said Charlie. 'I do hope you're not in a hurry to get rid of us.'

Francine laughed.

'I know better than try and hurry through any meeting with you two. I've cleared my diary for the next couple of hours.' The three settled themselves in Francine's cosy sofas and she poured coffee into delicate china cups. 'Right,' she said, 'We've already talked about Sunshine Supplements when you phoned from the States, so let's start with our friend Michael Hawkins.'

'Well, it all began with a stroke of luck, really,' Charlie began. 'We knew Hawkins had last been heard of in São Paulo, and we hoped we'd be able to locate him, but Suzanne certainly thought it was a bit of a long shot and, if

I'm honest, I wasn't too sure. Then Damien gave us a brochure for the marathon and we came across a picture of Mercy Gove Hawkins.'

'So we went looking for her and found both of them,' continued Suzanne, 'at the pre-race day, as soon as we arrived.'

The sisters went on to tell Francine the whole story. There were some details Charlie hadn't felt able to share previously and both Suzanne and Francine were shocked to hear of the risks she had taken in order to get close to her prey.

'But in the end, what do we have?' said Suzanne. 'We have Charlie's word that Hawkins confessed to changing his identity and possibly committing bigamy, if his first marriage was even legal. We have the recording taken in the car, but a clever lawyer would probably be able to discredit that. We know where he is, but he's not moving from Brazil and we know how long an extradition would take, even if anyone would believe us.'

'And,' said Francine, 'you have the backing of a government member who knows that everything you say is true—and who has fallen foul of Michael Hawkins herself.'

'But do we know where he is at the moment?' asked Charlie. 'Felix was very vague when we asked what was going to happen to Hawkins after Demetrio and Benji drove him away.'

'Yes, I've had an update from the Embassy in Brasilia,' said Francine, smiling and nodding her head. 'Two days ago, during the night, there was a disturbance in the street outside the compound. A vehicle drove up, pushed a large bundle out of the back, right on their doorstep, and drove away.'

'Terrorism?' asked Charlie. Francine nodded.

'Yes, that's what they thought at first. So they went into red alert mode and used a remote camera to check out the bundle. And that's when they realised it was a person.'

'A person? Dead or alive?'

'Very much alive—but out for the count. They think he'd been drugged. But they only realised that afterwards. Once they were convinced there was no booby trap involved, they pulled the bundle through the gates and into the yard. And they found it to be an elderly man, smartly dressed, drugged and with his hands and ankles bound with plastic ties.'

'How strange,' said Suzanne, starting to smile broadly. Francine grinned back at her.

'But it gets better! There was a label pinned to his jacket. It said *You may need to check with the Foreign Office before you let me go*. So, they fingerprinted the man and it threw up a strange anomaly. He doesn't exist! He died back in 2005. And his name is...'

'Sir Fredrick Michaels!' the three women shrieked together.

'So, he's back on British soil, for the moment,' continued Francine when they'd calmed down. 'He's been put into custody for the moment until they can decide what to do with him.'

The three turned the facts around a few times more. Finally, Francine looked at her watch and grimaced.

'I'm sorry, guys, but I'm going to have to bring this to a close. I have a cabinet meeting I must attend. And the PM gets really testy if anyone's late.' She stood and the three hugged. Suzanne reminded Francine it had been a while since they'd all had supper together.

'I'll ring you next week,' said Francine, 'and we'll fix a date.' As the sisters walked to the door, she was already back at her desk pulling papers out of a pile and stuffing them into a briefcase. But she looked up as they reached the door. 'Charlie, you've done a brilliant job,' she said. 'Don't worry; we will get him in the end.'

Once the regulatory authorities confirmed the nature of the samples the sisters had obtained from the Sunshine

Supplements factory, things started moving very quickly. The FDA contacted the Brazilian authorities who descended on the company, seizing their stock and forcing a recall of all batches in the marketplace.

Nigel Atkinson continued to protest there was nothing in his product that could have caused an allergic reaction. He produced a recipe sheet which listed a cocktail of harmless ingredients, common to most health foods and energy drinks. However, as a 'gesture of goodwill' he agreed to cease manufacture for the time being until 'this misunderstanding' was resolved.

But this didn't have any effect in convincing the authorities of his innocence and a detailed analysis of Super Fit confirmed the presence of psilocybin. Two weeks later he was arrested and held in custody pending extradition. Several countries issued arrest warrants and initiated proceedings, but when they realised the FDA and the FBI were well ahead of them, they decided to sit back and see what happened. It looked as though Atkinson was going to be spending a long time in an American jail.

Early in April, Suzanne was in the office, preparing for her trip to Armenia. The kick-off meeting for the project they'd won back in January had finally been organised for the following week. As she pulled her packing list up on the laptop, Charlie strolled in with the post in her hand and a puzzled look on her face.

'Bit of a mystery, sis,' she said, 'look at this.'

'This' was a postcard showing an ornate church on a hillside, with blue and yellow mosaic walls and a clutch of gold-covered onion domes. It was postmarked *Kharkov* and addressed to *The Jones Partnership*. The message was short and to the point: *Rose, hope you got back to England okay. How's the headache?* It was signed *MGH*.

One week later Francine Matheson received an email from the British Embassy in Brasilia: *Extradition application will not be lodged. Michael Hawkins has been released from custody. His current whereabouts are unknown.*

She grabbed the phone and stabbed at the numbers as though trying to drive them through the handset and out the other side. It didn't help make the connection any faster, but it did serve to absorb some of her immediate anger. By the time Rico Martinez, her contact in Brasilia, came on the line, she had calmed down somewhat and was able to speak normally to him.

'Rico, your email. Please tell me it was a mistake. Tell me Hawkins has just been moved to another part of the Embassy. Or has been taken into Brazilian custody. Anything...'

'Francine, it's no mistake. I'm sorry. Our hands were tied.'

'But how...? Why...?

She heard the young man at the other end take a deep breath and she could imagine him running his fingers in frustration through his long dark hair.

'There were complications...'

'What complications?'

'It seems your Mr Hawkins has managed to acquire dual nationality.'

'How on earth did he do that?'

'No idea; but I saw the documents myself.'

'Well, they must be fakes.'

'And there seems to be some doubts about his real identity.'

'But the fingerprints...'

'And the Brazilians weren't at all happy about the circumstances surrounding his forcible removal from São Paulo to Brasilia.'

'But that doesn't alter the fact that we've got proof the man living as Michael Hawkins is actually Sir Fredrick Michaels.'

'Apparently it does. This is a man who seems to have friends in high places.'

Francine stared into space, her fingers tapping a rapid tattoo on the desk. Finally she exhaled sharply.

'Well, I guess there's nothing we can do for the moment. It's all a bit of a cock-up, isn't it? I hate to think what the Foreign Office is going to say.'

'Er, you don't know, do you?' said Rico tentatively.

'Know what?' Francine felt a frisson of apprehension run through her.

'The order to release Michael Hawkins came from someone at the Foreign Office.'

'What?'

'Listen, Francine; you didn't hear this from me, right?' There was a pause then he started again, speaking even more quietly than before. 'There are some high level talks going on over here at the moment. It's supposed to be a commercial trade delegation, but between you and me, there are rather a lot of people with a military bearing around.'

The penny dropped. Or rather, it rolled down the slope, flew across the room, ricocheted off the bookshelves and hit Francine right between the eyes.

'The Fastscape project!'

'Precisely. I understand we're close to a signature and no-one's willing to risk losing the deal. Too many jobs and too much money at stake. And as Michaels is supposed to be dead anyway...'

'So we just rolled over and handed him back?'

'That's pretty much it. I'm sorry, Francine. I'll put out some feelers with my contacts in Rio and São Paulo, but I'm not holding out much hope. The villa seems to be locked up. Has been ever since we received this little bundle last month.'

In a daze, Francine concluded the call and replaced the receiver. She picked up the email and read it through once more. Then knowing she had no other option, she pressed the intercom connecting her to her PA's desk.

'Marjorie, can you put a call through to the Jones Technical Partnership, please? I need to speak urgently to Suzanne Jones.'

ENJOYED THIS BOOK?

Reviews and recommendations are very important to an author and help contribute to a book's success. If you have enjoyed *Deception!* please recommend it to a friend, or better still, buy them a copy for their birthday or Christmas. And please consider posting a review on Amazon, Goodreads or your preferred review site.

ABOUT THE AUTHOR

Elizabeth Ducie was born and brought up in Birmingham. As a teenager, essays and poetry won her an overseas trip via a newspaper competition. Despite this, she took scientific and business qualifications and spent more than thirty years as a manufacturing consultant, business owner and technical writer before returning to creative writing in 2006. She has written short stories and poetry for competitions—and has had a few wins, several honourable mentions and some short-listing. She is published in several anthologies.

Under the Chudleigh Phoenix Publications imprint, she has published one collection of short stories and co-authored another two. She also writes non-fiction, including how-to books for writers running their own small business. Her debut novel, *Gorgito's Ice Rink*, was runner-up in the 2015 Self-Published Book of the Year awards. The first in the Suzanne Jones series, *Counterfeit!,* came third in the 2015 Literature Works First Page Writing Prize.

Elizabeth is editor of the Chudleigh Phoenix Community Magazine. She is a member of the Chudleigh Writers' Circle. Exeter Writers, West of England Authors and ALLi (The Alliance of Independent Authors).

For more information on Elizabeth, visit her website: www.elizabethducie.co.uk; follow her on Goodreads, Facebook, Twitter or Pinterest; or watch the trailers for her books on YouTube. To keep up to date with her writing plans, subscribe to her email list: elizabeth@elizabethducie.co.uk

OTHER BOOKS BY ELIZABETH DUCIE

The Suzanne Jones series:
Counterfeit!

Other fiction:
Gorgito's Ice Rink
Flashing on the Riviera
Parcels in the Rain and Other Writing

Co-written with Sharon Cook:
Life is Not a Trifling Affair
Life is Not a Bed of Roses

Non-fiction:
Sunshine and Sausages

The Business of Writing series:
Part One Business Start-Up (ebook only)
Part Two Finance Matters (ebook only)
Part Three Improving Effectiveness (ebook only)
The Business of Writing Parts One—Three (print only)